THE BEGINNING THINGS

Bunny Goodjohn

Underground Voices
Los Angeles, California
2015

Published by Underground Voices
www.undergroundvoices.com
Editor contact: Cetywa Powell

ISBN: 9780990433163

Printed in the United States of America.

For my mum, my dad, my sisters, and for Bill.

And I shall have some peace there,
for peace comes dropping slow…

Yeats, "Lake Isle of Innisfree"

1

Mirrors can be tricksters. Sometimes, when she was getting ready for school and checking her reflection in the bathroom cabinet, Tot Thompson allowed herself to think about Gareth Strand and to trace their initials inside a heart in the air with her finger. If she focused on her finger, then the letters and what they signified made sense to her. If she focused on herself — on the girl in the mirror — the heart and its contents were jumbled, gibberish, blurry.

Some mirrors have no glass.

Gareth Strand's bedroom was the exact same size as her own — 8'6" x 10' — and held the same furniture: a single bed; a chest of drawers; and a bedside table, although his had two narrow bookshelves whereas hers had a cupboard. The room was a mirror image — flipped: when she stood at his door, the wall with his chest of drawers was on her right rather than her left, the built-in wardrobe on her left rather than her right. But face down on the bed, with her head turned to the wall to escape the hot crush of his pillow on her nose and mouth, it all made perfect sense.

*

The first time his body had pressed her hard into the mattress, she had been surprised more by the dead weight of his body than by her acceptance of his hands roaming across her shoulders, along her shoulder blades, the sides of her waist, her hips. He had kept the fabric of their clothes between them as if that somehow defused what was happening up there in his room. The light from the lamppost at the corner of Willowswitch Lane fell across the windowsill, bleaching the back of her hand and illuminating a flotilla of tiny, brilliantly coloured boats printed on his sheets. The hull of each boat was brown, but the sails were vivid: crimson, yellow, green. She counted each boat in the group that sailed around her hand. Seven, their sails full of wind.

She could hear seagulls screaming out there in the night. There were always gulls, night and day. The dump at the back of the housing estate fed them. It was where they scavenged, squabbled, fucked and laid their eggs. It was where they lived. She focussed on the pressure of his hand on the back of her neck, the way it supported all his weight, and let loose a tiny moan inside her head, the kind she had heard come from naked actors in late night television plays, the kind of moan that sifted in through the thin wall that separated her own room from the one her parents shared…before her father had left for America. The moan sounded good inside her head, like the sound a real woman might make, and she risked another, this time out loud. Liberated from her imagination, the moan morphed into the noise an animal — or a small scary monster — might make. The boy's hands froze on her neck, and she stayed very still, keeping her breath tight inside her body.

In that stuck silence, the tiny banging began again. It had started when Gareth Strand had stuffed his little brother, Melvyn, crying inside the wardrobe. Tot knew its terrain from the one in her own room: the wide shelf along the top, the hanging rail that ran below, the way things seemed to get lost or forgotten if pushed too far to the back. She pictured the boy, younger than she, in the closet's hold, knowing the darkness would be touchable, that if he opened his mouth to cry out, it would creep inside him whether he wanted it to or not. Metal hangers would be cold and clattering around his ears, and by now, the soft sides of his hands would have begun to hurt. His fists continued to hammer, and yet he didn't shout or cry out. He was as mute as she now, as if he, too, was afraid of letting that darkness in, or maybe he was unsure of exactly what sound he should be making, or even of how to make it. She pressed her own fists softly into the pillow.

Melvyn's banging stopped and Gareth began again. His hands left her neck, the full weight of his upper body now jamming her, empty breathed, into the bed, to stroke her bare calves. His touch was tentative, as if he were writing difficult words onto the thin skin on the backs of her knees. Little spells and incantations. Stories. Tiny gifts. She felt the breeze from the open window move across her as he pushed the folds of her skirt up above her waist. She felt the soft rub of his smooth corduroy trousers on her thighs. She tried another moan, and this time, it slipped out long and low and powered his hands faster, his fingers forgetting the story and easing her legs apart. His touch became firmer, more assured. He knew where everything was and where he was going. He knew her body and how it worked. He knew this room and the titles of all the books on its shelves. He knew his brother as he knew himself. He knew how it would be inside the closet. Even in the dark, this boy knew all these things. His knees slipped between hers, and he gripped her tight above her elbows. Hot and bony, his hands pressed the scratchy lace trim of her short sleeves against the soft skin on the inside of her arms. He was pounding into her harder and quicker, as if he were riding a rocking horse free of its wooden runners.

And then he moaned. The moan was a new-born, a sound that needed no practice, the kind that was his and nothing at all to do with her. It twisted in her ears as he stopped rocking, as she felt his body arch upwards, off of hers, his weight supported entirely on the hands that gripped her arms, the sudden lifting of weight pressing her inexplicably ever deeper into the mattress.

And then, when the moan was gone, dragged away like a wooden box along a pathway, he fell forward, covering her with heaviness. His breath on her neck smelled like fresh dirt on a shovel. The whole room smelled like a kitchen garden before planting, when the rows have been turned over earlier in the day, and it's getting dark and everyone has gone in, leaving the garden to itself and to the night birds. Tot lifted her head from the pillow, arching her own back, desperate to catch more of the smell, to file it away as evidence with the rocking and the banging and the dark, and the honest-to-goodness truth that this was her first boyfriend, and that this — all of this — was love.

2

Elaine Thompson spat a mouthful of pins into a saucer, pushed back the sewing machine, and emptied a tin of sewing paraphernalia onto the dining room table. Wooden spools of thread, their ends caught in a messy, multi-coloured snaggle, a faded fortune cracker motto, a lump of beeswax as yellow and misshapen as an old man's toe, a linty mint, and a silver Monopoly token — the coveted dog — all tumbled out across the table. Things that didn't belong always appeared in her sewing tin. Strange about the motto, though; it had been a long time since anyone in the Thompson household had been out for a meal, even a Chinese takeaway. She resisted unfolding the scrap of paper; whatever fortune its blue letters spelled out, it was all a fantasy, a fairy tale. Red numbers on the bill from the electricity company and the gas board provided the only reliable forecasts for her future.

She stroked the dog's shiny fur. "Lost, huh?" she said, dropping the game counter into the saucer of pins. "Join the club."

She fished out the spare spool of red cotton from the heap on the table and re-threaded the machine. Repositioning the length of scarlet velour beneath the machine's foot, she completed the seam, turned the piece right side out, and shook it smooth. The design was her own: a child's skirt in the style of a strawberry: its red surface dotted with black buttons, its wide braces fashioned from green felt leaves. She placed it on the pile with the fourteen others she had already completed for the Treeverton Baby Buds Dancing School's Valentine Recital. Beethoven's *Missa solemnis* finished on the ancient record player, the arm lifting and returning to its stand with a brisk click. She pushed her chair back and wandered into the kitchen. Time for coffee before she listened to the other side, stitched two more skirts, and let out Tot's school blazer yet again. The girl was growing like a weed.

She filled the kettle and watched the lone lamppost outside the kitchen window cast down a dull orange light. Every year, despite her complaints to the council, the lamppost remained out of synch with its neighbours: today, its oval bulb had stuttered into an orange glow in the middle of a still bright January afternoon, and it would give up the ghost at around 3:00 a.m., plunging the house into a darkness so complete, Elaine often fancied she could feel its blackness push against her blankets.

She plugged in the kettle and mapped out her evening. She had the house to herself and would sew for another hour or so, or at least until the news came on or the kids came home: Tot was out playing at Stacey's — or was it Keesal's? — and Dorothy and the baby were at Christopher's. The boyfriend was a nightmare: old enough to father a child but not old enough to be of any practical use in his kid's life. Even so, Elaine made sure that Dorothy took Trampus to see his father. A boy needed a man in his life. A good man would be a bonus.

Through the glass, the darkening garden looked forlorn: a lone thrush rain-danced on the hard-packed lawn in the hope of fooling worms; dead weeds strangled last summer's lavender; and the laburnum by the gate was dead, blight of some sort, its bare branches smooth and crossed like swords. She caught her reflection in the window. If she unfocussed her gaze, the tree grew up from her throat, its branches spreading across her cheeks and tangling in her hair.

She jumped when the telephone rang from the end of the hallway. She wanted to ignore its black ringing. It would say nothing she wanted to hear: she had a dire need but no desire for more sewing orders — her fledgling business *Collette's Creations* wasn't busy, but she was sick to death of strawberries and tutus; there was no friend's voice she expected to hear; and if it was her father-in-law calling, they would both choose to talk of nothing rather than deal with the demands her mother-in-law's terminal cancer would surely place upon them all.

"Hello?" She could hear tired Christmas music from a jukebox and laughter in the background. She hoped the caller wasn't Dorothy. "Who is this?" she asked, a thread of annoyance lacing her words.

"Sorry, sorry!" the voice came on the other end of the phone. "Is that Colette?"

"No, I mean, yes. I mean, who do you want?"

"I want *Colette's Creations*," said the man on the phone.

"That's me. I mean, I am *Colette's Creations.*"

"But you're not Colette?"

"No. Does it matter?" The man's voice competing with the music irritated her. She fiddled with the telephone's tangled cord and caught a glimpse of her face in the mirror that hung above the hallway table. She saw her dead mother scowling back at her: the namesake of her home sewing business. As if a daughter's naming of a business could placate the ghost of a mother who had ceased living years before she finally died. Elaine tried to dislodge the spectre by grinning at herself in the mirror. She looked like a lunatic. And now the man on the other end of the phone had said something and she had missed it.

"I'm sorry." She turned her back on the woman in the mirror. "Please. What can I do for you?"

"I need something made up. A costume. And I saw the card. Here, by the phone. At *The Dog and Partridge*."

Elaine could see the pub, a little brick inn on the corner next door to the newsagents. Last week when she driven out of the car park, the pub's hanging baskets had been full of rare snow. New Year's Eve had seen a storm rush through the Chilterns, dropping four inches of fine icy snow that had settled and lingered for days. "Right," she said, pulling her mind back from the image of snow and from the random calculation of just how many months had passed, years perhaps, since she had been in a pub for fun rather than to tape business cards next to pay phones.

"Well, can you do it?"

"Can I do what? What do you want?"

"Damn. Sorry. A spacesuit. Not a real one. I mean, I'm not an astronaut or anything."

"What kind of a spacesuit?"

"Lurex. I already have the helmet. Trousers, braces...maybe some new hoses. Like off a vacuum cleaner. Loads of Velcro." The noise from the bar got louder. "Look, I'm sorry. It's bedlam here," he said. "Fifteen drunk women on a hen night. Can you do it or not?"

Elaine thought about the strawberries. Just two more and she was finished.

"Lots of Velcro," he repeated. "Or some kind of easy fastenings. I'm a stripper — with pyrotechnics. It all needs to come off ... in a flash."

A stripper. "What's your name?" she asked.

"Simon," he said.

"Simon, the stripper? Are you winding me up?" She glared at the receiver. "If you're taking the piss, I've got better things to do—"

"Flash Moron, Space Stripper."

"Oh, right. I'm sorry, Mr...."

"Simon. Simon's fine."

"Well, I've not done...I've not done much in Lurex and...hoses before, but if you have a drawing, I can give you a quote..."

"Great. No drawings, but I've got an old costume. It's a bit big. I've lost some weight. Weight Watchers and all that."

She fought yet failed to dispel an image of an overweight Neil Armstrong in a posing pouch.

"So," he said, "can you do it? I need it by March. I've got a gig in Wales — Penryth. You still there?"

"Yes."

"Yes, you're still there, or yes, you can do it?"

March. Her fortieth birthday was in March. In two months.

"Hello? Are you still there?"

"Yes. I mean yes, I can do it. I'll need the old costume for a pattern. And I'll need to take measurements."

"No worries. What are you doing Wednesday night?"

"I'm sorry?"

"Wednesday night. I'm opening up at *The Firkin* in Breckett Wood. I'm not stripping. It's just comedy. But it's the same outfit. You could come along, watch me open, see the costume up close. Are you doing anything?"

"I don't know…" She knew exactly what she would be doing: she'd make dinner at six, decamp to the front room to watch TV at seven, and by eight, she nod off. Thirty-nine years old. Very nearly forty.

"Free ticket. Come on, it'll be a laugh."

"Wednesday, you say?"

"Eight o'clock. I'll buy you a beer."

She worked it out. It had been over three years since Donald had left, since she'd stood in a bar with a drink in her hand. One that a man had bought her. And she had nearly finished the strawberry skirts. "How will I know you?"

"I'll be the one in a space helmet. See you then, Colette."

*

The foyer was packed, the stairs a snarl of people queuing for the show. Elaine joined the line's slow snaking to the second floor. At the top of the stairs, pinned to the wall, was a poster advertising the show. It showed a slim, blond man wearing a sparkling jumpsuit and space helmet. She leaned forward to study the picture — the man as much as the costume.

"Just one?" A girl sat at the ticket table, her magenta hair whipped into Medusa dreadlocks. "That'll be a quid. Seventy-five for members."

"Er, yes. I mean no. I'm a guest. Of Simon's." Elaine pointed at the poster, and the girl ran her finger down a sheet of paper.

"Colette?"

She was about to correct the girl but stopped. "Yeah. Colette."

Medusa stamped the back of Elaine's hand with a rubber stamp. "Go through," she said. "Next!"

Elaine pushed through the double doors. A fog of cigarette smoke and noise hit her. The brightly lit bar area she stood in was lost behind a storm of drinkers trying to either attract the two bartenders' attention or carefully carry drinks away towards the seating beyond the alcove. At the far end of the main room was a makeshift stage. The space was dark, but she could make out people crammed into wooden pews that ranged in rows across the room. The noise around her was deafening, and she hung back by the door. She leaned against a pillar, happy for its solidity. She wondered what her customer would really be like. She wondered if his photograph had been kind. She wondered why she cared.

The PA fired up, the dim lights went out, and notes began to pound slowly from the ceiling-mounted speakers. The crowd erupted into applause as a tiny spotlight, spreading a circle of light no larger than a teacup, lit upon the stage, illuminating a scrap of something gold. As the pace of the music increased, the circle of light widened, identifying the scrap of gold as the groin of a man at the microphone, his hips grinding in time to the music. The crowd stood, clapping like crazy, the spotlight's beam growing wider, revealing the man from the poster dressed in baggy Lurex chaps over a gold thong, a Perspex space helmet, and a tangle of hoses. He removed the microphone from the stand and stomped across the stage, glaring at the audience.

"All right, all right, all right," he shouted, shaking his fist, his voice distorted through the helmet. "Who wants some, then? Eh? Who bloody wants some?"

The crowd's regulars, seemingly privy to an old joke, brayed and screeched as the man took handfuls of candies from his pockets and hurled them into the audience. Shiny wrapped toffees and mints ricocheted off the walls, lollipops smacked into tables, and a storm of *Hubba Bubbas* bounced off the bar, scatter-shotting one of the barman and smashing the pint glass in his hand. Unable to stop herself, Elaine reached to catch a tiny roll of minty *Fisherman's Friends* mid-air.

She fiddled with the roll of mints and pictured its linty cousin in the sewing tin. She saw the strawberry skirts hanging from the front room's picture rail. She saw her empty chair across from the television where she had sat almost every evening for the past three years, waiting, and she began to laugh, its sound at first like water forcing its way up old plumbing. Hearing her own laugh was like not recognizing herself in a mirror. She listened harder and caught fragments, tiny memories, snagged in its sound. She untwisted the roll and popped a lozenge into her mouth, the hot, peppery mint dissolving on her tongue. On stage, Flash Moron, having run out of ammunition, removed his helmet, pulled a sheet of paper from his pocket, and announced the running order for the evening's comedians before abandoning the stage to the opening act, a heavyset man in rubber waders and an oversized mackintosh.

The mint left a medicinal sweetness in her mouth. She needed a drink. As she made her way through the crowded alcove back towards the bar, someone grabbed her arm. She turned to find Flash Moron, his space helmet tucked under his arm.

"Colette? Ah, shit!" He was jerked backwards, his space man/vacuum cleaner tubes tangled around the handbag of a girl leaning against the pillar.

"Let me help." Elaine and the owner of the handbag struggled to unhook him.

"Bloody tubes!" he laughed, taking her elbow and propelling her forward. "Come on, let me get you that beer I promised you."

*

"How did you know it was me?" she asked as they stood at the bar. The space had thinned, its customers now packed into the hall beyond where the overweight comedian held court.

He unclipped the tubes and rammed them into his space helmet. "Woman on her own at a comedy night with a tape measure hanging out of her handbag — dead giveaway." He leaned across the bar, waving a five-pound note at the barman who was kneeling on the floor, restocking the shelf with bottled lager. "Come on, Eric! How about a little service over here?"

The barman continued to load the bottles methodically, four at a time, onto the shelf. "You might be the spaceman, Dolan," he said without looking up from his task, "but I'm the bloody barman. You'll have to wait."

"Very nearly funny, Eric. Very nearly."

"Fuck off, Dolan."

Simon tucked the note into the waistband of his chaps and turned back to Elaine. "You've got to measure me, right?"

She nodded.

"Then stuff the bar. I know where there's a bottle of Merlot with our name on it."

He led her out of the double doors, down the stairs and through a door in the foyer marked "Private: Staff Only."

*

Simon, six-feet-two inches of oiled skin and silver cowboy chaps, swept a pile of old Christmas decorations off a sagging couch. "Sit. Grab a seat before they all pile in."

Elaine retrieved a plastic Santa from between the seat cushions before sitting down. "All pile in?"

He nodded, retrieving an Adidas bag from behind the sofa and pulling out a screw-top bottle of red wine and a stack of paper cups. "This is the management's sorry excuse for a Green Room…where all the acts are meant to pace around and stress out before they go on stage." He poured the wine. "And then get hammered when it's all over."

"So where is everybody?"

He took the Santa from her, replacing it with the wine. "They prefer to stress out at the bar, slag off the competition, and talk crap. Comics aren't funny. We're the saddest bastards around until we get a mic in our hands. Shame, isn't it?"

She nodded and sipped.

"I haven't just blown away your fantasies then? About comedians?"

She shrugged. "I didn't really have any."

He sat back against the arm of the sofa, his legs stretched out under the beaten-up coffee table. "So, Colette…"

"Elaine."

"Sorry. You look like a Colette. A bit French around the eyes…"

"Oh, please!"

19

"So, if you're not into compliments and you're not into comedy, what do you like? Aerobics? Macramé?" He was smiling at her. The kind of smile that starts way back, nowhere near the mouth.

"I've got two teenage kids, an eighteen-month-old grandson and a mother-in-law with terminal cancer. I like to sleep, Mr. Dolan. And if I can rustle up a nice dream at the same time, all the better."

"Ah."

They were silent for a moment and Elaine looked around the room. The green room was also the pub's store room, and they sat wedged between the past and the future: menu boards propped against the walls advertised "Santa Specials" and "St. Valentine's: Share a Champagne Cocktail." Boxes marked "Staff Hats — Paddies Day" supported a plywood Easter chick with a pint glass in its claws. She knew the stripper was looking at her, could almost hear his eyes upon her. She put the cup down on the coffee table, fished about in her bag and retrieved a battered cigarette case. As she clicked open the clasp, Simon pulled a lighter from his pocket and snapped it alight. She shook her head and took a photograph from the silver case.

"I gave up in '73," she said "after my grandson was born." She handed him the photo. "These are my girls. Tot and Dorothy. At Camber Sands two years ago. We rented a caravan." A small girl with orange hair grinned from the yellow caravan's window, and an older version of the same girl, sullen and hugely pregnant, sat on the steps below Elaine, who stood, noncommittal in red shorts and a bikini top, in the van's doorway.

He took the photo and relaxed back into the cushions. "How old?"

She leant over the photo. "Dorothy would have been thirteen and Tot about nine. Maybe ten."

"Cute."

"Yes, they are, aren't they? Even when they're grumpy as hell."

"I meant their mother." He placed the photograph on her knee.

She left it there and picked up her paper cup. "Do you have kids, Mr....Mr. Gordon?"

He laughed. "It's Dolan. Simon Dolan. But please...," he topped up her glass, "call me Simon."

She put the photograph away in the cigarette case, her fingers fumbling at the catch. "It's getting late. We'd better get on with these measurements." She stood and pulled the tape measure and a pad of paper from her handbag. "You say this one's a bit big?"

He nodded and tugged at his waistband before draining his wine and standing. "Too much breathing room," he said. He pulled a bundle of silver Lurex from the Adidas bag. "I'll leave you to get the Velcro and thread and stuff. But remember: quick release. It has to be a quick release." His smile grew. "So...you'll be needing chest, waist...inside leg?"

She unrolled the tape measure, warming its tin ends in her palms. "I'll need everything, Mr. Dolan."

He slipped the braces off his shoulders and, with a flourish, yanked at the waistband of the chaps. They split theatrically at the seams, leaving him standing before her in a spangled gold codpiece.

"Colette," he said, stretching his arms out wide, "I'm all yours."

3

Tot Thompson told her best friend, Stacey, that the Valentine card had not been there when she packed her school bag at home that Friday morning. But in Mrs. Spearling's English class, the first lesson that followed assembly, she had fished out her copy of *Great Expectations* and there it had been, stuffed between the book's pages: a large, bulky, white envelope with her name on the front.

"He'd drawn a heart instead of an 'o.' In my name. In 'Tot'."

The girls were sitting on the ancient canopied porch swing at the bottom of the Wright's back garden. The swing was draped with its transparent winter cover, and the garden beyond looked strange and alien through the thick plastic, the late afternoon dark creeping up over the roof of the house, the evening getting ready to settle around them all. Tot leaned hard against the cold, cushioned back of the swing, causing it to rock slightly. She pulled her scarf tighter around her neck, its wet wool chill against her skin.

When Stacey answered, Tot couldn't make out her face. "That's romantic," her friend said. "It's probably an Indian thing."

The garden swirled beyond the plastic — oily and fragmented.

"But what am I going to do? Keesal's not a BOY-friend. He's a friend-friend. He's been a friend since we were eight. We go fishing together down the canal. We watch stupid films on the telly. He's squeezed my back spots, for God's sake." Tot spun the muddy card between her fingers. "He's ruining it all."

"He's dishy...in a mystic kind of way," said Stacey.

"I don't want him to be dishy. I want him to be my friend. How can he be my friend when he draws hearts instead of 'o's?"

"What did he do in the woods?"

22

Tot didn't answer.

"Did he try and kiss you? Oh, my God! Did he French kiss you?"

Tot bit her bottom lip and opened the card out flat on her knees. She shook her head.

"What did he say, then? Did he say he loved you?"

She shook her head again, and a tiny, green paper heart fell from inside the card onto the wet patio slabs underneath the swing chair. The green darkened to black.

"What DID he do?"

Another heart, this time red, tumbled from the card and disappeared. She turned to Stacey, a frown across her face. "He threw a handful of confetti at me," she said.

"Confetti? Where did he get that from?"

She shrugged. "I dunno. Confetti shop?"

Both girls swung in silence, the evening pulling in above the garden, and the rain pattering against the swing's cover, a barrage of drops beading on the plastic.

"Do you think that was a declaration?" Stacey said.

"A declaration? About what?"

"Like a proposal."

"Stacey, I'm twelve. 'Course it wasn't a proposal. Jesus!"

"Then it was a hint. What did you do when he handed you the confetti?"

"You mean when he threw it at me? I ran off."

"You ran off? Where?"

"Down Spanley Way, round the back of the garages, then in here. Through the gap in your fence."

"Good job I saw you through the window. Did he follow you?" Stacey leaned forward to peer towards the fence.

"No."

"Did you keep any of the confetti?"

Tot closed the card, slipped it back inside the envelope, and tucked it down the front of her gabardine mackintosh. "No."

Stacey huffed on the swing's plastic cover and drew a heart in her breath. "I think he's dishy."

Tot lifted the edge of the cover. The rain had stopped. "I'm going in now," she said, crawling out onto the dark crazy-paved patio. Stacey followed and the two girls walked up the garden path towards the house. Stacey paused on the back step as Tot unlatched the gate at the end of the alley.

"Tot," Stacey called.

"What?" She rocked the gate backwards and forwards between her fingers, looking out across the patchy grass in the middle of Stanley Close. The light from the lampposts cast small puddles of orange on the road that circled the Green.

"He is."

"He is what?"

"Dishy. In a mystic kind of Indian way."

"If you say so."

"I do. Night, Mrs. Patel."

"Bog off, Stacey."

*

She had thought the card was from Gareth Strand. From the point of finding it in her bag at the beginning of Mrs. Spearling's English class right up until lunchtime, she had been sure it was from him, and she was beside herself with hope. A card meant that he was moving forward — that *they* were moving forward. She had never been in any doubt that what she felt for him was love. From that first meeting in the woods at the back of the park, when he had been sweet and inquisitive about her, had ignored the fact she was such a kid, that she had orange hair like a clown and was unable to meet his eye without the blood gathering thunderous in her cheeks, she had known. He had cast his wide-mouthed net across her world, and inside was trapped everything that was good, and the bad fell through the mesh and disappeared from view. She had no reference, but this was love. She was sure of it. She thrust her fingers through his net and held it close around her.

The card, his first love token, unlocked everything. It moved them out of the secrecy of his bedroom, of the sharp-edged sedge grass, from the derelict Martello tower on Tom's Lane where they met if his mum was home. The padded satin card meant the secrecy was coming to an end: he had sent her a Valentine's card; the card was the key and he had given it to her.

They would take it slowly. He would come to her and they would talk. He would become the boy he had been that summer afternoon last year when they first met in the park — bold, but a touch clumsy at the edges — and she would again be the girl — but this time buttoned and zipped. He would tell her how he was tired of the secrets, how he was proud of her and wanted everyone to know she was his girlfriend. There would be hand-holding walks from the school gates to the bus stop. He would move from the back of the bus to sit next to her; Keesal would give up his seat and shake Gareth's hand. Tot and Gareth would sit together and ignore the chaos around them. He would stay on the bus past his stop in the village, would stay on until the bus reached the far end of the estate, and then he would walk her to her front door. He would come round for tea, and her mother would bring out the china that matched, and he'd be awkward, but they would make him feel at home.

At lunchtime, she had waited for him to come to her so they could talk about the card and plan this future. It was raining, so she sat under the eaves of the gym, within sight of the bike sheds and the boys who, every day, gathered there, and pulled her mac around her to keep her and the card dry. She decorated the edges of the oversized envelope with pencilled vines and leaves, careful to keep the paper from getting wet. She wanted him to look over from the huddle at the bicycle sheds and see how calm and poised she was, how grown up, to realize he had made a good decision about her. She could hear him, rocking backwards and forwards on a borrowed bike, holding court with the other boys from his year, laughing and smoking cigarettes. She forced herself not to look over. Now that he had taken the initiative and sent her the card, she wanted him to carry on at the head of the relationship. She wanted him to come to her.

She held the point of her pencil towards her palm, the same way he held the lit end of his cigarette, and waited. At first, when he didn't come, she dug the point into her palm. Then when she had run out of palm and couldn't help herself, she looked over to where she knew he would be sitting on another boy's bicycle.

When she caught his eye, he had done the head shake thing, the thing that flicked his heavy fringe back from his forehead. She had held the card up high in the air, twirled it between her fingers, and risked a large public smile. He had seen the smile and the card spinning in her hand, and nothing good had crossed his face. No recognition. No smile. Nothing. Just another flick of his fringe, the customary wheelie, and a momentary frown.

The card had not been from him.

*

It was on the school bus heading home that Tot had found out the identity of the card's sender. She had taken her usual window seat next to Keesal, mindful of Gareth's voice from the back of the bus. Pressing her forehead to the glass, she listened to the C-stream girls in the seats behind her, all of them giggling and shouting, noisily ignoring the off-color comments from Gareth and his friends.

She leaned back in her seat and tried to smile at Keesal. "It was in my bag," she told him. "I found it after English. It's a nice one — padded and everything." She pulled the envelope from her holdall and slid out the card. "See? It's got roses and a puppy on the front." She held up the card so he could see it, and that was when the hand appeared from nowhere and snatched the card from her fingers. It disappeared in a wave of passes over the headrests towards the back of the bus.

Tot leaped up and twisted on her seat. "That's mine! Give it here!"

The card had already reached the back, where a knot of boys were braying and stamping it into the floor of the aisle. A blond boy, one whose name Tot didn't know but whom she recognized from the bicycle sheds' smoking gang, picked up the card and pretended to wipe his behind on it.

Tot went to scramble across Keesal, but he was already standing and blocking her way. She watched him stride up the aisle towards the back of the bus, his trousers a little too short showing too much sock, his hand-me-down blazer's hem unravelling, its shoulders shiny and bluish. He reached the back of the bus and the stamping boys, looking very thin and light.

"Give me the card," she heard him say.

"Or what?" the blond boy asked, looking back across the seats behind him to grin at his friends.

"Just give it to me."

"Why?" The boy faced Keesal and opened the card. He read the words inside aloud. "Says, 'To Tot, Be My Valentine and Gate Crash my Heart'." He turned back to his friends. "What the fuck does that mean?" They all laughed. "Aw, it's got a little heart instead of an 'o.' Says T-heart-T. Aw, how sweet!"

27

"Give me the card," Keesal said again, still standing in the middle of the aisle.

"Little Paki wants Carrot to gate crash his heart. Gate crash his knob, more like!"

Gareth Strand grabbed the card from over the blond boy's shoulder. The rest of them fell into a squirmy hush of expectation and looked at him, wondering what he would do, how he would up the ante. Keesal stood silent and still. Gareth opened the card and read the words for himself. He looked down the length of the bus and held Tot's eye. She didn't look away. He rubbed the silk card on the front of his shirt as if to clean it, then handed it to Keesal. "The heart's a bit naff," he said. "In the name. The heart's fucking naff."

Keesal took the card, and Gareth sat back down. Pulling a transistor radio from his pocket and holding it to his ear, Gareth looked out of the window, tapping the side of his hand against the sill in time to the tinny music.

Keesal still stood in the aisle, the card in his hand, facing the blond boy. Neither spoke. Their faces were close, just inches apart.

"Sit down, Fieldy," said Gareth, still looking out of the window. "Little fucker's not worth it."

The blond boy hesitated a moment and then sat down, play-punching the lad who was sitting quietly next to Gareth on the shoulder as he did so. "Arsewipe!" he shouted, and the two began to fight, more bluster and show than real aggression.

Keesal walked slowly back down the bus to his seat. Tot was still kneeling up on hers and facing the now quiet C-streamer girls at the back. She slid round in the scratchy upholstery. She didn't know what to say. He handed her the card, and the pair of them sat in silence as the bus reached the end of Toms Lane and the driver turned left into the village. At the church with the stained glass saints, the boys from the back of the bus, Gareth bringing up the rear, flowed down the aisle and got off. Gareth didn't turn to acknowledge either Tot or Keesal. He just shouldered his bag and strutted down the coach steps.

At the far end of Willowswitch Lane, Tot and Keesal got off at their usual stop. They hadn't spoken since she had told him about finding the card in her bag during English. She had counted through the silence. Four-hundred and-thirteen seconds. She realised he must have slipped it in there on the bus that morning. She should have realized there was no way that Gareth could have done that. More than that, she should have realized there was no way he would have.

She stopped counting, tightened her scarf around her neck, and stuck her hands deep into her mackintosh pockets. On the lane, it was cold and almost dark and rain had begun to fall. The walk down the lane and into Stanley Close would take an eternal ten minutes.

Keesal rested his hand on the top of her holdall. "Carry your bag?" he said. She shrugged in the broken silence, and he slipped the bag off her shoulder onto his own. "Let's cut through the copse."

He walked a little ahead of her and took the footpath through to the trees and into Tenner's Wood. She followed. Just inside the copse, where the scrappy bushes gave way to the first real trees, he stopped. He leaned back against an oak, whose low branches seemed to sweep at the ground, and studied her. It was the tree all the Stanley Close kids learned to climb first, its lower branches thick and evenly spaced, kind and solid.

"What?" she said. She looked up at the tree where light from the early evening moon slipped through the uppermost branches. "Keesal, it's too cold and I'm too old to be climbing trees."

He didn't reply, just stuck his hands deep into his pockets.

"I mean, thanks for the card and for getting it back and everything," she said. "It's lovely. The puppy and the silk and all the padding. It's…lovely." She bit her lip and wished he would say something or do something. "I just didn't think it was…I mean we're friends, yeah? I didn't think you'd send me a Valentine." She pulled the card from inside her coat and opened it, re-reading the words. "I don't think the heart's naff…"

In one fluid movement, Keesal pulled his fist from his pocket. She thought he was going to hit her, and she flinched as he unfurled his fist and a cascade of confetti pattered down on her head and onto her shoulders. Tiny paper hearts and lucky horseshoes.

She ran. She grabbed her bag from his shoulder and ran through the trees, down the lane that skirted the back of the dump. She ran for home but knew she couldn't face its noise and the fact that there, all would be as it had been before — the wireless would be tuned to Radio 4, the oven would be on, Trampus would be playing on the floor under the kitchen table — when for her, nothing could be as it was before. She ran down through the row of garages to the barbed-wire-topped chain link that marked their perimeter, veering off to slip through the hole in the fence that opened into Stacey's back garden. She squeezed through and dipped under the plastic cover of the Wright's ancient garden swing seat.

In the cold, still evening, she could hear dinnertime pans clattering inside the Wright's kitchen. She reached inside her mackintosh and pressed her finger into the padded silk of the card as if she were testing a bruise.

4

Dan Thompson had always had a thing — a bad thing — about feet and fowl. He was certain his wife had been aware of his phobias, and it was this certainty that allowed him to cite his dead wife and her cruelty as the deep and tangled root of all his problems. And if Millicent and her meanness had been the root, their marriage had been the stem from which sprouted all the day-to-day demons and difficulties which had dragged him down. It would all need grubbing out if he were to stand any chance at all.

She had tormented him with her feet. On the sofa after supper, she had taken pleasure in kicking him with her terrible mauve heels to wrest him from his book. She'd point at crime on the television's evening news with her bunioned big toe. On Sunday nights, in her dressing gown, her hair wet and wild from the bath, she served up her feet hot and pink on a towel, like trotters on a platter; she liked him to trim her tough spade-shaped toenails with the clippers. Later, at *The Hook and Parrot*, their smell — talcum and dead skin — accompanied each sip of his beer, regardless of how many times he washed his hands. Even in sleep, her feet would horrify him, her cold heels rubbing against his thighs under the covers. He could recall the rasp of her feet in more detail than he could the touch of her fingers.

Millicent was also connected to Dan's second fear since the flock of chickens at the bottom of the garden had been hers. She kept the birds for eggs and meat, selling that which they didn't use through the local farm store. He tried to keep his distance from the hens, but when the aftermath of chemotherapy pinned Millicent to her bed, and her birds needed tending, he had taken on both feeding and fear.

Filling the galvanized bucket from the feed sack under the sink, he'd head down the stone-flagged alley towards the back garden and the coop. Those late winter walks down to the hens had been cold and quietly dark. The trees that rimmed the yard were enormous in the pre-dawn, each merging seamlessly with its neighbour, forming a colossal wall more grey/black than green. Song birds, invisible in the branches, called to their incarcerated cousins in the coop as he walked by, short snatches of song, little snippets of solidarity.

Each time he reached the coop door, he'd pause with his ear against the plywood wall, imagining the hens listening to him as he listened to them. He'd knock. Then knock again. Three times in all. Hollow raps that told them he was there, that he was about to open the door, and that they were not to rush him…that there was no need for panic. At the sound of his rapping, the birds began to shift down from their perches into the deep litter in a procession of solid thumps. Waiting on the floor of the coop, most were silent, but through the wood, he'd hear one or two call out to each other and, perhaps, to the birds in the trees along the fence. Soft throat clicks, sounds of dusty anticipation. Dan needed to wait until they were all down on the ground before he risked opening the door and entering the low-roofed hut to refill the feed hoppers: the thought of being hit in the head by the light feathered fullness of a descending hen made his stomach twist.

He also waited because of the other sound — the clicking of claws on wooden boards, a noise that built as more birds left the perch and landed in the litter, a noise that combined both fears: twenty pairs of horny, yellow feet, kicking up clouds of sawdust and old feathers, scratching in the thick black of the coop. In the moments spent before the coop's latched door, he would tell himself there was nothing evil inside that darkness — merely hens. He had studied bird anatomy at the library — their claws, spurs and shanks. It was in these pages that he realized it was the intersection of feather and scale that bothered him the most. It was as if that transition — from feather to scale — needed watching. It seemed to him that a shift like that should worry a man.

And yet the pausing made him feel no easier. Those moments spent listening at the door allowed him to acknowledge the source of his dread; it did not allow him to dismiss it. He'd unlatch and pull open the door, then quickly stand aside on the narrow planked walkway as the birds spilled out to jump off the deck into the dawn, to peck and scratch at the hard-packed ground below. Once the birds satisfied themselves that there were no treats to be had, no fruit or vegetable peelings, they would bustle off towards the hedge and the oaks at the perimeter of the yard, their ruddy brown bodies blurring to dark rounds, their orange shanks the last colour before the darkness of the garden's edge.

Time had taught him not to believe the coop to be empty; there was always a straggler, some feathered teenager up there on the perch, reluctant to relinquish her sleep. In feeding these birds on the mornings his dying wife could not, he had learned that his fears were not always groundless, that sometimes it was wise to hope for the best but to prepare for the worst: it could take a moment or two for a waking hen to realize she was on her own on the perch and, suddenly desperate for company, explode from the dark like a champagne cork, to narrowly miss him before landing in the midst of her own kind.

The bird's need to be in the middle of things, inside the group, made sense to him. He, too, had a fear of the solitary, of being alone, of being left behind. He met his fear in the same way the straggling bird met hers — by catapulting himself into life, into the midst of people he thought, perhaps mistakenly, might be like him. He had found them in the public bar of *The Hook and Parrot*, and in the beginning, the companionship, the warm beer, the odd game of darts or dominos, had made him feel part of something. But recently, he had found himself looking at his companions at the bar and not recognizing himself in their features, in their good-natured banter, in the way they sipped their beer and munched their way through packets of potato crisps and peanuts. He had begun to stay indoors, to drink at home, alone on his perch, his fear of loneliness fighting paradoxically with his fear of people and what they might think of him.

*

It was Valentine's Day that he woke to find the bed wide and cold beside him and assumed the maelstrom of chemotherapy had calmed and that Millicent had risen early to reclaim the hens and their feeding for herself. He had pulled the blankets up to his chin, grinning like a boy into their warm wooliness. But his happiness quickly turned to guilt as he tried to discern its basis. Was he grinning because his sick wife was feeling well enough to feed her beloved birds, or was he just happy that he didn't have to? Unwilling to deal with the question or its answer, he had put on his dressing gown and shuffled downstairs in his slippers to make tea. As he filled the kettle, he saw through the kitchen window that the coop door was still closed. It was then that he noticed the feed bucket still hanging from its hook by the stove. He took it down and filled it from the sack below the sink. Abandoning the warmth of the kitchen, he headed to check the coop and its birds.

The morning was already underway, the outline of last night's moon a biscuit cutter in the pale sky. The birds would be hungry, he thought, and down in the litter by now, even the straggler, all scratching for yesterday's leavings. Perhaps Millie had decided to make an early start on plucking yesterday's culls and forgotten to let out the living. At the coop, he unlatched the door without knocking, and the hens swarmed like monster bees around his feet before they jumped down and scattered towards the fence. He filled their feeder with scratch, deciding to leave the egg collection to Millicent.

He had found her in the quiet plucking shed adjacent to the coop, the bare light bulb hanging bright and picking out the hut's detail. She sat with her back to him and the open door, her thin shoulders criss-crossed with the blue straps of her apron, slumped over the plucking bench as if she was sleeping and using a fat, brown-feathered hen as a pillow. Another bird was lying in her lap — just its orange legs visible to Dan. Three more hung from hooks above the bench. They, too, looked asleep. The metal hooks bent their necks into angelic curves, and their eyes were closed, wattles bright red against the wooden wall. Their claws were furled, short feathers tightly packed against their bright, scaly shanks. He had spoken Millicent's name, knowing as it formed in his mouth that his wife was dead. Feeling like an intruder in church, Dan backed out, shut the door with a click, and returned to the kitchen to telephone for an ambulance.

5

Dan's wife had never taken to Elaine. It wasn't the younger woman's fault. Millicent wouldn't have liked any woman loved by her son; it was as if the boy's love for another leached love from her portion. And yet, she blamed Elaine for accepting this affection rather than Donald for offering it. Even after he ran away to America, abandoning them all, he had remained the perfect lone star in Millicent's sky.

On the rare days she was feeling magnanimous, she might have described Elaine as sly or perhaps aloof. On bad days — and these were much more common, especially towards the end — she described her as a good-for-nothing bitch. As far as she was concerned, her son hadn't deserted his wife and children; he had been run off. Right up until her death, she had worked at unravelling Elaine's reputation as a woman might unravel knitting gone wrong: then she reworked the yarn until her daughter-in-law was nothing but a money-grubbing whore who had never deserved Millicent's only son, a good man who was seeking (and finding) his well-deserved fortune as a musician in the United States of America.

Dan was left alone with the bald truth that had arrived almost three years earlier in a letter bearing a Scottish postmark. It was from his son, a man Dan had always considered to be an unrealistic romantic who had left his wife and kids to chase a dream he was neither quick nor constant enough to catch. The letter was a long, rambling affair which catalogued regrets and wrong-doings. Donald wrote that when push came to shove, lack of money and courage had kept him from leaving the country. Ego and shame, which he referred to as his "filial inheritance," had kept him from returning home. He was living with a singer called Carol and hadn't played the trumpet since leaving Bishop's Croft. He swore his father to secrecy, wanting only news of Elaine and the children. And Dan, because his son reminded him of himself, had kept the secret from both his own wife and from his son's.

*

It spoke of character that his son had not attended Millicent's funeral but that his daughter-in-law had. Not only was Elaine there but she had plucked responsibility for planning the entire sad event from Dan's stooped shoulders. Not knowing who else to call, he had dialled Elaine's number from the pay phone at the hospital where the ambulance had taken his dead wife. She had picked up the phone at almost midnight on Valentine's Day and listened to him, his words rolling and tumbling through great quaking sobs. Then she had told him to go home, that she would speak to the hospital and make all the arrangements for the funeral.

The funeral had been a quiet affair. In fact, if Elaine hadn't driven down the previous night with the kids, the house and the crematorium would have been almost empty. The few people Millicent had counted as friends — her son's old headmistress, the woman from the farm supply shop, and an old school pal — came back to the house after the service and hovered in the kitchen. There wasn't much to eat or say. Neither Elaine nor Dan had had time to make food, but the landlord from *The Hook and Parrot* had dropped off a tray of ham sandwiches and a small bottle of sherry that morning. Elaine had cut the sandwiches on the slant and set the sherry on a tray she had found in the larder. Once the bottle was empty and the sandwiches gone, the few mourners followed suit, and the sorry event was over.

As the light outside began to fade, Elaine and her eldest bundled black suits and dresses into carrier bags, ready for the dry-cleaners. Then they trailed from room to room, picking up possessions and packing and repacking

37

suitcases while Dan sat at the kitchen table awkwardly bouncing his great grandson Trampus on his knee and racking his brain for horsey nursery rhymes. The clock on the wall ticked down the day like a stop-watch. He studied this woman and her girls, none of whom he really knew, as they moved about his house. His daughter-in-law seemed to know where everything was and what to pack and what to leave behind. He let her get on with it, happy to sit with the few remaining minutes he had left of his old life. He was aware that as soon as he had agreed the previous night to head North with Elaine for a few weeks, until, as she said, "things settled down," his life would change, and he could feel fear, familiar but undefined, waggle its fingers in the pit of his stomach. His relationship with change was complex: he put great store in its powers of renewal, with all its fresh perspective and opportunity, and part of him was anxious for this new start. But the rest of him — the part he knew well — wanted the opportunity for change to leave with his houseguests so he could head back to bed and pull the covers up around his ears.

"You ready?" Elaine stood at the kitchen door, his bulging and tatty suitcase at her feet, spare blankets and pillows under each arm. She looked with difficulty at her watch. "If we set off now, we'll be home by midnight."

He passed Trampus to Dorothy — his granddaughter and the child's teenage mother — and picked up his own small bag that he had packed early that morning before the funeral. "No time like the present, I suppose," he said. "Can the young 'un ride with me?" He looked across at Tot who sat dozing in a chair, a glossy wooden tea caddy lodged securely in her lap.

"I don't see why not. Tot, wake up, Lovey." Elaine gently shook the girl's shoulder. She stirred and yawned, running her fingers through a tangle of short red curls. "You go with Granddad, Sweetie."

Elaine opened the back door, the blankets and pillows still lodged under her arms. "Dorothy, take our case and Tramps, and get him strapped in the back."

Elaine and Dorothy, lugging blankets, bags and toddler, and Tot, carrying the tea caddy full of Millicent's ashes, trailed slowly down the dark and unfamiliar alley to the two cars parked in the driveway. Dan balanced his case on his knee as he double-locked the back door. He turned and paused a moment on the step to look out across the garden with its tall trees and its vegetable garden which had been neatly tilled for the winter. In the coop, the birds would be sleeping and would wake to the fearless Mrs. Phemister, the next-door neighbour, opening their door and filling their feeder. He tightened his scarf and, adjusting his grip on his suitcase, joined the women loading cars in the driveway.

*

The drive from Sleaford north to Bishop's Croft was uneventful. Tot had been quiet in the car as he knew she would be. She was a thoughtful child — as in full of thought rather than particularly selfless. Millicent had never warmed to her, preferring instead the showiness of her sister. Dan had taken a shine to Tot from the moment he first saw her in the maternity wing of Treeverton General. His son's call had come early in the morning, and he and Millicent had driven up, the first of many visits to young grandchildren still wrapped in novelty. Lying in her hospital crib looking up at him, she seemed to inspect his soul. Her smile at what he perceived to be the things she found there had made him feel that all might be saved, might be different. He had been calmed, almost horse-whispered, by a grey-eyed baby.

As she learned to speak, she spoke her mind, much to the alarm of her parents. The ugly, the fat, and the unkind were all identified, after a pause, loudly and clearly. As were the beautiful, the kind, the lovely. It was this slight hesitation that had sealed the deal for his heart, the way she paused before she spoke, before she answered questions, as if both the question and its answer mattered equally, as if there were always options, choices worthy of careful consideration. Her pauses had become longer and deeper of late. Elaine had put it down to her age. Dan put it down to the fact that her father had deserted her, and that Trampus, her sister's unplanned baby, had pushed her off the family stage and into the stalls with the empty sweet wrappers and sticky paper cups.

Another bond between the two was her early affinity for Dan's spoonerisms. There was something about the clean muddling of words that appealed to them both. The mundane became magical. Instead of merely buttoning a shirt, one *shuttoned a birt*. A standard man poured himself a mug of tea, but Dan sat down to a *tug of me*. The word play had always driven Millicent mad. She saw it not as magical but as childish — ridiculous even. He had confined himself to private or silent spooning…until Tot had come along. She was a natural, renaming her parents *Dummy and Maddy* from the very first. Elaine and Donald had been worried that Dan would confuse the child and tried to put a stop to their word games, but Tot was hooked. Words spelled in alphabet blocks on the carpet were quickly jumbled. Big Dog shuffled to *Dig Bog*, her quick hands swapping the blocks, her face bannered with a huge smile. The realization that her name Tot Thompson could not be spooned brought a torrent of tears until Elaine turned to the telephone, calling Dan in order that old man and toddler might talk it over. In the years since, the element of game had all but disappeared for Tot. Instead, she seemed to self-medicate with transposition. She would use it to verbalize the difficult, the tough. When she spoke to him on the telephone in the weeks following Donald's disappearance, she didn't say her father had left home; he had *heft lome*. She *hissed mim*, she *honted her waddy*. But on darker days, she said clearly and simply that she hated him for not coming back.

Their connection, her way of looking at and dealing with life and its challenges, had been behind his suggestion that she occupy the passenger seat on the long drive from the South Coast to North London. He had also thought that it would somehow be easier for him to drive away from this old life to a new one with a warm body in the seat beside him.

The whiskey, mixed with a little ginger ale for appearance sake and decanted back into the empty soda bottle, had also helped. That is, it had helped once he had managed to silence the nagging voice in his head. This voice, a voice which seemed to be growing fainter with time, told him that drinking whiskey while driving was foolhardy, dangerous even, especially with his granddaughter in the car. But he had become an expert at ignoring the voice. After all, he told himself, there was no alternative. At least, not at the moment. Not until he got away from here, from his drinking buddies, from the memories of Millicent, those birds, all that stress. Not until he got things straight.

*

Things had not been straight with Dan for some time. Peace, and increasingly the ability to cope with the things that needed coping with, no longer came as it had before with two pints in *The Hook and Parrot*. Those days seemed a long way back in his past. He looked at that past with nostalgic affection, as a husband might look back on his wife's long-gone habit of leaving love letters in a lunchbox. The idea that just two pints of beer with friends could ever have brought him peace of mind, or anything other than a gnawing craving for more pints, seemed ludicrous. He could remember in sharp clarity the moment at which the two pints had ceased to deliver peace, when he had picked up his glass and left the group to sit alone at the bar.

There had been something indefinable but difficult about that Friday night at the end of the summer, a feeling of anxiety and irritability that the company of friends failed to dispel. From his seat at the bar, two stools down from the hot cabinet, perpetual home to a lone pork pie and a wrapped sausage roll, Dan held on tight to his pint and studied his friends in the mirror that ran along the length of the bar's back wall. The reflection returned his friends as they sat together, squashed arm-to-arm along the padded bench, the straight lines of the optics and bottles dividing the scene as if watched through bars on a window. Other men, too late in arriving to secure a place on the bench, had pulled up chairs and little tables to sit at the edge of the group, their bulky bodies leaned forward into the chatter and bustle. Smiles rounded out their faces, men talking to men, men calling across men to other men at other tables. Jokes about three-legged dogs and midgets and mariners marooned on desert islands bounced across the tables, punch-lining into the cigarette smoke that settled above their heads. Men bought men beers, and men complained of their wives and of their bad lives, nodding at each other like cows at the fence, outdoing each other's misery, then commiserating, then taking it all back and outdoing each other with stories of marital bliss. Now and then, they would lift their glasses and sip their beer, dip fingers into packets of peanuts, spear prawns purchased from the seafood man who made the rounds of Sleaford pubs every Friday night. Dan watched the men as they shifted easily from conversation to conversation, scootching up on the bench, making room for each other, groups splitting and forming, growing and shrinking, and all the while, he held onto his beer and to his reflection in the mirror. Bonhomie was at his back. A glut of smiles, good nature wind-blown around the room. It was all behind him and it was suddenly incomprehensible. Unfathomable. He ordered a double rum and poured it into the dregs of his beer, spirit sinking to the bottom in an oily swirl. He stood and checked his pocket for his car keys, his wallet, his glasses before downing his drink and slipping out of the side door into the silence of the night beyond.

*

He had tried, once or twice in the weeks that followed, to rejoin the group. He had come armed with new jokes he had heard at work and with stories to tell them about Millicent, but each time he had found himself moving towards the solitude of the bar and its stools. After a while, he preferred the reflection of companionship to the real thing. He watched its performance in the glass, his two-pinter evenings becoming three-pinters, then four, always lacing his final beer with rum before topping up his hip flask for the long walk home. He no longer brought the car.

Once or twice, Dan had woken up in the alley with no recollection of the evening or the journey home. Several of his friends refused to speak to him anymore; they turned away when he entered the pub, spreading out on the bench, making the bar stool a blessed necessity rather than a choice. The landlady's smile became forced, and the barmaid seemed sad when she pulled his pints. Between rounds, the two women stood in the doorway between the bar and the kitchen and whispered about him. The mirror whispered, too, but Dan couldn't hear what it said. He had no memory of what had or had not happened during those blacked out evenings, and he was too proud — and scared — to ask. So Dan began the solitary and slippery habit of drinking alone at home in the kitchen in his chair by the stove, while Millicent watched soap back-to-back in the front room.

Peace came slowly if it came at all. Each morning, it hovered on the edges, like hope, as he stumbled his way, trembling and sick, out of bed to the bathroom to stand beneath the shower until the hot water ran tepid, until his morning shakes could be explained away as the result of too much cold water on an old man's body. He hadn't deviated from the habit, even after Millicent's death; it was as if habit held him together. The shower, the keeping down of breakfast and strong coffee settled the shaking into a constant bee-winged vibration behind his rib cage. Peace didn't arrive until he gave in: a glass of wine, beer, cooking sherry...it didn't care back then. Today, it was pickier. Today, Dan's brand of peace demanded a bottle of Bells. What had happened? He had asked himself the question time and time again. What had caused the shift from his being a peaceful two-pint-a-night man to a drunk who couldn't drive without a bottle of whiskey under the seat?

Peace or no peace, he told himself, as he had every morning for as long as he could remember, it had to stop. And it would. In Bishop's Croft. New town. New life. New future. It would all change when he left here and arrived there. He had told himself this at 3:25 a.m. that morning as he decanted whiskey into the ginger ale bottle in the dark kitchen, as his daughter-in-law and family slept in the spare room above, before he put on his suit and got ready to cremate his wife.

6

When her grandfather had told her to hang onto Grandma tight, especially over the speed bumps that slowed their departure from Sleaford's town centre, Tot hadn't needed telling twice. From the moment he had handed her the tea caddy containing her grandmother's ashes, she had been both honoured and horrified: honoured that he trusted her to be the keeper of the ashes and yet horrified that he had handed her death and that she held it there, heavy in her hands.

Even at twelve years old, Tot understood that a tea caddy was no fitting container for a dead woman, but she also understood that when push came to shove, it was the Thompson's lot to make do with what they had. As Sleaford's grey office blocks, DIY and cut-price furniture centres, all lit up like Christmas trees, gave way to the ghostly frost-rimed fields and low stone farm buildings of the Sussex countryside, she ran her fingers over the tea caddy's hand-tooled flowers. They reminded her of those carved on the ancient grey tombstones that flanked the doors of St. Lawrence's church.

While the church had stood in the village for four hundred years, it had only figured in Tot's memory for the previous three. Up until her graduation to Waterford High, Tot had attended the village school, a low slung modern building painted in bright primaries. It made an odd pairing with St. Lawrence's which stood next door. When the school opened its doors at the end of the day and its children streamed out and down the hill towards the estate, Tot had to head for the church to wait with her mother and Baby Trampus for Dorothy's school bus. On the days she craved a little peace, she would leave her mother and nephew on the church's low flint wall for a few moments to think inside the quiet of the dark church porch and slide her fingertips along its tombstones' chiselled patterns.

Sometimes, her mother noticed neither her departure nor her return.

And yet, back then, it seemed to Tot as if her mother was desperate to keep them all close, as if she were intent on keeping track of everything that was left. And there was something in their waiting for Dorothy that brought them all a little closer, something in how she and Tot shifted in unison on the wall's hard ridge, staring silently for what seemed like hours towards the corner where the cream and blue school bus would appear, in how her mother said, "Here she is," in how Tot was relieved when Dorothy proved her mother right by jumping off the double-decker's platform. And in how they would set off down the road for home, Dorothy yards in front, ignoring them all with the sullen disregard of a teenager who came home not only to homework but also to a baby son.

Later, when news of the baby's existence had caused Treeverton Grammar to suggest Dorothy graduate early, and after her mother had buried herself in the business of sewing, Tot returned to the church even though there was no one to wait with or to wait for. Waiting with her mother for Dorothy, the low flint wall had been a symbol of the enduring nature of family love in spite of a father's desertion. Waiting alone, she considered the church an escape from the people she loved, when the noise of family life and of her father's absence proved unbearable.

And lately, the wall provided a vantage point. If she climbed on top and edged along to where it was interrupted by the pathway, if she stood on her tiptoes and used the gatepost for support, she could just make out the roof of Gareth Strand's house, the second semi-detached from the village end of Willowswitch Lane. If she tried really hard, she could imagine she could see through the bay windows at the front into his room, that he would be sitting on his bed reading a hard-backed book, transformed into the boy she knew he really was, the deep boy who lurked beneath all that bravado and bluster.

*

Sitting in her grandfather's car, lulled by the rhythmic rumble of the car's tyres on the road's smooth unwinding, she might have drifted into a daydream of Gareth's transformation and of his resulting public declaration of love delivered to a rapt and enthusiastic audience behind the bike sheds if her grandfather had not dropped his bottle of ginger ale and if it had not rolled underneath the brake pedal. His manoeuvre to retrieve it slewed the car from side to side and threatened to wrest the caddy from her grip. With one hand, she jammed the caddy down between her knees, and with the other, she grabbed the steering wheel. Her grandfather slammed back in his seat, stepped on the brake, and miraculously, the car straightened.

"What?" he said, looking at her and slipping the bottle back down the side of the driver's seat. "WHAT?"

Tot shook her head, her heart pogo-ing in her throat. "You nearly killed us! We nearly...we nearly... *DUDDY BLIED!*"

"Oh, for goodness sake! A little swerve, that's all. Just a little miscalculation on the steering front. If you hadn't grabbed the wheel—"

"We'd be dead. We'd be *duddy bled.*"

"Oh, hush!"

For the rest of the journey, her grandfather drove with the rapt attention of a novice, like a man on his driving test. His lips moved as if he were reciting the highway code, his gaze darting from the road ahead to the side mirror, from the side mirror to the rear view mirror, then back again to the road. From time to time, he shot a nervous glance in her direction.

"Tot, if you drop your bloody grandmother, you'll not sit in the front of my car ever again." He pulled the bottle out from the side of his seat, his manner defiant, and took a long swig. "Watch yourself!"

"Don't you worry about me, Dangrad," she said. "Just don't drop that bottle again." She settled the caddy securely on her lap. "Can I have a swig?"

"You've got your own," he replied, jerking his thumb over his shoulder. "In the bag on the back seat."

Keeping one hand firmly on top of the wooden caddy, she twisted around in her seat and leaned over the headrest. She could see the figures she knew to be her mother and sister in the car behind, and thanked God she wasn't in the car with them and having to listen to Radio 4, to her sister's nagging, and to Tramp's whining. She grabbed a can of Fanta from the vinyl shopping bag on the back seat, then settled back, running her palm across the smooth, warm sides of the wooden caddy. Her mother had been fussy about the container for her grandmother, which was confusing considering the relationship that had existed between the two women. From as far back as Tot could remember, there had been accusations: Tot's grandmother had never forgiven Tot's other grandmother for an imagined slight. Old Mrs. Gardner, Tot's mother's mother, had worked as a tailor for a high-end clothing company in Golders Green and, as a result, had built up a clientele of rich Jewish women, many of whom, in addition to paying their bills, would present her with last season's furs and dresses as tokens of their appreciation. She had taken one of these dresses and altered it as a surprise gift for her daughter's mother-in-law-to-be. Unfortunately, she had miscalculated and the dress was far too big for Millicent, who read this "miscalculation" as an inference that not only was she too poor to buy her own dress, but also that she was as fat as a pig. From that point on, Grandmother Thompson referred to Grandmother Gardner as a jumped-up seamstress. Tot's mother had retaliated by complaining about the money Tot's father had "lent" his parents over the years. It was never a huge amount — a hundred here and there perhaps. Occasionally, Tot's father bought "treasured items" from his parents for hard cash — an old 78 record player with no needles, a cracked-leather settee, the piano on which Tot and Dorothy had learned to play — transactions which allowed him to bail them out without, in his eyes, bailing them out. And so the disagreement over a suitable container for Grandma's ashes had come as something of a surprise to Tot.

The tea caddy hadn't been the first choice. Initially, they were going to buy a nice funerary urn from Coleman and Blakelock, the undertakers. But the urns were expensive, and her grandfather wasn't sure if he was going to keep or scatter the ashes. He said it seemed a waste of money to pay out for an urn if he wasn't going to keep Millicent on a shelf. He wanted to use a tall tin that had contained a bottle of Balvenie, a fine single malt. It was at this point that Tot's mother went on a search of the house and discovered the tea caddy in the loft. It was fashioned from a coconut, its surface trellised with strange flowers and leaves. Granddad said he had picked it up at a car boot years ago down in Crediton, and that Grandma had liked it but had consigned it to the loft when they went over to tea bags. Her resting place, albeit temporary, was decided.

Tot had not been allowed to attend the funeral: her mother had deemed her too young for such things, and she and Trampus had been left behind. A neighbour, a Mrs. Phemister, had spent the morning desperate to entertain the "poor wee babes" and had enlisted a medley of building blocks, plastic cars and jam doughnuts in her quest to "take their minds off it." She had proved a big hit with Baby Trampus but had scored lower with Tot who declined the wooden blocks and cars and took two doughnuts outside to share with the chickens. Being left behind in a wake of funeral cars and black suits and dresses had filled her head with questions about the dead, the dying, and its processes.

The caddy felt warm beneath her fingers, and she fiddled with the lid, gently twisted it to the left. "Righty tighty, lefty loosey," she murmured, though once the lid was squeaking loose, the idea of spilling Grandma on the floor of the Morris Marina made her twist it quickly back to the right. As it tightened, her stomach relaxed.

"Dangrad?"

"Yes, Lovey."

"Did Gran die straight away, or did she..." Tot searched for the right word, "...linger?"

"Straight away, Lovey, I think." His voice was low and flat.

"How do you know she died straight away? Were you there?"

"No," he said, steering with one hand and pulling the road atlas out from the glove box with the other, his gaze chopping from the road to the open map on his lap and back again. "But the doctor said it was quick. A heart-attack in the plucking shed."

Tot had hidden in the plucking shed's darkness during a summer's game of hide-and-seek and had seen her grandmother's dead chickens hanging from their hooks. "So she was plucking when she died?"

He nodded. "At first, I thought she was asleep. She had her head resting on the bench and a half-plucked chicken in her lap. That was how I knew." He indicated right and turned onto the A23, merging into spare late night traffic.

"That was how you knew that she was dead?"

"Aye. Millie would never have slept halfway through a hen. Wouldn't have been respectful, you see. She loved those birds. Saw the plucking as some kind of...farewell. Never understood it myself. How a woman could wring a bird's neck with a few twists of the wrist one day..." he let

50

go of the steering wheel and demonstrated, "...and cry like a girl when she plucked it the next is beyond me." He blew his nose into a handkerchief. "A good woman to her hens, Tot," he said. "Dust to dust, ashes to ashes. Some things just don't spoon, and there's no getting around it."

Tot had seen enough movies to know the phrase, and yet she couldn't understand how someone's body might burn to dry ash. She'd been witness time after time to her father's abortive attempts to light the garden incinerator; each time, it was the dampness — of leaves, of privet clippings — that defeated him and filled the garden with plumes of grey smoke. And then there was the front room's temperamental Baxi-Burner that had to be coaxed into sustained flame through the use of a pair of tiny brass bellows and much swearing from her mother.

But if it was possible — and it obviously was: the proof was in her lap — to turn a damp body into dust and ashes, what would that look like? She could accept the crematorium's fire turning old skin and hair — even bones — to dust, but what about the dampness of flesh, of blood? And what about those really big bones? Like the pelvis? What about Grandma's gold tooth? What about the screws from Grandma's hip replacement? And the hip itself? Would it have melted and smooshed pink all over the ashes like plastic bottles did in the garden incinerator?

Why would she think it would be pink? What would be the point of pink?

Her grandfather handed her the road atlas. "Be a *Dittle Larling*, and remind me what happens after the A23."

She settled her grandma in the foot well between her feet and by the light of the glove box traced the A23's thin yellow ribbon up the centre of the page to where it became a broader blue ribbon and the M23.

"Keep straight on, Dangrad," she said. "A23, M23, M25, home."

He nodded and reached down the side of his seat again for the bottle of ginger ale.

"Careful, Granddad."

She measured the journey. Just two inches, a staple, then another five inches, and they would all be home. Mum, Dorothy, Trampus, and now Dangrad. And Grandma, too, she thought, pulling the caddy up onto her lap, trying to put the old woman back together again, and wondering why she thought the things she thought and how she might stop it.

7

They had arrived in convoy back at the house in Bishop's Croft a little before midnight. Tot had fallen asleep as they passed through Slough, the tea caddy held tight between her knees. Dan pulled in behind Elaine's car and sat there in the warm for a moment, watching her search her bag for keys on the pavement in the weak, yellow moonlight. Dorothy stood impatiently on the front door step, holding Trampus on her hip like a seasoned professional. She had thickened, hardened. The girl on the step was nothing like the gap-toothed child in the school photographs back on the kitchen dresser at home. Where did everyone go?

He nudged Tot. "Wakey, wakey," he said. *"Home Heet Swome."*

She stirred, one hand curled tight around an empty can of Fanta. Wordlessly, in the newly split sleep of a child, she leaned over and opened the car door. Leaving the can on the passenger seat, she got out and carried the caddy carefully to the front door step, sat down at her sister's feet, and fell back into a moment of sleep. Elaine had found the key, and waking Tot, she ushered her girls through the front door.

Dan pulled his one case from the boot of the car, then followed the women into the house. He found Elaine alone in the kitchen. Like Millicent, her first task, irrespective of the occasion or the hour, was to fill the kettle. For his wife, making tea had been an opportunity to pause before action. He assumed that making instant coffee served the same purpose for Elaine.

The two hardly knew each other. In Dan's book, daughters-in-law had always been the province of their husbands' mothers — whether they were liked or not. And yet here was this slight woman — who'd be attractive if she would only pack on a few pounds — taking charge of him, his dead wife, and the mess that death invariably leaves behind.

The mess had begun to make itself known to him when Millicent was first diagnosed with stomach cancer in '73. Both debts and cancer had been aggressive, and husband and wife could discuss neither. Dan would go with her to the hospital and wait in the family room, lose himself in *Woman's Own* and *Home and Gardens*. They never talked about what happened after she walked off with the nurse through the swing doors. This inability to communicate about sickness, pain, and the inevitability of death bled into his decision to burn the official manila envelopes addressed to Mrs. Millicent Thompson that had begun to fall like autumn's leaves upon their doormat.

He had begun to tell Elaine of his concerns over money the night before the funeral. The kids had gone up to the guest room early, leaving the pair of them alone, Elaine in Millie's rocker, he in his armchair by the Aga. The silence that followed Dan's fears was punctuated only by the sound of coals falling through the grate and by the clock ticking from the wall.

"You'll come to us," she had said, more statement than question, but he had felt obliged to answer.

"For a while," he said. "Until we know what's what."

She had stood and begun to dry the dishes that lay stacked on his draining board. As she spoke, she took a long time finding a place for the plates in the cupboard above. "For as long as you need, Dan. The girls ... and Tramps ... they need a man about the place. You'd be good for them."

He had sipped at his tea, feeling the smooth roundness of its surreptitiously added shot of whiskey. "If you say so, Elaine. For a while."

She had closed the cupboard door and shook out the tea towel, just as Millie had always done, before hanging it to dry on the rack over the cooker. "That's settled then," she had said before heading up to the guestroom, leaving him alone in the kitchen in his chair.

Now, just twenty-four hours later, she stood in her own kitchen, pulling cups from the drainer and polishing them with her own tea towel. Dan stood in the doorway, unsure of where to go, what to do. She turned, as if sensing his unease.

"We didn't really know what was happening," she said, wiping her hands on the cloth. "So you can have Tot's room for tonight. We'll sort out a room for you... maybe we could turn the dining room into a bedroom... Oh, well, whatever we do, we'll do it tomorrow." She took the whistling kettle from the gas ring and poured hot water on top of the instant coffee in the cups. "Sugar?"

He nodded, his suitcase still in his hand, his back resting against the larder door. "Could I take it up with me?" he said. "The journey ... the funeral ... I'm bushed."

She nodded and walked out with him to the hallway, his mug of coffee in her hand. "Tot," she called up the stairs, "you're in with Dorothy and Tramps tonight." She turned to Dan. "Follow me."

Only one door was open off the small upstairs landing, and Elaine ushered him inside. "It's not tidy, but it is clean," she said.

The room was small. Ten by eight, perhaps. A single bed was pushed up against the far wall under the window, and he put the case down on it with a heavy thump. Above the bed head was a narrow shelf which held a collection of snow globes. The glass sparkled in the glare from the room's ceiling light, and he stretched forward to get a better look. The shelf held at least twenty globes, souvenirs from stately homes, from zoos, from picturesque towns across the country. One, the largest, contained a blue unicorn, the snow thick and forming in heaps around the creature's hooves.

"Our youngest is a collector." Elaine placed the mug next to the tea caddy that Tot had left on the low bedside table. "Welcome to our home, crazy though it is," she said. "If you need anything…" She stopped mid-sentence to bend down and pick something up that was poking out from beneath the bed. It was a greetings card. She opened it, her lips moving as she read the words. "Oh, how sweet," she said, and passed the card to Dan. "I can't believe how quickly they grow up nowadays."

Dan read the card then stood it on the bedside cabinet. "Happy Valentine's Day," he said, reading the words on the front of the card aloud. "Trust Millicent to pop her clogs on the most romantic day of the year."

"Oh, Dan. Are you okay?"

"You mean now that I've swapped Valentine's cards for Sympathy cards?" He laughed, a little snorting laugh, took down the unicorn globe from the shelf and shook it. Glittering silver snow swirled inside the unicorn's world. "I'm fine, Elaine." The storm took only seconds to resolve, the snow settling back in a glistening layer at the unicorn's hooves.

She paused at the door and turned to look at Dan, concern drawn across her tired face. "You sure?" she asked.

"Sure I'm sure," he said. "I'm fine, really!" He patted the pillow. "Comfy bed. Cup of milky coffee. Unicorn. What more could an old man need? Go on, away with you!" He began to unbuckle his belt. "Unless you want to see an old man in his underpants?"

She put her hands over her eyes in mock shock then, laughing, headed back down the stairs to the kitchen and to her own cup of coffee.

Dan sat on the bed until the house grew quiet around him. He still had the unicorn globe in his lap, and he ran his hand over its smooth cool glass as he studied the tea caddy on the bedside table. He sat for what seemed like hours before picking up the tea caddy and placing it outside the door on the landing. Back in Tot's room, he leaned heavily against the closed door, the snow globe with its unicorn still in his hand. A new start, he had told himself in the car, away from the pressures of sickness and death, from his old drinking buddies, from all his demons and difficulties. He shook the globe again and again, raising the snow to a frenzy each time it looked like it might settle and began to cry, great silent tears hitting his cheeks and lips. Because the truth was, he wasn't fine. He wasn't fine at all. He had driven two-hundred miles in order to leave the problems behind and had brought the biggest problem — himself — along for the ride. He needed more than a comfy bed, milky coffee, and a unicorn. He needed a drink and he needed it badly.

8

When Tot needed to think, to push back the world and its players a little, she headed for Bishop's Croft park, to the place at the back where a line of trees marked a transition from public to private property, where the big houses — mock Tudors and low-slung bungalows — began to spread out along the back of the village and down to the canal. There, in a narrow secluded strip, the uppermost branches of the oaks and beeches gathered in a high canopy, and the park's mown grass gave way to deep leaf litter. Squat bushes and dense clumps of sedge grass sprang up in the filtered light. She adored the space's narrowness and the way it never changed back there, as if the filtered light maintained a steadiness of season and place, fixing the space as if it were a landscape painting into which she could escape whenever she needed constancy.

It was there, one late spring afternoon the previous year, that Tot met Gareth Strand. It was a Friday and she had chosen to walk the long way home from the village school, and she was loath to arrive. Back then, home had been too full of her sister — full to bursting with reluctant parenthood and bad mood — and of her mother — angry and worried, her mouth perpetually full of dress making pins. Its doors had been hangers for sewing projects — dresses for Cinderella, dresses for ugly sisters, a fairy Godmother's wings — all of which made Tot feel as if she were living in a theatre that had no audience, no opening night. So, rather than cut through the copse off Willowswitch Lane, she headed instead for the park.

Inside the park's fence line was a series of freshly painted swings and roundabouts, their bright colours garish below a cool blue sky. The playground's asphalt gleamed cold and black from an afternoon downpour which seemed to have rinsed the entire park clean and to have wrung from the still-bare trees the smell of wet bark. Tot set out across the damp grass, skirting the cricket pitch with its white backboard and cutting down the narrow dirt path that ran along the edge of the two tennis courts. That afternoon, the trees broke the back of the wind, leaving the air cold but still. She stepped through a gap in the oaks onto leaf litter that still wore a thin glaze of ice, a reminder of the morning's low temperatures. The tussock-sedges, which sat like sage-green scatter cushions around the roots of trees, were wet and heavy. She noticed the boy's school blazer before she noticed the boy, its mauve a shocking blotch against the dull, quiet green. It had been four o'clock, St. Lawrence's bells ringing four peals, and he had been leaning against a tree, smoking a cigarette.

It had been a lifetime ago.

She would learn that the boy was what her father — if he had been around — would have called "a bad 'un." He was fourteen years old and already sported a faint moustache. She would learn that he was the kind of boy who broke rules, grabbing them by the throat and squeezing them until they choked. For this boy, regulations were mere suggestions; his trousers were Waterford-Technical-High-regulation grey, but held up by a brown leather belt with a skull and crossbones buckle; and the white stag on his blazer pocket had been transformed with black pen into a rampant, horned zebra. Gareth Strand was bad news. He was also the most gorgeous boy who had ever smiled at her.

In the hour that followed, Tot took her rightful place on a stage. Gareth fed her lines and she ate them like candy. He quizzed her about her parents, her home, her sister, and she gobbled up his sweet interest like a diabetic. She said yes to a seat on his blazer spread across the wet grasses, to his evaluation of her father as worthless and of her mother and sister as uncaring and selfish, to his arm around her shoulder, to his need for secrecy. She said no to a drag on his cigarette but took it anyway, his fingers against her lips, the filter wet and hot, the smoke like a canopy of crows against the roof of her mouth.

*

So, when she arrived at Waterford Technical High School the previous autumn wearing her brand new big-enough-to-grow-into school uniform, it came as no surprise that Gareth ignored her; his disregard was merely the second act in the absurd theatre of their love affair. On rare evenings in his bedroom, he wanted her. But in the corridors of Waterford Tech, in its dining hall, in the Quad, and on the bus back to Bishop's Croft, he was a stranger. When she realized their relationship was to be a secret of this magnitude, she learned to love words like *clandestine* and *illicit*. She saw them as beautiful and disregarded the others — the ugly words like *furtive* and *sly*.

She took to hanging around the bicycle sheds where the older boys smoked at lunchtime. She sat a little distance away — far enough so it didn't look as if she was angling for inclusion, but close enough so she could hear their voices. She ate her sandwiches, inhaling both the boys' words and their cigarette smoke. Gareth was the loudest, and he held court astride an appropriated racing bike, one hand on the back of the cycle seat and the fingers of the other clasping a cigarette, the burning end turned palmwards. The other boys hunkered around him in a circle, passing a group cigarette and sharing stories of detentions, of near misses with parents and authorities, and dirty jokes. Gareth Strand didn't contribute. He just smoked his own cigarette and rocked the bike backwards and forwards on its wheels. Now and then, he looked over the heads of the hunkered boys towards the orange-haired girl in the too-big blazer. He'd jerk his chin upwards, the action flicking his long fringe back from his face, and raise the bike into a static wheelie. It was shorthand...semaphore. It was recognition. It was a caress.

Gareth Strand had style. He had sailboats on his sheets.

9

No one knew where to put her. At around 1:15 a.m., her husband, unable to handle sharing the dark of a strange room with his dead wife, opened the door and slid her out across the carpet where she came to rest by the airing cupboard. Around her and the caddy, the house hummed and clicked, adjusting to the redistribution of unfamiliar bodies. At 6:00 a.m., her daughter-in-law, stressed not only at having her father-in-law in the house but also at finding funerary ashes out on the landing, tucked the tea caddy under her arm and headed downstairs, fully resolved to find out what Dan intended to do — both in the short and the long term — with his dead wife. But, distracted by the need to coax life from the Baxi-Burner and by the memory of a leather G-string, she left the caddy and its ashes on the corner of the red-tiled hearth. At 9:20 a.m., Trampus, the great-grandson, opened the caddy to sprinkle his great grandmother with tiny grey plastic World War II soldiers. Dorothy, the favourite granddaughter, found the boy strangely ashy-handed and, on her way to wipe his hands, relocated the caddy to the top of the piano in the dining room.

*

Which was where Tot had found her grandmother. The wooden caddy sat on the upright piano which itself sat alone in the middle of an empty room, a room that had been full of furniture: chairs, a table, a bookcase, Trampus's box of toys, her mother's sewing machine, a padded dressmaker form — the usual detritus of family living. Only the piano, the footstool, and the tea caddy remained. Tot sat on the stool with the caddy in her lap and listened to the conversation echoing from the kitchen next door.

"I don't understand the problem, Dan," she heard her mother say. "It's quite simple, isn't it? Either Millicent can go in with her parents in Jersey — you could take the ferry, make a day of it — or you could scatter her in Sleaford. Unless there's somewhere else?"

Tot placed the caddy on the floor by the window. Out of earshot. Her mother began loudly making tea, clattering spoons and cups.

"There's no problem," her grandfather said. "I just haven't decided yet."

"So why did you leave her on the landing?"

"She's dead, Elaine. She doesn't care where she is.

Tot moved the caddy behind the thick orange velour curtain with her foot. She lifted the piano's cover. The sheet music for *Greensleeves* lay open on the stand.

"Yes, but to leave her on the landing…with children in the house."

"They're just ashes, Elaine. It's not Semtex. It's not bloody cocaine."

Tot slowly played the opening bar with one finger.

"Dan, watch the language."

"Sorry."

The kettle whistled, the china and spoons rattled, and Trampus whined for more Coco Pops. The fridge door clicked open then sucked shut. Tot made her way through the next few bars.

"Maybe you could keep her in the dining room…in your room, I mean. Once we get the bed in from the shed. It'll be your room then. For as long as you want it."

Tot stopped playing. So that explained the empty room and the missing furniture. Where had it all gone?

"I'll make a start then," he said. "I'll get that mattress in from the shed."

She closed the piano cover and wandered into the kitchen where her mother was at the table pinning a paper pattern to a folded length of glittering silver Lurex and where the answer to her question regarding the missing furniture was piled high. The dressmaker form stood behind her mother, a black vacuum cleaner hose looped around its headless neck. The dining room table, its legs unscrewed, leaned against the larder door, its chairs jostling for space with those of its smaller cousin, the kitchen table. Cardboard boxes of magazines, bags of knitting wool and needles, two seashell-encrusted table lamps, and the telephone were piled haphazardly onto the kitchen counter. The toy chest and bureau blocked the exit to the back door. Her grandfather sat at the table, his chair pushed back, swapping his slippers for a worn pair of trainers. Neither mother nor grandfather appeared to notice her. She took a mug from a cupboard and poured herself a cup of tea.

"Of course, you could always see this as an opportunity to put down some roots."

Tot sidled across the room and fiddled silently with the lid of the biscuit tin.

"Roots?"

Her mother rummaged in her workbox for her shears. Finding them and polishing their blades on her apron, she continued: "You could scatter the ashes at the church in the village. They have a lovely rose garden and you could…you could take a walk up there every day and sit with her, maybe make some friends up there."

"In the graveyard?"

"No! In the village!" She began to cut the silver fabric.

"You mean stay here permanently?"

"Why not? We're all family. It's home." The scissors made a shearing noise, repetitive and harsh.

"It's my son's home, and he buggered off. Remember?"

Tot took a biscuit from the tin, her mother handing her a look that declared crumbs or tea a very bad idea around her sewing, and hoisted herself up onto the counter between the seashell lamps and the bags of skeined wool. She nibbled her biscuit in careful concentric circles.

"You could get your own place," her mother continued. "Go on the council list. There's some new one-bedrooms at the back of the spinney. You'd be close to the shops and the pub...and the 'bookies. Why not? Where else is calling you?"

"What's a spinney?" Tot asked, taking out a skein of wool and stretching it across her knees. She found the end and began to wind a tight ball.

"A wood. A *thittle licket.*" Her grandfather continued to lace up his shoes: "I don't know, Elaine. Let's just leave it as it is for the moment. We'll...I'll stay here for a week or so, get my head straight, and then make a decision about where we're all going to end up. I'm not even that sure about hijacking your dining room."

More tea gurgled into china. "And a doctor's visit, Dan. You could see our doctor while you're here."

"There's nothing wrong with me," he said. "I don't need a doctor."

"How can you say that? What about that kerfuffle last year?"

"What the hell's a kerfuffle?"

Her mother waved the shears at Dan. "I'll tell you what a kerfuffle is! I'm called at 11:30 p.m. by Tommy Preston in a panic who tells me my sixty-year-old father-in-law picked a fight with a young lad in *The Hook and Pirate*—"

"Parrot."

"What?"

"It's *The Hook and Parrot.*"

"Picked a fight in *The Hook and PARROT* and, after being sat on by three of his friends, had to be driven home by the landlord's wife because he couldn't remember where he had parked his car. THAT'S a kerfuffle. And you're telling me that's normal? Nothing to be worried about?"

"I had a few to drink. It was grief. Tommy shouldn't have called you."

"He couldn't get any answer at your house, and Donald's…mine was the only number in your wallet."

"As I said, it was grief. Isn't a man allowed to push the boat out when his wife dies?"

"She wasn't even dead then. We didn't even know she was sick at that point. And anyway, Tommy thought we should know."

"Foreshadowing. I had a premonition. I was upset."

"Foreshadowing? Dan, healthy men don't lose their temper AND their memory on the same night unless there's something…wrong."

This time, he was the one to hold up his hand, like a man stopping traffic. "Okay! I was drunk. Can't a man get drunk once in a while?"

Her mother leaned across the table and took his outstretched hand in both of hers. "Of course he can. But humour me. It might be something else."

"Like what?"

"I don't know. Stress?"

"Okay," he said, pulling his hand from hers and draining his tea.

"Or maybe it's your age. You need to see a doctor, so he can work out if there's anything wrong."

"OKAY!" He pushed the cup away and stood up, the chair screeching on the lino, and let himself out of the back door. Tot slid out of the kitchen, leaving her mother sitting at the table with her sewing, and returned to the calm of the dining room. She could see her grandfather through the window. He had opened the shed door and begun to haul out garden furniture. The spare bed frame and mattress were at the back, so everything would have to come out. The patch of lawn under the kitchen window filled up with deck chairs. It began to rain.

Tot retrieved her grandmother from behind the curtain and returned her to the top of the piano before opening the cover once again and playing Greensleeves, this time right through to the end.

*

It had taken all morning to transform the dining room into Dangrad's room. Tot had stayed at the piano until the politeness between her mother and grandfather shimmied like a feral cat preparing for the pounce. Unwilling to engage in the drama unfolding between the two as they moved in and out of the house with a bed, a mattress and other furniture and linens borrowed from various rooms, she decamped to her own room ostensibly to gather her grandfather's few belongings but more to guard her own against relocation and to consider the past week with all its shifts and turns.

It had been a big week crammed with big things that needed serious consideration: death, a funeral she had been deemed "too young to attend," her grandfather moving in, her spluttering relationship with Gareth, then Keesal and his confetti. In an effort to slow her thoughts and their stormy confusions, she took down her snow globes from the shelf with the intention of polishing them one at a time as if that might steady or slow the week's frantic jinking. She picked up her favourite and began to buff its curve with the edge of her counterpane, the silver snow swirling around the blue unicorn like the questions that howled inside her head.

She put aside the globe and its chaos and reached down to retrieve a cardboard box from under the bed. She upended the box, shaking it violently, the contents that spilled across the counterpane telling her story more eloquently than any words read from a diary: a flyer for tonight's Youth Club "Valentine — Better Late Than Never — Disco," a cigarette end in a screw of tissue paper, bus tickets to Skegness, two acorns, passport photos of her and Stacey making faces, some buttons and badges, a crunchy grey sock. A host of important things. Everything was strewn upon the biggest thing in the box: the Valentine card. She didn't need to fish it out from under the other things, to open it, to read its words. She knew them by heart.

On one hand, she was horribly sad the card had not been from Gareth Strand. If the card had been from him, it would have brought everything into focus, made everything sharpen into something that could be understood and explained and told to people. Things between them had happened back-to-front, and *that* she had thought was at the root of their problems; they should have seen each other across a crowded room — at tonight's youth club disco perhaps — then smiled, chatted, danced once or twice, gone to the pictures … and *then* locked his little brother in the wardrobe before they did the things they did on his bed. If the card had been from Gareth, it would have shown that he wanted these beginning things — the smiling, the talking, the dancing — as much as he wanted the ending things, the things that happened in his bedroom. A card like that, with its padding and its silky roses, should have been one of the beginning things, one of the things that came at the start, before all the rest.

But on the other hand, she was glad to have received a Valentine card from anyone at all.

When both of those hands were put together, they held a card from Keesal, and she had never thought of him in that way. He was just a friend. He was the boy the Stanley Close kids had christened Mowgli. He was the skinny kid her mother called "the Indian lad at number ten." He was the boy she had turned to when her father left, when she had needed to be with someone who was not a best friend, not Stacey, not someone who knew her inside out. She had needed someone who didn't realize the difference between who she was when she had a father and who she was without one.

Keesal became that someone on the day she got stuck in the oak tree in the copse. She had gone there to be alone and had forced herself to climb to the top, as if that might bring her some clarity, might help her make sense of why her father had left. She had found nothing there, just more branches above, and below her, their tangle of limbs and leaves and pure panic at the thought of staying and more at the thought of returning to earth. As she sat in the crook of the highest bough of her bravery, Keesal appeared like a wild thing from the branches below: first his hands, fluttering in space, searching for a hold; next the top of his head, his hair as glossy as the leaves that parted; finally his dirt-smeared face, triumphant for a second but then full of dismay at finding her there above him. His dismay seemed to speak to her, as if he too was trying to find some other place to be.

For the rest of that summer, they scaled other trees and fished in the canal. When her house became noisy and difficult, she spent autumn evenings sitting at the table in his kitchen just a few doors up on Stanley Close. Stacey was *her* best friend, but Keesal had been her place when she craved invisibility. In the time since that first summer, Keesal had become something more than "the Indian lad at number ten." He was comfort, a constant in her life. That he was a boy gave him an extra dimension, gave their friendship an extra layer. But she had never thought of him as boyfriend material. Never. Never. Ever.

And yet, when she pictured him standing in the aisle of the bus demanding that Gareth's friends return the Valentine, she couldn't help feeling a tight bubble of something else, something not just friends, bouncing about behind her ribs.

If the card was from Keesal, and if he liked her in that way, could she like him back? Could she be his girlfriend? And if she did, and if he became her boyfriend, what about Gareth? What if Gareth wanted to be a real boyfriend but was scared or clueless about how to do it? What if she turns up with Keesal as her boyfriend, and Gareth — who would then never have the chance to do all the beginning things they should have done as well as the bedroom things they shouldn't have — what if he got angry and told everyone what she had done and what she was?

And what *was* she to have done all those things with him anyway?

She took down Princess Anne and Captain Mark Phillips and huffed on their glass dome before polishing it with the corner of her pillowcase. White snow swirled around the couple. It was their wedding day, and they were nowhere: Buckingham Palace was merely a picture on the inside of their glass. She held the globe close to her face.

"So, Captain Phillips…Do you mind if I call you Mark?" The plastic groom stood smiling in the snow. "What would you have thought of Anne if she'd let you do all the Ending Things before the Beginning Things?" He didn't say a word, just smiled. She shook the globe, the snow a blizzard around the happy couple. They both looked at her, the bride's plastic hair very yellow, and the groom's suit glossy and black with gold piping. She held the globe to her ear to hear Princess Anne tell her she wasn't that kind of girl; she was a princess and had held out for the talking at polo matches and the dress and the wedding cake. Tot slid the happy couple under her pillow like a lost tooth.

She went back to the blue unicorn that pawed at a rock planted in silver snow. She had believed what her dad wrote in the letter, that he was sending it to her from America, until her sister pointed out the words "Made in England" on the base. It was the last thing her father had sent. Below in the dining room, the muffled voices and sound of squealing furniture had stopped, and she could hear her mother preparing an early dinner in the kitchen. She could hear the radio and that nice man from *News Week* talking about the traffic backed up on the M25. She could hear her grandfather playing *Nobody Knows* softly on the piano. It was her father's favourite song. Her grandfather was playing it very badly.

She returned all the snow globes back to the shelf, even the prince and princess, and picked up the Valentine card, her other Important Things scattering across the counterpane and catching in its crocheted holes.

*

The dining room looked embarrassed, like a fat woman wearing a bikini and wishing she had packed her one-piece. The piano was pushed back to the window, and in its place, along the wall that ran between the dining room and the sitting room, was a narrow bed. Next to the bed stood a dining room chair that did double duty as a nightstand, and in the corner, behind the door into the kitchen, a single wardrobe. A stack of shirts and trousers and a pile of wire hangers lay on the bed.

"Shall I put these away for you, *Dangrad?*" she asked him. He had his back to her and was marking the wall with a pencil. A framed seaside photograph of a man buried in sand up to his towel-draped neck was propped against the wall. A little behind the man sat a woman on a deckchair.

"You're a *dittle larling.*"

"And you're a *grovely landdad.*"

She pulled a shirt from the pile and hung in on a hanger. "Who are the man and the lady?"

"Me and Millicent. 1948. Bognor Regis." He hammered a picture hook into the wall and hung the picture. "What do you think?"

She went to stand at his side. "I don't think you look very happy," she said. "You look sort of scared."

He leaned in to the picture, peering at it through the bottom section of his bifocals. "You know, I think you're right. I think it's my proximity to her feet."

Tot nodded. "Feet can be a problem. Dorothy strangles me on the stairs with her toes. Or she used to. Before Trampus."

"Ah, yes. BTE. 'Before the Trampus Era.' A turn up for the books, eh? And how is life in the Years After Our Lord Trampus?"

She returned to the bed and continued to hang shirts and trousers on hangers.

"It's hard," she said, "when things change. It's hard to know what to do when things aren't what you think they are." He joined in, teaming trousers with matching shirts and ties, the entire outfit bulging on one hanger. "It's a *mucking fess*," she said.

He looked at her, this time over the top of his glasses. "No, Tot. It's just life, and some things — mucky words included — are no better even for the spooning."

She pulled the Valentine from inside her shirt and handed it to her grandfather. He sat down on the bed and smoothed his hand over its padded puppy and roses, smiling. Then he opened it and read the words, his mouth moving silently as he went.

"Ah, yes," he said. 'Gatecrash my heart,' eh? Quite poetic. Do you know who sent it?"

She nodded.

"Boyfriend?"

"Yes. No. Not really. Oh, I don't know. That's the problem."

"Ah."

She took back the card and set it on the floor by the bed. "You see, the boy I wanted the card to be from isn't the one who sent it. The one who sent it is just a friend. Or I thought he was just a friend. And the one who didn't send it…well, I thought he was my boyfriend. Or could be. It's complicated."

"You were right. Sounds like a *mucking fess*," he said.

"Yeah."

"Can I help?"

She picked up three full hangers of clothes and hung them in the wardrobe. "I don't know."

"You could talk to your mum."

"No. She's goes off her rocker if I talk about boys. It's the Dorothy/Trampus thing."

He pulled a stack of clothes towards him and continued to match shirts and ties, occasionally looping a belt from the neck of the hanger. He passed them to Tot so she could hang them from the wardrobe's rail. "No friends you could ask?"

She thought about Stacey. "Yeah, but I don't want to. It would make things...uneven."

He nodded. "Just left with your old granddad then. Sorry about that."

Tot shut the wardrobe door and went back to the photograph on the wall. "When you met grandma, did you...did you do it all the normal way round?"

"How do you mean?"

"Well, did you meet her somewhere and then like her and then ask her out and then maybe dance with her or something, before...before...?"

"...before I kissed her, you mean?"

"Kind of. Do you think you did it the right way round?"

He patted the space next to him. Tot sat back down, and he put his arm around her shoulders: "It was summer. I was nineteen years old. A merchant navy man. Lad, really. My friend Archie was going out with a girl called Evie who lived next door to your grandmother. Archie was a sailor, like me, and we had a few days off, and he wanted to see his girl, and I was the only one with transport. A bike. A Norton Commando with sidecar." He stopped for a moment, as if remembering the bike, or maybe the girl, or maybe both. He went on. "Millicent Murrell and Evie...Spinner, I think...were friends, and we met up down by the river at Oxhey. We hit it off and the next time I had a few days leave, I came back down and took her to the pictures. Millie and me."

74

"Millie?"

"Millicent. She used to like Millie better. Anyway, we courted a while, I met her family, we got engaged, we got married, we got into debt. Is that the right way round?"

She nodded and wriggled out from under his arm. "Me and this boy...."

"The one who didn't send the card?"

"Yeah. We might not have done things the right way round."

"Ah."

"And now I don't know if he just wanted the end stuff, and not the beginning stuff."

"The end stuff?"

"Yeah."

The room was quiet. A fly buzzed from behind the curtain. Her mother was searching channels on the radio in the kitchen next door, the stations surging in and out of earshot. The whistle on the pressure cooker signalled the potatoes were ready and that dinner was only moments away.

"Is it bad to do the end stuff without the beginning stuff? I mean, is it bad if you just do the end stuff and never do the beginning stuff. Does that make you bad?"

"Not bad, Tot. If I've got you right, it's just sad. It's the beginning stuff that lets you know if you really want to do the end stuff. You might not want to. If you knew."

The two of them sat side by side on the narrow bed.

"If they don't want to do the beginning stuff with you, does it mean they don't love you?" Tot asked.

He shrugged, and the pair of them looked at the photograph he had just hung on the wall. "Who knows, Pet? Who knows?"

A voice from the kitchen told them tea was ready and on the table and that they both better have clean hands.

"What's this other lad — Card Boy — like?" he asked.

She shrugged. "Stacey says he's dishy, in a mystic way."

He nodded. "Well, you know what they say about a bird in the hand."

"It's worth two in the bush?"

"That's right. Seems to me you've done the end stuff with the other lad. Maybe you should try the beginning stuff with this one." He stuck his hands out in front of him. "Pass muster?"

She looked at them hard and nodded. "Mine?" she asked, holding out her own.

He took them in his and kissed her palms. "Good enough to eat off."

10

Elaine put the last of the plates away in the cupboard and turned off the radio. She forced herself to stand still before the kitchen window inside the room's heavy silence. The quiet flowed into the space that Radio 4 had filled and its pressure threatened to bury her. She found herself pressing her palms to the sides of her face and staring wide-eyed into the dark garden beyond. Saturday evening loomed and the house was as quiet as…as quiet as what? A mouse? A grave? She fought the urge to turn the radio back on and, instead, sat down heavily at the kitchen table. Where were they all, these people whom she had told herself needed her. Why were they — the old and recently bereaved, the young and insecure — all out enjoying themselves while she, available and not a bad catch by anyone's standards, sat alone in her kitchen?

She gave in and turned the radio back on, easing the station finder back through the channels until she found a news show. This was not an evening for music—she needed a voice…and she needed to get on. The clock above the stove read five-forty-five, and Mr. Dolan, her spaceman, was due for a fitting at six. She just had time to get this space straight before he arrived. Grabbing the dressmaker's form around its waist in a bear hug, Elaine walked it into the tight space between the stove and the back door. This was the dummy's last chance before banishment to the hallway. She stood back. There was more room there…but there was no peace of mind. None whatsoever; she couldn't help but worry that one of the girls would come charging through the back door and send both dummy and spacesuit into orbit across the cluttered room. There was no getting away from it: if Dan decided to stay, she would need to find a new home for all the ex-dining room stuff and to sort out new operating space for *Collette's Creations*.

If her kitchen was a nightmare, the old dining room, newly transformed that morning into Dan's room, was a serene dream. In fact, when she had visited after tea to put an extra blanket on the bed, the room itself seemed happier, more cheerful somehow, as Dan's bedroom than it had ever been as a dining room. Dan wasn't there. He had offered to visit Bishop Croft's pubs and village stores to check that Elaine's business cards were still stuck above payphones and in shop-front windows. She had encouraged him, relieved he wasn't planning on spending his first real evening moping in his room, and had lingered after dusting the mismatch of chest of drawers and nightstand, thinking back to the early days when she and Donald had first moved into the house on Stanley Close. Their furniture, which had seemed reliable and solid in the tiny maisonette they rented from Donald's aunt, seemed shabby and small in the big semi-detached on the Bishop's Croft Estate. *They* seemed shabby and small, like little children playing at house.

And there had never been enough money to buy the things they needed to fill the space, let alone to pay for the treasures they wanted. That first Christmas, when her in-laws came to see their brand new grandchild, she remembered throwing a sheet over the ironing board and using it as a serving buffet in the front room. Later, when both two girls were big enough to sit in proper chairs at the dining room table, there weren't enough proper chairs, so Donald had to sit on a wooden tray set atop the upturned laundry basket. She still had the tray.

When she saw Dan's seaside picture of Bognor Regis, she was taken back to the time before Donald had left them all, when the walls of the dining room had been home to a flock of framed photographs chronicling Thompson family events: their wedding photos, the babies, the babies grown into children, the awful school photographs, the picnics, the holidays in Bournemouth. Now, Dan's photo was the only one that hung there. If it hadn't been for the tiny holes peppering the wallpaper, she might be forgiven for thinking that no other photos had ever hung there, that none of the milestones in her life had ever really taken place or had warranted recording.

She had taken the photographs down long before Dan moved in when she realized that Donald was not coming home. Dorothy had come home from the hospital with baby Trampus, and Elaine had taken a photograph of them both in the back garden on a blanket under the sumac tree. Trampus was bundled up against the chilly spring weather and was the same happy child he was today. Dorothy had looked cold and exhausted. Shell-shocked even. Regardless, Elaine had had three prints made. One she had framed for the dining room. The other two she had mailed to Millicent: one for her mother-in-law to keep, and one for her to forward to Donald. For some reason, she felt sure that Donald's mother had his address in America. She also felt sure that even though he had been able to walk away from her and the girls, a grandson might prove too much for him to ignore. She was ready to try again, to do whatever she needed to do to make her marriage work. After all, she had done nothing wrong, and therefore, guilt did not stand in her way. She knew she had enough forgiveness in her to mastermind a reconciliation. But clearer than that: she felt she couldn't manage much longer on her own, without a man in the house, without a man for the girls.

But the photograph had not brought Donald home, and she had never mentioned the matter to her mother-in-law again. Instead, she had taken down all the pictures and put them in a box in the attic. The framed print of Dorothy and Trampus had never made it onto the family wall.

The sitting room seemed like the best bet for her sewing. She manhandled the dummy down the hall and into the front room, positioning it in the bay window. Then she pulled a fold-out table from under the stairs and set it up alongside the dummy. When she added the full length chevalier mirror from her bedroom, the work space was complete. She had been loath to allow her sewing to take over the only room in the house fit for entertaining. But it had been years since she entertained anyone, and if they were going to eat, the business of sewing had to take place somewhere.

She took the almost-finished costume from its box and dressed the dummy, smoothing the silver chaps into place, pressing Velcro hooks to Velcro loops, and snapping home the poppers down the fly front. She attached the gold leather braces and stood back to see how the outfit looked before she tackled the problem of the vacuum cleaner hoses. Dan had offered to spray them silver, so they would look right. But she had held off; she still wasn't sure if they would attach securely enough.

She didn't know whether to lodge the braces between the dummy's breasts or stretch them either side. Her decision was interrupted by the ring of the doorbell. He was early. She tidied her hair in the reflection in the window's glass.

When she opened the front door, Simon Dolan stood smiling on the top step. His blond hair stuck up in a cow lick at his forehead. He wore a baggy off-white cotton sweater under a neon Puffa jacket, faded army fatigues, and a pair of deck shoes sans socks. In his hands was a white cardboard box bearing a sticker that marked it as coming from Creasey's, the bakers in the village. On top, two Styrofoam cups of coffee balanced precariously. She took the box from him.

"I'm claiming this as a business expense," he said, pulling a taped receipt from the tray and stuffing it in his pocket. "The tax man kicks at beer, but coffee and doughnuts might get through." He stepped inside and shut the door behind him. "Nice place."

"Thank you. Please, go through there. We're in the sitting room."

She showed him into the lounge, where he sat messily on the sofa: he was a sprawler, a man whose legs were far too long for neatness. Setting the coffees on the edge of the coffee table, she watched him lean forward and rifle through the magazines on the slatted ledge below.

"I'll put these in the kitchen." She tapped the top of the doughnut box. "House rule. No snacks near the sewing." She turned for the kitchen, pausing briefly in the doorway to watch him select one of the magazines, then thump a cushion into shape before settling back to read. He made himself comfortable in someone else's home very quickly, she thought. A little too quickly.

"Please, make yourself at home, Mr. Dolan," she said.

"Thanks. And it's Simon." He picked up one of the coffees, pulled off its lid and blew across its surface.

When she returned from the kitchen, Simon was kneeling in front of the dummy, inspecting the poppers on the trousers' fly front. "May I?" he asked, turning back to face her.

"Be my guest."

He pulled sharply at the fly, the fabric giving way with a staccato series of pops. He swivelled round and smiled at Elaine. "Nice!"

"The back," she asked. "Is the back alright? I wasn't sure…"

Simon got to his feet and leant over the dummy's shoulder.

"Oh, yes! That's ace." He picked up the dummy by the waist and spun it around. The sparkling chaps exposed the dummy's dingy canvas buttocks.

"Hope mine looks better than hers!" he said, bending down to pinch the faded beige cheeks. "You could come," he said, still inspecting the dummy. "To Wales. Let me know what you think of all this in action. Give me your expert opinion. "

"On your show?"

"Of course. What else?" He knelt down and tested the strength of the waistband's Velcro. "You could be my guest." He pinged the braces with his finger. They snapped back hard on the dummy's breasts with a dull thwacking sound. "It all seems a bit more...perverse on her, don't you think?"

"I'm probably not the one to ask," replied Elaine. "I don't go to many strip shows. I'm not sure what's considered ... perverse."

She pulled the lid from the remaining coffee cup.

"It's not sugared."

"I don't take sugar. I just can't stand these plastic lids." She sat down on the couch and sipped, her elbow resting on her knees, her fingers playing in the saucer of pins on the coffee table.

"Perhaps you're sweet enough?"

"For a comedian, that's a really lame line."

He stepped away from the dummy and sat down next to her. "I'm a better stripper than I am a comedian. And I'm not funny in my spare time."

"No?"

He shook his head. "No." He, too, traced a pattern in the pins, his thumb circling close to hers.

"What are you in your spare time?" she asked.

"Twenty-two," he said, his teeth clamping onto his bottom lip. His thumb hooked around her finger and stopped.

She let her finger stay there, in the saucer of pins. He said nothing, just looked at her, his eyes dark like unskinned almonds.

"We don't know about the fit," she said. His thumb was hot against her finger.

"We'll need to find that out. Before Penryth." His voice was low and when he smiled, she could see the faint impressions his teeth had left on his lower lip. "Ease in. Gently."

She pulled her hand back, pins spilling onto the coffee table's tiled top. "I meant the costume."

He smiled, wider this time and stood up. He grabbed the hem of his sweater, pulled it up over his head, then dropped it to the floor. "So did I," he said.

*

She could hear him changing into the spaceman outfit in the dining room. In fact, his bumping around the furniture and the rip of the Velcro as he adjusted the fit of the chaps were the only sounds she could hear. Six-thirty on a Saturday night and a man nearly twenty years her junior was standing almost naked just ten feet away beyond the door. She wondered if he had taken off his shoes. The idea of his naked feet on the bedside rug made her stomach clench.

She sat at the sewing machine in the window and fiddled with the tension dial. Penryth. Had he meant it? Could she go? The furthest West she had ever been was Brecon Beacons when she was a child, a car journey that seemed to take a lifetime of mountains and motorways, the journey fuelled by endless egg-and-cress sandwiches that her mother pulled from a basket with the aplomb of a magician producing white rabbits and scarves. What was she thinking? It was a five-hour drive to Penryth. She could stay in a guest house, maybe find one with a view of the sea. They might meet over breakfast, talk in close whispers, and in the evening, she would wear her best dress and sit in the front row of a theatre and watch him move in the costume he was trying on this very moment in her dining room. Of course, later, he would appear in her bedroom, proposing a

night of passion, the kind that starts with timid touches —
fingertips on earlobes, stray hair brushed from eyes,
butterfly kisses. And afterwards, after the show was over,
she would drive home alone, the car radio silent, the
mountains like anvils in her rear view mirror, a comedy
programme on the seat next to her bearing his scrawled
telephone number, a number she would never call.

"Da-dah! How do I look?"

He stood in the doorway. The chaps were tight, the
waistband barely covering his hips, a wave of coarse gold
hair lapping up to his navel. The silver braces strained
against his chest, the space helmet tucked under his arm.

"You look…very astronautical," she said, pulling a
box from under the sewing table and hauling out two
lengths of black vacuum hosing. "Head over to the mirror,
and let's try these. I've glued hooks on every four or so
inches and there's matching eyelets on the braces, but I'm
still not sure." She moved towards him, but he reached out
and took the tubing from her.

"I'll need to be able to do it myself," he said.
"Precious few helpers in green rooms." At the mirror, he
attached the hosing tube to the front of the first brace,
latching the hooks into the metal eyelets. "Guide my hands
to the ones at the back," he said. He put the helmet on.

She stood behind him and lifted the concertinaed
hoses over his shoulders. He reached his hand up and back,
his knuckles knocking awkwardly against the helmet's
plastic curve. She reached up and took his hand. It was hot,
and the whorled copper hair that extended just past his
wrists felt alien under her fingers. His hand was quiet in
hers, and he allowed her to guide his fingers down the
braces to locate the top eyelets. He didn't blink, his smile
behind the helmet's convex glass steady in the mirror. She
watched his fingers locate each tiny hook and
corresponding eye. She tried to help him with the last one,

but he flicked her fingers away, and persevered until the last hook was latched.

"Just the legs need hemming," she said. "Let's head into the kitchen and you can stand on a chair."

Still wearing the helmet, he followed her down the hall into the warm kitchen where he climbed onto a chair she had pulled out from the table. She eased a line of pins carefully between her lips before hitching up her skirt and kneeling on the cold linoleum. She studied his bare feet, long and pale-nailed, his big toes curved slightly upwards like turtle heads.

She had double folded the front of one chap hem to length and was about to pull a pin from her lips when the back door flew open and Tot, with Stacey in tow, erupted into the room, the pair of them a flurry of dresses on coat-hangers, hairdryers, and make-up bags. Tot, head down and single-minded, made straight for the larder, and Elaine could hear her rummaging about among the shelves' tins and packages.

"I'm still starving," her daughter yelled from inside the larder. "Why can't I find the biscuit tin?"

Tot's friend Stacey stood open-mouthed in the doorway, her bag dropped to the floor, her hairdryer held like a crucifix before her, staring at the near-naked man standing on the chair.

"His bum's hanging out!" Stacey cried, pulling Tot from the pantry by the arm. "Your mum's got a man on a chair and his bum's hanging out!"

In one fluid movement, Simon spun on the chair, took off the space helmet, stowed it under his arm and executed a deep bow. "Flesh Gordon," he said. "Exotic dancer, at your service, Ladies."

Stacey shrieked with laughter and ran out into the hallway and up the stairs, but Tot stuck out her hand. "Tot Thompson. Adolescent. Crap at dancing."

He leaned down from the height of the chair to shake her hand.

"Nice bum," she said, before grabbing two doughnuts from the box on the kitchen table and following her friend up the stairs.

Simon made as if to step down from the chair.

"Stay up there!" mumbled Elaine, her mouth full of pins, and her fingers clutching at the trouser hem.

"My, my, Mrs. Thompson," he said. "What a sharp mouth you have."

11

Only those who have travelled too far from childhood define it as a place of simple innocence. For the adolescent caught inside its perimeter, the close of childhood is a confusion of shifts — of mood, of mind, of like and dislike. At one edge of the kingdom, in a garden say, on a sunny day, a girl is captivated by make-believe, her teddy dipping his stitched mouth to an acorn cup of tea. But minutes later, bear abandoned, the girl drops to crawl soldier-style beneath childhood's white picket fence into a field of adolescent gin snares.

But as quickly, the lure of the dark turns dreary. The child crawls back to the trivial — the trifles in her toy box: dolls without their shoes, knitted dogs and kittens, strings of pearls and plastic rings. Girls turn to each other, to myth and magic to spin sense from the confusion of these worlds: Prince Charming lives in a house behind the butcher's shop; a girl's hair will grow into a rope ladder long enough to scale the wall of Grownup; a father is a chain-smoking King; the boy from down the road a baron, his bicycle a horse with magic painted on its hooves.

In myth and magic, a girl's best friend is her champion, but in a land of snares, she is competitor, and its hard packed ground is best covered alone.

*

The playground was very dark and almost empty. Just two little kids, a boy and a girl, huddled in their coats on the roundabout, their mothers sitting on a nearby bench smoking cigarettes in the harsh glare of the security lights. Tot pulled her make-up case from her handbag and fished around for her pot of lip gloss. She found it, dipped a finger in "Luscious Berry" and touched it to her mouth. Stacey checked her watch.

"What time can we go in? I'm getting cold!" Stacey shivered in her anorak and best going-out dress, a cotton frock from the previous summer, her bare legs mauve and blotched.

Tot dropped the lip gloss back inside her make-up case and checked the clock on the pavilion wall. "We can't go in until eight. Ten minutes."

"Why can't we go in now?"

"Because of the rules. Only spazzers who dance with their brothers go in before eight. And anyway, none of the boys will be there. They KNOW the rules."

"Keesal'll be there."

"Keesal will be there because Keesal's mum is in charge of chairs and tables. Keesal doesn't count."

"But he sent you the card..."

"Stop it, Stacey!"

The mothers on the bench called their children over from the roundabout and bundled them deep into knitted scarves and hats. The bigger of the children, the boy, clambered onto his bike and took off across the dark park, his backside out of the seat and his legs pumping hard. The smaller one, the girl, grabbed her scooter and tried to follow him out across the grass. Her mother grabbed the hood of the little girl's parka without breaking conversation, and as the two women began a slow walk to the park gates, the girl trailed after them, looking back longingly at the boy on his bike as she walked.

"What boys will be there at eight?" Stacey asked.

"The boys from the back of the bus."

"Your bus?"

"Yeah."

"That boy you like?"

Tot nodded and fished her hairbrush from the depths of her bag. She leaned her head down between her knees, letting her hair fall forward, and ran the brush hard through her curls. They sparked and writhed in the nylon brush's teeth then spread like an orange cloud. Gareth Strand would be there. He would be there with his friends — the blond boy with the buck teeth, the older one from Queens, the two brothers he played "Knife" with — and she would be there, too, in her elasticated boob-tube and blue-and-white striped skirt, both thieved from Dorothy's wardrobe. He would see her dancing — swaying and waving "Bye, Bye, Baby" to the Bay City Rollers — and she'd be laughing and confident with Stacey and looking like she didn't need him, and he'd come over as a slow one came on — maybe that one about the lonely girl *("...my lonely girl...")* — and ask her to dance and she'd think about it for a moment. Then she'd nod and walk into his arms. He'd be a bit stiff and formal for a moment or two, but then he'd pull her closer. She'd rest her head on his shoulder, and he'd run a hand through her hair, and it would spark in the dark (because it would be gone eight o'clock and the lights would be off apart from the big, round disco ball covered with mirror tiles) and he'd tell her that he *had* bought her a Valentine card after all but was scared to give it to her because of the Commitment Thing. But now he wasn't scared anymore, and he was doing the Slow Dancing Thing and wanted to add in the Beginning Things: the Out-In-The-Open Dating and the Holding-Hands-at-School Things.

The mothers had almost reached the park gates. They were standing in the car park, the one woman's hand still in the hood of the little girl's jacket. The other woman was calling to the boy who was no longer pedalling but who sat astride his bike at the far edge of the park, on the edge where the floodlit clipped grass met the dark trees. Tot watched him turn away from his mother and towards the trees before he shifted his bike around and pedalled slowly back across the park.

The hand on the pavilion clock had crept around towards the eight. She held onto the swing's chains and walked back until she was on tip toes. Then she pushed off, swinging up and back once, twice then three times, each time higher than the last, the wind catching inside her skirt. On the fourth swing, she jumped, and despite her heels, landed perfectly on the concrete.

"Come on then," she said. "Let's get this show on the road."

*

"Hands, please!" said the woman taking money at the entrance. She inked a small wooden block on a pad by the side of her cash box. Tot held out her hand, palm down. The woman pressed the block hard against her skin. As the woman stamped Stacey, Tot studied her own stamp: a green Christmas tree. She heard the woman say to Stacey, "We couldn't find a love heart. But you kids don't mind a Christmas tree, do you?" Tot did mind, but Stacey hadn't answered; she was looking apprehensively at the double doors that led into the hall. The woman kept talking: "Ladies' toilets on your left, telephone to ring your parents on the right, one free fizzy drink and a packet of crisps. No smoking, no drinking, and no sliding across the floor on your arse."

They pushed through the heavy fire doors into the hall beyond. The room was noisy and dark, apart from a shower of mosaic light that spun across the deserted dance floor, empty save a tight circle of girls dancing and giggling at the stage end of the room. In the circle's centre, a girl bopped around a mound of discarded shoes and handbags. As she finished her solo, she merged back into the circle which pushed another of its dancers into its centre.

Braver girls began to leave the ring to dance with each other, the foot or two of space between them vanishing as they clinched and whispered, laughed, then separated again. They looked like amoebae shimmering and dividing.

Clusters of boys loitered nervously along the hall's walls. Some — the ones wearing too-new shirts and trousers, their hair still damp from the bath — were more edgy than others and covered up their nervousness with loud laughs and horseplay. A few — including Gareth Strand and his blond friend with the buck teeth — leaned easy against the stage, watching the girls dance. They didn't talk to each other. They stood with their Cokes in their hands and watched.

Gareth stood out from the others. He had embraced punk and was wearing torn jeans and a tattered black and white striped mohair sweater which made him appear long and skinny. Someone, his mother perhaps, had sewn straps and buckles onto his jeans. To Tot, he was the epitome of cool. She watched him lean in to whisper something to the buck-toothed boy. They both laughed.

Stacey prodded her. "I'm going to get something to drink. Coming?"

Tot nodded.

She was dismayed to find Keesal's mum serving at the kitchen hatch. Mrs. Patel handed Stacey a can of Coke and a packet of crisps and crossed through the Christmas tree on her wrist with a felt-tip pen. She smiled and waved Stacey away from the hatch, and Tot moved to the head of the queue.

"Little Tot!" said a smiling Mrs. Patel, her accent heavy, her sentences, as ever, full of strange order and missing articles. "How pretty! But cold, no? Little Tot is cold with her shoulders all out in the world?" She bobbed down for a moment, then reappeared with a brown cardigan in her hands. She held it out across the counter. "You want cardi?"

Tot shook her head. "No, thanks, Mrs. Patel. Just a Coke and some crisps, please."

Mrs. Patel still held the cardigan by its collar. "Sure? Good cardi," she said. "100% wool!" she said, showing Tot the label.

Tot shook her head again.

"Okey-Dickey. Keesal is up the back getting toilet rolls. I tell him Tot is here?"

"No!" said Tot, quickly grabbing her Coke and crisps in one hand and threading the other through Stacey's arm. "We're off for a dance. I'll see him later."

As they reached the dance floor, Mud's "Tiger Feet" came on, its beat stomping from the speakers. The floor filled around them. Even boys left the safety of the walls to risk the polished wood floor and its girls. The circle of dancers by the stage disintegrated into the beginning of an extended line of girls that soon reached across the room to the serving hatch, and was, as if by plan, mirrored by a shorter and stragglier line of boys.

Tot and Stacey broke into the middle of the girls' line, catching up with the dance's repetitive steps. Each line tried to out-dance and out-sing the other. *"That's neat, that's neat, that's neat, that's neat, I really love your Tiger Feet."* The girls were winning, their dance steps tight and matching, their voices hitting all the right words and notes. They linked arms, an unbreakable cord of nearly-women, and the boys' line began to break as its dancers retreated to the walls to drain their Cokes as if their cans contained beer, as if they were men and therefore not meant for dancing.

Just two boys remained on the floor: Gareth and the blond boy. Their dancing was smooth and fine and they hadn't linked arms. They danced as a team, as naturally as if they were playing football or running a relay. Gareth's chain and buckles clinked and flashed in the lights from the mosaic ball. Tot and Stacey faced them in the line, and Tot was close enough to see tiny lines of sweat forming on Gareth's upper lip. The sweat had darkened his hair at his temples, and he was smiling, grinning almost. He was grinning at *her*, his head cocked to one side, and he was singing the words out to everyone, but especially to her, and she made herself listen to the track as she danced, trying to keep to the steps and trying to work out the words, aware that both were equally important: Forward, cross to the left, back, cross to the right, *"I know you're achin' to be makin' me tonight, I got a feeling in my knees, a feeling only you can please"* and he was singing these words to her because he wanted her and her alone from this long string of dancing girls.

When the track came to an end and the DJ put on a slow dance, the floor instantly emptied. It was her favorite — *Lonely Girl* — and Eddy Holman was wringing out the words. Even Stacey unlinked arms, leaving Tot's side and hurried back to the edge of the floor; none of the girls wanted to wait in vain to be asked to dance, and none of the boys had the courage to ask.

Except for Tot…and Gareth.

She stood alone in the middle of the floor as Gareth Strand walked towards her. She could see the blond boy and Stacey watching from the edge. When Gareth reached her side, he whispered something unintelligible in her ear. She hoped he had asked her to dance and she nodded. He took her in his arms, and they began to sway to the music — a little mismatched at first until they were able to stop concentrating on the act of asking and accepting and able to focus on the beat. The blond boy shuffled towards Stacey and, without asking, took her in his arms, propelling her back out towards Tot and Gareth, and then they were two couples dancing on the light-scattered dance floor. Other boys, suddenly attentive, stopped their horseplay and set off into that first bravery of a boy's walk across a hall to ask a girl he doesn't know if she would like to dance with him.

Tot leaned into Gareth and tried to inhale everything about him and the moment, so she could fix it in her head and memory. She watched the room over his shoulder as they slowly inched around in a circle. She saw

93

girls prettier than she standing alone by the wall. She saw Keesal, his arms full of toilet rolls heading for the Ladies', his mother still serving cans of fizzy drink and packets of crisps, the plainer, shyer boys still pushing and punching by the stacked tables, and the DJ fingering through his boxes of records. She felt Gareth's breath on her cheek as he leaned in to whisper in her ear.

"I'm sorry," she said. "What did you say?" She craned her neck so her ear was close to his mouth.

"Outside. Can we go outside?" he asked.

She wasn't sure. It was warm here, inside the hall, on the dance floor with the music, with all the pretty girls watching her dancing with Gareth Strand. Outside there would be nothing but cars and swings and the cold dark trees, and out there, who would know that she was a girl who danced, a girl who was danced with?

"Come on. Let's go outside." He pulled away, grabbing her hand. She tried to find Stacey in the mass of couples that now shuffled around in circles on the dance floor to let her know she was heading outside for a moment, but couldn't. Gareth was pulling her across the polished floor, past Keesal and his mother, out the double doors, past the Ladies and the Gents and the plump woman who was still inking Christmas trees on the hands of the latecomers.

Outside, the park's flood lights had been turned off and the air was dark and sharp with the smell of petrol and rain. Gareth didn't say anything. He just held her hand tight and pulled her across the grass towards the swings, where she and Stacey had sat and watched the mothers, and the boy with his bike, and the pavilion clock hands. They passed the swings, and the park got darker and the security lights outside the community centre stopped being a dazzle and became soft yellow disks. They reached the spot where the little boy had sat on his bike and looked at the trees. They slipped through the gap in the oaks and reached the sedge grass where Gareth gently pushed her down into its tufty softness. He threw his jacket to her — his *jacket* — and she wrapped everything it meant around her shoulders.

"I need a leak," he said. "Just a minute. I'll be back."

He disappeared into the darkness behind a deeper line of trees, and Tot lay back in the cold sedge grass and closed her eyes and tried to bring back the memory of the dance floor with its waxed polish smell and the way the mosaic ball kept spinning, kept throwing light, like bright confetti, down upon the dancers.

She could hear his shoes on the damp leaves. They said "shush, shush, shush" and she complied, her eyes closed. He was a press of weight on top of her, and his hands were clumsy around her waist. She could feel the prick of the sedge against her skin. He tugged up her top until it was bunched under her arms, then roamed his hands back down to the wire ridges of her pointless strapless bra and pushed that up too, the wires coming to rest cruelly for a moment across her tiny breasts until he reached back and undid the clasp with one hand and released the pressure. His hands were, for the first time ever, on her bare skin, and she was aware that if she was going to stop him, the moment was now, and the moment was very thin and fragile.

"Do you love me," was all she could say as she handled the thin moment and tried to decide what could be done with it. "Do you? Do you?"

He mumbled something, his words lost in the tangle of her clothing, and they could have been "yes" and "yes" and "yes." She laid back, her eyes tight shut. His hands were grasping at her shoulders, his mouth on her breasts, and she felt the moment begin to break up into stretched seconds. In her mind, she could see mycelium-like runs of brightness that pulsed — disconnecting and connecting, flashing and surging — in her brain and down the length of her body. It felt like salt and urgency. He moved one hand down across her stomach and, reaching under her skirt, encountered the narrow, elastic stretch of panties, and all the jagged zaggy lights in her head began to connect and form 1000 watt neon stripes, so bright and crazy, they buzzed and burned like thick, gaudy electric eels that sparked throughout her body. The intensity scared her enough to open her eyes, and she looked up as a waxy yellow moon crawled out of the grip of branches above. She looked down and ran her hand through his hair.

His blond hair.

His blond hair.

His blond hair.

It wasn't Gareth.

She grabbed his shoulders and pushed on them hard, and the boy fell backwards into the damp, deep leaf litter. It was the buck-toothed blond boy. The friend. He lay back on the ground in the dark and began to laugh, a high-pitched, almost girlish laugh. Tot tried to rehook her bra and pull down her top, and still the boy laughed. She refused to cry, instead straightening her skirt and standing up from the sedge.

She went to kick him hard in the stomach with the pointed toe of her shoe, but he curled away from her and, grabbing her foot, pulled the shoe off.

"Give me back my shoe, you bastard!" she said, trying to stomp him hard with the other foot.

He rolled out of reach and scrambled to his feet, the shoe held high like a trophy. "What's it worth? What are you going to give me for it?"

"Fuck all. Give me back my shoe!"

"Aw, come on, little girl. Don't be like that," he said, smiling in the moonlight. "You give it to Gareth, don't you? Give it to me. Come on." With his free hand, he tried to grab at her waist, but she jumped back. "You even give it to the little Paki fucker!" He wasn't smiling any more. His face was turning harder, a scowl setting like stone around his mouth. "I've seen the pair of you on the bus, heads together, closer than knives."

"Give me my bloody shoe!" Tot held out her hand, trying to look bigger than she was, trying not to look scared.

"Close enough to get his hand down your knickers. Is that why you're always smiling on the bus?"

"My shoe. Give it to me!"

"Little tart." He moved towards her, his hand grabbing again at her wrist. She pulled back with her free hand and slapped him hard on the side of the face. He let go and stumbled back, clutching his cheek.

"Stupid little bitch! Little cock tease!" He hurled the stiletto high up out above the rushes, into the trees beyond. "Go get your fuckin' shoe!"

He pushed past her and strode off across the grass towards the community center. She fell back on the mound of sedge-grass and closed her eyes, trying to slow everything down, trying to work out explanations, ways that all this might be put back neatly in its bag. But there was no tidying up. Gareth and the blond boy had planned it. They had danced with her and Stacey to break them apart. He had asked her outside because he knew she would say yes, that she would let him pull her to wherever he wanted her to be. And he had wanted her to be with the blond boy.

She took off the remaining shoe before beginning the walk home across the park's dark cricket pitch. At the mid-way point, she looked back towards the community center. She could hear the disco's tinny treble. If she had her shoes, she could have gone back in, found Stacey, made a decision whether to brazen it out and dance as if nothing had happened, or to confront Gareth and slap his face like she had slapped the blond boy's.

But she didn't have her shoes. One was in her hand, the other lost in the trees.

She turned away from the yellow lights outside the Centre and towards the street lights on Willowswitch. She didn't know what she was going to do about the shoes. They were Dorothy's.

She didn't know what she was going to do about any of it.

12

In the lamppost's harsh light, the high privet hedge looked like a woman who had let herself go. It slouched across the pavement, its dense bulk obscuring the garden whose perimeter it marked. But here and there, dead leafless branches afforded glimpses through to the house beyond with its black windows, glass reflecting the lamp light, revealing nothing. The hedge seemed to absorb all available light, leaving the garden and the house in a cold, anonymous darkness. When Tot's father had been king, he had tamed the hedge with shears. He had planned to clip peacocks or rockets or love hearts from the square towers at either end and had spent spring nights sketching plans on the backs of envelopes. But nothing had come of it. Tonight, the hedge was shapeless, a straggly mass of common-or-garden privet. Like the house beyond, and like those who remained inside the house, the hedge had been left to fend for itself.

Which was why no-one noticed when Tot came home early from the disco. No-one noticed that she was barefoot, that her skirt was damp and grubby, and that her face bore a thin scratch from her eyebrow to the lobe of her ear.

She unlocked the front door and stepped quietly along the hallway, pausing at the entrance to the front room for a moment to watch her mother who was wearing a bathrobe and sitting on the rug in front of the fire. The coal stove, its enamelled doors open, played wild shadows and red light across the room. James Taylor, her mother's favorite, played quietly on the record player while she played Monopoly with no one. A spread of money fanned out around her on the rug, and an insane number of green houses and red hotels populated one corner of the Monopoly board. She watched her mother slide two counters — the racing car and the boat — from one square to the next, her fingers shuffling them into a tight pair as they crossed from one property to the next. The standard lamp spread a puddle of light onto the board and onto the armchair alongside, home to a sleeping Trampus, his white cellular blanket wrapped around him, its corner threaded as ever through one hand's fisted fingers. His other hand gripped a length of black vacuum cleaner hose.

Tot wanted to run in there and grab the arm of the record-player and gouge its needle across James Taylor's smooth vinyl. She wanted to kick the Monopoly board into the bay window and shake her mother. She wanted to steal Tramps' blanket and wrap it around her cold shoulders, to crawl into her mother's lap like a toddler, like a little girl, like someone who didn't know how things were.

Instead, she pulled the door shut with a quiet click and went upstairs to wash her face.

The bathroom door was locked. She pressed her ear against its wood and closed her eyes. There was the ever-present *drip drip drip*; the cold water tap had been leaking for as long as she could remember. They wrapped a flannel around its mouth to muffle the noise, but the water soaked through until the cloth could hold no more and the tap resumed its dripping percussion. No light leaked out from under the door. She pressed her ear more firmly to the wood, the pressure numbing her ear. There was no sound save the steady drip and gentle slap of water. Inside, there would be candles: Dorothy liked to cry in the near dark.

She leaned against the banister. She felt unable…or unwilling to move. She knew she should tell someone what had happened back there in the trees, in the sedge-grass, that she needed to tell someone that she had said no, that she had pushed a boy away. If she had met someone on her way back from the trees, if maybe she had met one of the mothers returning to look for her little girl's lost gloves, or perhaps a man taking his dog for a last walk of the day, she would have told, and the thing would be done.

But that period of time, the window of opportunity with strangers, had passed. She was away from the trees, and she wasn't quite sure if the story she would have told to the woman with the gloves or to the man with the dog would have been true. What had really happened out there behind the trees? What *did* she feel? If the boy in the dark had been Gareth, and they had finished the thing the blond boy had begun, would she have needed, in the same aching yet numb way, to tell someone about it? Or would she have held the moment to herself, delicious and clandestine? Would she have run to Stacey tomorrow morning and dragged her out to the privacy of the garden swing and its plastic cover, and told her every single detail of what it was like to almost lose one's virginity? Would it have been almost? Would she have handed over everything to Gareth? Would she have told Stacey about it? Or would she have held the night's culminating moment to herself alone, rearranging all their other moments into order and placing this one, this star-studded moment, at its very zenith.

She didn't know.

But it hadn't been Gareth. It had been the blond boy with the buck teeth.

If her mother had been sitting sewing in the kitchen rather than locked into herself in the living room, could she have told her? Could she have sat down at the table and told her mother exactly what had happened with the blond boy and that she was entirely innocent? Was the blond boy right? Was a tiny part of her already spinning the event, turning it to the light, to display it in such a way that it might become somehow luscious, something she might hold onto, something that might make her somebody else, somebody important, someone not her?

Dorothy might have understood. If there had been bright light spilling from under the unlocked bathroom door, then maybe she would have walked in on her bathing sister and, with her hand over her eyes, sat down on the cold edge of the tub. She might have started out with some sister-questions. She might have asked if it was possible to be scared on the outside, but inside to feel a beautiful wildness boiling up fast and furious like milk in a pan. She might have asked if it was okay to love one boy, to want another for a friend, and then to have a third put his hand between your legs and for just one second, not want to push him away.

But light had not spilled out onto the hallway carpet, and she was left leaning against the bannister, pushing hard against it until her back hurt.

She heard the squeal of skin against bathtub. Dorothy was getting out. In a few moments, she would have towelled herself dry and would appear damp and shiny on the landing, demanding to know why Tot was "snooping" outside the door. She decided her sister was not the person to talk to and trailed down the stairs, kicking her bare heels against each step, feeling the rough paint-grain of the bannister rail under her fingers, thinking, of all things, about the lost shoe.

In the kitchen, she nosed around in the larder for something to eat. As she lifted the lid to the bread bin, she heard a noise from her grandfather's room. She pulled the crust from the end of a fresh loaf and stuffed it into her pocket. She knocked on his door.

"Come in." The voice seemed buried in sleep or blankets or both. "In," it said. "Come in."

She opened the door. "It's me, Dangrad," she said. "Can I talk to you?" There was no reply, but she walked in anyway and stood at the end of his bed.

It took a moment for her eyes to make sense of the shadowed room. Her grandfather was burrowed under the covers, the bedspread pulled up around his ears. She tried again. "Can I talk to you about something?" she said. "It's … kind of a boy thing and everyone is…well, there's no one else at the moment. Apart from you."

The covers shifted like slow animals.

"Can I turn the light on?" she asked.

He mumbled what sounded like no, so instead she pulled the curtains back a crack, allowing the street lights to illuminate the room just enough so she could see her grandfather. He had sat up in bed and was still wearing his shirt and jumper, his tie loose and skewed below his ear. He reached out and picked up a bottle from the wooden chair beside his bed. Light reflected off its glass. "Home early?" he mumbled, taking a long drink before cuddling the bottle down below the bedclothes.

She nodded and felt inexplicable tears begin to form and a hard, cramping band tighten across the back of her throat.

"No Fred Astaires ask you to dance?" His voice was thick and stumbled across the words.

"Can I lie down?" she said, quickly cutting him off. She knew her tears would silence her, and she had a sense that there were answers here in this room. She didn't wait for him to respond but crawled onto the bed and snuggled down alongside him on top of the covers. She burrowed her feet underneath the dressing gown that lay across the foot of the bed.

The house eased down around them. She listened to the hot water tank refilling and reheating; Trampus gave a short cry from the living room then fell silent; James Taylor finished singing for a moment ... then began again from the beginning.

"He danced with me. Gareth Strand. He danced with me in front of everyone." She trailed off and remembered how good that had felt. To see all the pretty girls stand still for just a second while the fast dance finished and the slow one began, waiting but not wanting to be seen as waiting for boys to ask them to dance. And she had been about to follow Stacey back to the chairs when she realized that a boy — Gareth Strand — was walking towards her. Towards *her* and that he was going to dance with her in front of everyone, and that would let all the Beginning Things happen, and they would be in a real boyfriend/girlfriend relationship after all and everyone would know that she, Tot Thompson, was a girl worth dancing with.

She chewed her lip then began again. "He danced with me like a real dance, Dangrad, you know? Like really slow and with his hands on me — not on my hands, but on me, properly — like a boyfriend. Not like a cousin or a dance teacher ... or a dad."

She tucked her head underneath the crook of his arm. She felt him shift a little beside her, then heard him sipping from his bottle again. She knew that if she wanted the answers, she had to move from the wonder of the shiny dance floor into the park and through the narrow band of trees into the sedge-grass. "So we had a Beginning Thing, Dangrad. We had a Beginning Thing right there with all the girls from school seeing us dancing with each other and him whispering in my ear like...like we were in love or something. Then he said he wanted to go outside..."

Had she been wrong to go outside? Should she have made him give her more Beginning Things before she went with him back to the Other Things? Maybe the blond boy was right and she wanted the Other Things more.

"People do that, Granddad. People go outside when they're in a...relationship."

The word felt heavy and grown-up. Like Responsibility, or Menstruation, or Divorce. It didn't seem to fit what she had or where she was. She remembered the way the security lights had dimmed in the distance to yellow plates hung over the cars, how the park had seemed dark but inviting. How she hadn't felt scared.

"But it wasn't him, Dangrad. It wasn't him...outside." Her grandfather didn't stir. She continued. "I waited in the grass, and it wasn't him. It was the blond

104

boy. The one who danced with Stacey. But I didn't know. I didn't know it wasn't the right one, that it wasn't Gareth."

She waited. Part of her wished she was snuggled on her sister's bed asking questions. Dorothy would have given her the answers, then moaned about the lost shoes. Dorothy's answers would be Sister Answers — little truths from inside her head, things Dorothy was able to fashion from her own experiences in parks, in cars, behind bike sheds, in the woods. The handing over of Sister Answers wouldn't change anything between them.

But asking her grandfather questions about boys and why they did what they did would result in Real Answers. His answers would come from the insides of boys' heads. And the handing over of Real Answers would change everything between them. Because by asking, he would know the insides of her head.

"He put his *ningers down my fickers*."

It was nearly asked.

"And I didn't stop him."

And it was out. Not a question after all, but a fact.

The bed began to shake. Her grandfather's shoulders were shaking under the covers. He was laughing at her.

"I liked it," she said, suddenly angry at his laugher and at her miscalculation. He continued to shudder beside her. "Quite a lot, actually," she said, her voice rising from the pillow, louder this time. "I LIKED IT A LOT!"

This time, the words cannoned across the bed. Her grandfather sat bolt-upright and snapped on the bedside light. His face was red, angry and creased, and tears laid bright streaks across his cheeks and chin. The empty bottle fell from the bed onto the floor.

He grabbed her by the shoulders and shook her hard. "What do you expect? Going out dressed like a little whore. Look at you! What are we meant to do? Eh? Eh?" He held her at arm's length. "...with your body all tight and wrapped up like a Christmas present? And your face all painted. Like a bloody warrior. It's a war, young lady. It's a war out there and people get..." His voice trailed off and he loosened his grip on her shoulders. "...hurt," he said. "They get hurt." His tears came noisily this time, and he pulled her to his chest, pressing her face into his shirt. "We get hurt. We all get hurt."

She couldn't breathe, but she stayed where she was, wedged against the pillows with her grandfather. His hands were rocks on her shoulders.

As suddenly as he had grabbed her, he let her go and jumped out of bed. In the middle of the bedside rug, he struck a comical boxing pose, his fists up and ready, trouserless, his bare legs bent at the knees, ready to pounce. "Where does he live, eh? Where? WHERE?"

"Who?" she asked, holding a pillow in front of her, to her chest. "Where does *who* live?" Her voice shook at the things her grandfather knew about the insides of boys' minds.

"Gareth. The blond kid. Either one of 'em." He cycled his fists in the air, swapping his stance, jabbing with one fist and then the other. "I'll show 'em. Treating my Tot like a little whore. Teach 'em some respect. Give 'em the old one-two. Give 'em what for..." His voice fell away and he dropped his fists to his sides, his body limp. "Give 'em ... give 'em ... a seeing to?"

His last words were a question rather than a threat, and he crawled back into bed without waiting for an answer, and pulled the covers over his head.

13

Tom's luminous hand, not the one holding the sledge hammer, was pointing to the two, and Jerry's short, thin mouse tail flicked at the five. Sunday. 5:10 a.m. The house ticked, quiet and still. Dan burrowed his arm beneath the pillow and buried his face in its hot feathers. He felt shaky, sick, useless. A failure. His big plans for a new start had come to nothing: he had lasted just seventeen hours before insanity arrived in town, guns cocked, and shot his plans to hell.

Or was it even seventeen? He was, as ever, unsure of the moment when his plans for a new life slipped into plans for a resumption of the old. Perhaps it had arrived yesterday as he nailed the hook for the photograph into the wall. Or when he realized there weren't enough hangers for his shirts. Perhaps insanity had picked up his trail before he even left Sleaford, polishing its pistols on Dan's soft new resolutions. He thought, if he were honest, that he had been able to hear the jangle of the gunslinger's spurs in the back seat.

*

Yesterday, after an early tea, he had returned to his room with its pile of clothes and empty hangers, his granddaughter trailing behind him, to complete the task of moving in. But he and Tot had ignored the undertaking, choosing instead to sit side-by-side on his bed — the skinny twelve-year-old with kinky red hair, and the old man with bony hands. They watched the sun set through the open curtains, its red glow acing the streetlights' sulphur wash. As it dropped lower, the sun set fire to the peaks of the dump's rubbish heaps that ranged beyond the garden's fence. The windows had been slightly open, and they had listened to the last of Saturday's dustcarts: their gears grinding, the distant swoosh of rubbish finally laid to rest, the black plastic bags buried for eternity. Dan's hands had shaken slightly in his lap, like two swarms in the crook of a tree.

"Are you alright?" Tot asked, not moving her gaze from the window and the dark activity beyond.

He stood, stretching, and crossed to straighten the photograph on the wall. He pulled the curtains closed. "Just tired, my pet," he said. "Just tired. Do an old man a favour though … before I finish unpacking and hanging up my stuff?"

"What's that?"

"My bottle of ginger ale. I left it in the car last night. Under the seat. Could you get it for me?"

She nodded, but was distracted with the hanging of a shirt, sliding wire shoulders into its sleeves and buttoning its neck.

"Now, Love? Can you get it now?" He nodded his head in encouragement.

When she returned, he had been standing by the window, one curtain looped back, looking out at the night. The sun was lost, and all that remained was a cold streetlight glow that gave way first to a thin strip of cobalt, then to the wide black of a February night. There were no stars. There was no moon.

He turned away from the window to watch as she placed the bottle on the chair by the bed and bent to retrieve a hanger from the metal tangle on the rug by the wardrobe. "Leave that now, Pet. Granddad's a bit tired." He had taken the bottle and unscrewed its lid.

"Okay, Dan," she said.

"*Dangrad* to you, *Snipperwapper.*" He winked.

She smiled. "Wish me luck for tonight."

"Luck?"

"Me and Stacey are going to the disco."

"Ah. It'll work out, Tot." He saluted her from the bed. "It always does."

108

He had tipped the ginger ale bottle to his lips and forgotten her before she had even closed the door.

*

The clock by the bed now showed 5:15 a.m., his critique of last night's final act having taken a mere five minutes to complete. He pulled the covers up to his chin and even though he knew he could never win, he couldn't help but play the "What If?" game, the same pointless game of choice he had been playing his entire life: What if instead of spending last night drinking in *The Crooked Staff* he had taped Elaine's business card above the pub's phone as he had promised and headed back to hang the last of his clothes in the wardrobe? What if he had hugged his grandchildren and decided against the pub? What if he driven Tot and Stacey to the disco like a good granddad? He had played the same game late last night too sitting on the edge of the bed with the bottle in his hand. How about a cup of tea instead of this…or a hug…or some late night TV? He had weighed all his choices, rejecting the good and choosing the bad.

As always.

Of course, if his resolution had been solid, if he had been able to muster any will power whatsoever, he would have directed the play differently from the very start. The beginning would have been the same: late Friday night, the two cars would have pulled into Stanley Close, and the mother would have ushered her girls into the house and filled the kettle. But then, a better director would have called "Cut!" and thrown the old script away. He would have improvised, made the grandfather stand alone outside in the moonlight, on the front door step, listening to the people moving around inside the house, putting their bags on the stairs, talking softly the way women sometimes do late at night. The grandfather would have stood listening to the mother getting cups down from hooks, milk from the fridge, a sugar bowl out of a cupboard. Then, the Director would have told the grandfather to step away from the open front door, to walk back to the car. There, the grandfather would have pulled a bottle from under his seat and, crouching down in the dark, would have emptied it into the gutter. Then, he would have joined the mother in the little kitchen in the house on Stanley Close. Where they lived. Where they *all* lived. Where the grandfather would star in a brand new performance playing the good grandfather, the good father-in-law. The good man.

But that wasn't the way it had played out. There was no director. Just Dan doing what Dan did. What Dan always did.

The hot pillow was suffocating him, and he could feel tiny fingers of sweat gliding through his hair. He closed his eyes and rolled over, groping inside the open cabinet for the bottle. He found it and pulled it up and into the bed, cradling it against his chest as is if it were a long, cold baby. His hand moved up the glass neck to the cool lid, and he traced its embossed ridges with his fingers. Somewhere inside himself, somewhere deep and logical where he still cared, he knew that if he did this thing, if he took a drink before he even took a piss or brushed his teeth, then he would be moving across some kind of line.

He knew that this line — the one he had seen in the distance for some time — would be hard to step back from once it was crossed. He knew that. He knew that for sure. If he unscrewed the lid, put this morning bottle of whiskey to his lips, tipped the base and filled his mouth and swallowed, then he would have moved from the company of those on the safe side of the line — the good old boys, the lads in the mirror at *The Hook and Parrot* — to the other side where alcoholics waited for him with their arms open, their dirty mackintosh pockets full of empty brown paper bags.

On good days, the "A" word seemed too melodramatic, too harsh a diagnosis. Instead he defined himself as a "regular," just one of the lads at the bar, a man in search of companionship, a connoisseur of hops, that great British tradition. Even on bad days when the beer had kicked his arse and his memory had stormed off in high dudgeon, his self-diagnosis hovered around "piss head," entertained the idea perhaps of "problem drinker." Whatever the day, the four syllables of "alcoholic" were too much for him. It wasn't that the word conjured up visions of a dreadful and dangerous end. More, it made him think of the beginning of an end that started with the loss of home, of loved ones, and finished in parks, on benches, with only bottles of cheap wine for company. Ultimately, the word defined loss of self, a lonely madness.

But, still, his fingers unscrewed the lid. He held the bottle against his chest, the glass cool through the thin brushed cotton of his pyjama top. He placed the brassy bottle top on the bedside table next to Tom and Jerry. It was 5:20 a.m.

In one fluid movement, eyes still closed, he raised his head and guided the bottle to his lips. His tongue sampled the neck's old sweet thread. The line — his first ever morning drink, the dangerous solution to the sweats and shakes that had woken him every morning for the past year, to the wretched feeling that yet another displaced twenty-four hours yawned in front of him, that there was no joy left, just a barren mess of time — was about to be crossed. He tipped the bottle back, anxious to get it over with, to start the walk away from social drinker, across the line.

And nothing. He flicked on the bedside lamp and held the bottle up to the light. It was empty.

*

By 7:00 a.m., he was showered, dressed and sitting at the table in the cluttered kitchen. Elaine stood wedged between the table and the stove, burning toast and boiling eggs. Tot was quiet, trowelling through the butter dish with a knife, softening up the hard yellow mass, and Dorothy shovelled oatmeal into the moving target of Tramp's wet mouth.

Dan fingered a tiny soldier the boy had pushed across the table at him and saluted his thanks. But it was a quick salute, and he pulled his hand sharply back into his lap; if Elaine saw its shaking, she would be back on her Doctor tirade again.

"How many, Dan?" she asked, sliding burned toast from the eye-level grill onto a plate and trying again with four more slices.

She knew. He didn't know how, but she knew. "What do you mean, how many?" he snapped. "I don't know how many. I wasn't counting. Why would I count?"

Elaine looked at him, confused. "Toast, Dan. How many slices?"

The close call and the kitchen's charred smell made him queasy. "I think I'll just have bread…an egg sandwich, maybe. Is there any mayonnaise?" He made to stand, but Elaine waved him back down.

"Tot, get your granddad some Hellman's."

The kitchen still housed things that had no place there. Tramp's alphabet toy box stood in the corner next to the ironing basket. The neat little Formica-top kitchen table had been folded and stored away in the shed, replaced with the huge oak dining room table, and everything — from the rolling pin to the bread bin to the fridge door — was now within arm's reach of anyone who sat there. Tot, her chair wedged up against the fridge, scooted sideways, knocking into Tramps and setting him off into a torrent of wails.

Ignoring the boy, she pulled a glass jar from the fridge's shelf and dropped it loudly on the table. Elaine spooned an egg from the bubbling pan and held it under the cold tap's noisy stream before rolling it across the table like a cue ball towards her youngest.

"Make your granddad a sandwich, there's a good girl."

Tot snatched it up, tossing the hot egg from hand to hand. Once it was cold enough to hold, she rolled it backwards and forwards on the table. The shell's tiny crackling joined the room's cacophony as a brittle top note, and Dan felt the room begin to sway. But he knew from old that if he could eat an egg mayonnaise sandwich and keep it down, the room would steady and the queasiness that roiled in his stomach would calm. Then he could take some aspirin, some coffee. Then he could get through.

He watched Tot shell the egg and plop it, naked, into a teacup. It resembled a huge white eyeball. She spooned in a dollop of mayonnaise and a shake of salt from the cellar and began to chop noisily at the mixture with the butter knife. If the cracking of the egg shell against the table had been problematic, the clatter of the knife against the china cup was unbearable. The kitchen and its players mounted an attack on his remaining senses: Tramp's sunny smile, the smell of cooked eggs and burning toast, the drone of Radio 4's *Morning Show* was too much. He stumbled up from the table, pushing past chairs and the toy box, and hit the back door handle at a run.

He reached the outside privy at the far end of the alley in three strides, where he hung over its porcelain toilet bowl and heaved. He heaved until there was nothing left in his stomach, and then he heaved some more. Finally, when the retching subsided, he rested his head against the toilet bowl's cool rim. He shut his eyes and wished he was home. He wished he could stand up and move to his shower and sit down in the cradle of the bathtub and let the water cascade over him until the hot went warm then tepid then cold and washed these feelings away down the plughole.

There was a knock on the door. Not the normal tap-tap-tap one might expect, but just one loud rap. He ignored it and pulled down some toilet paper to wipe his mouth. It sounded again.

R A P !

"Who is it?" he asked, sitting back against the wall and dropping the soiled paper into the bowl.

"Me. I've done your sandwich."

He rested his forehead back down on the rim. "Leave it out there, Tot. I'll get it in a minute."

"Can't. It's raining. It'll get soggy."

"Then take it back to the kitchen."

"Can't. Mum's cleared the table for cutting out."

Dan reached up and slid the latch. The door creaked open. Tot stood outside in the alley, pressed up against the house, sheltering in the thin strip of dry afforded by the eaves. She carried a saucer that held an egg mayonnaise sandwich cut on the diagonal. She handed him one of the triangles, and he took a wary bite.

"You should wash your hands," she said. "I never do. But they say you should."

Slowly and carefully, he got up off the floor and sat on the toilet, his head resting against the wall.

"Fish and chips does it for me," she said.

"Does what?"

"When I'm sick. If I get fish and chips from up the village, I feel better."

Dan stood and flushed the toilet. "I'll remember that." He studied his granddaughter as she pushed the remainder of the sandwich into her mouth. Her eyes seemed red, and a thin scratch ran across her cheek from the corner of her eye to her ear. "What happened to your face?" he asked.

She pulled her hair forward and studied her sandwich closely. "If someone said I had to eat the same thing every day for the next fifteen years...or even thirty...I'd choose fish and chips. I could do that. And Coca-Cola ice-cream floats...if they said you were allowed a drink — the same one every day — as well." She stood and brushed crumbs from her skirt. "You'd be allowed a drink. They'd let you have a drink, I think. What would you have?"

He thought for a moment. "Egg mayonnaise sandwiches," he heard himself say.

"No," she said. "To drink. What would you have to drink every day for the next thirty years? If you could only have one thing?"

He didn't answer. He felt suddenly hot, the toilet wall spotty and wavy in front of him. He sat back down, rested his head on the wall, and closed his eyes, praying that the sandwich would stay put, that this day would begin, that he could play a proper part in it, and that it wouldn't just spin on and on without him. He heard her pick up the saucer, the grate of the china harsh against the rough concrete path.

"Cup of tea," she said. "You should have a cup of tea."

*

It had been a wake-up call. While he hadn't taken that first Morning Drink, it had been close. He had been a step away from becoming a card-holding member of the alcoholics club. The intention had been there. The action had been there. The only thing that hadn't been there was the whiskey inside the bottle. He had to be vigilant. He needed to be ready for when the craving came again.

He had eaten the sandwich, then managed to reach the upstairs bathroom without being stopped by Elaine. Once inside, he locked the door and cleared the tub of sponges, naked dolls, pink shower caps, loofahs, pumice stones, and Tramp's plastic dolphins. He picked them all up and dumped them in the laundry basket and ran himself a deep, hot bath.

Naked and with only the shallow plate of his face above the water, he made his decision. He would call Mrs. Phemister and ask her to open up the windows at the house and maybe to push the vacuum around a little, get some things in for the fridge: milk, cheese, a loaf of bread, some Jaffa cakes. Next week, he would take Millicent home and bury her ashes with her mother in the churchyard at Sleaford. Then he'd sell the chickens. All of them. Sell the bloody chickens, the ducks, the fifteen quail, and all their feeders and waterers. Maybe he could even find a buyer for the coops and the nesting boxes. Or he could burn those. Burn it all.

And then what? He could put his life together. He looked around the bathroom. It had nice new tile, a modern tub. By the basin, there was a line of toothbrushes, some flannels, pretty soap. Pictures of spouting whales broke up the white walls. This was a proper room. One that worked. He needed rooms like this. He could have a new bathroom. And a bedroom with a single bed, just for him. Maybe buy a new television set for the front room. Some books, perhaps. He could start reading Wilbur Smith again. He could spend his evenings eating home-cooked meals — ones he had cooked — at the dining room table, and then he could move into the front room and watch the news, or read some more Wilbur. He could sit on his sofa and watch the telly like a normal old man. He'd have a bowl of pistachios on the table, a little cork coaster to put his glass on. He might have a sherry before dinner. In a nice sherry glass. Then after dinner, he could smoke a cigar, one of those thin ones, and then have a glass or two of good Scotch. No more than two.

He could get rid of the chickens and cut back on the drinking and start living like a man ought to live. He could do that.

He braced his toes against the tap end and scooted up until he was sitting upright, leaning against the inflatable back rest. It resembled a pair of bright red plastic lips and reminded him of Mick Jagger. He was leaning back into a kiss from old Rubber Lips himself: *"I can't get noooo...satisfaction...."* Yes, that's what he would do. He could get this back on track. He would stay another week so Elaine would stop fretting about him, and then he'd go home and start putting his life in order. No more chickens. No more drinking until he fell over. No more shaky egg mayonnaise sandwiches in the morning.

He could hear music from down the hallway. Tinny transistor music from Tot's room. He soaped the loofah. He'd buy her a record player. That's what he'd do. He'd walk up the village tomorrow to Hancocks, and he'd buy the girl a record player. Funny little thing. Kinky orange hair. Like a clown. A bit lonely, he thought. He would buy her a record player, and the two of them would talk. Friends were important, he'd tell her. It didn't do to isolate. You needed to talk to people, and if you didn't know how, you needed to learn. You needed to find out what they liked and ask them about it. Their pets, their holidays, their families. Then they would think you were interested, and eventually, they might ask you the same questions, and then you'd be okay. You'd have people to talk to, people who knew who you were. He'd get one of those snazzy portable players, one with tartan cloth. A record or two. Maybe he'd get some 45s, some Queen. That Bohemian Rhapsody was a good one. A bit sad, but a good tune. Something a man could whistle along to. He'd get the player and some records, and they'd sit in her room, and he'd befriend her. Maybe he'd buy some Rolling Stones so she would know what music really was.

This was the week to show the family that he, Daniel Thompson, was fine and that he was just a run-of-the-mill grandfather, father, man. That there was nothing to worry about. Then he could go home.

He carefully climbed out of the bath and pulled the plug. As he dried himself with the pink and green fluffy towel, he made plans. He'd walk up the village and get the record player. Maybe he could borrow Elaine's push-along trolley. Maybe she needed some shopping from Bishops? He'd ask her. Be helpful. He'd buy her flowers anyway. A big bunch. Like his stupid son should have done. Not roses though. That's for love. Tulips. If it wasn't too early. Or Chrysanthemums. No ambiguity with 'mums. Big bold friendship – and – everything's – hunky – dory – with – me flowers. He'd walk back past that little flint library, maybe see if they had any Wilbur Smith. He could read a Wilbur in a week. And then skirt back through the park with its swings and slides. He'd call in at the Off-Licence. Get one last bottle of Bells. That should take him through the week if he was careful. It would help him leave this little family with its untidy shed, its bathroom full of toys and women's things, and help him get ready for his new life. A life without chickens, with a home-cooked dinner in front of the telly, the occasional glass of good Scotch. A life of balance and moderation.

In all things.

Maybe he'd get two bottles. And some Ginger Ale.

14

Tot's decision not to tell her best friend about Gareth Strand and the things they did in his bedroom had been an easy one, formed on the basis that Stacey's world seemed still to be one of skipping ropes and hopeful conversations that began with "When I grow up." Tot's world, given those afternoons in an upstairs room in a house on Willowswitch Lane, had split off from her friend's, had begun to move slowly into its own dark orbit, floating away like some rogue circle in a Venn diagram. Sometimes, she pressed herself against the cold curve of the old world and stared back at its toys.

That decision had made it impossible for her to tell Stacey the real reason for deserting her at the disco. There was too much ground to cover, too many things that had not been shared. So she stayed away for a week, time enough for the scratch on her face to scab and fade and for an almost truth to surface that might excuse her for leaving a best friend to walk home from a dance alone.

"So we had a snog and then he walked me back to my house." Tot kicked at the door mat on Stacey's front step and fiddled a strand of hair across her cheek, the scratch now silvery and pale. "He even lent me his jacket."

"But that Gareth's a third year at your school," Stacey said, as if this blew Tot's story out of the water entirely. She leaned against the jamb, holding the door more shut than open. She wore her mum's pink towelling bath robe, and her face was flushed red from the shower.

"I know he's a third year and that's why it's got to be a secret."

"So why are you telling me?"

"I tell you everything, Stacey." That was another lie, of course, the details of which still lived in that deep and dark circle, the silent lie that had split her away in the first place. "You're my best mate."

Stacey rubbed at her damp hair with a towel, her other hand firmly gripping the door. "Eventually," she said. "You tell me everything *eventually*."

"I had a really bad cold. Probably flu." Tot stooped down to rearrange the empty milk bottles on the door step, turning them so the dairy's embossed nameplates were perfectly aligned. They clinked and chimed against each other. "Give us a break, Stacey," she said, straightening up. "I felt really bad about leaving you there. But … it's what mates do, right? They move over a bit when a boy comes along."

"And he's your boyfriend?"

"No. I mean he…" Of course, he wasn't. And yet the idea that she could not share at least the shinier parts of their relationship with her best friend seemed unfair.

Stacey stopped rubbing at her hair with the towel. "It doesn't matter anyway. Moira's dad gave me a lift home."

"Moira from 1-D? The girl who plays the clarinet?"

"Yeah. She's great, actually. I really like her. She's got a brother at University and her own room. Her mum lets the dog sleep in her bed. IN her bed." Stacey gripped the edge of the door. "She's really funny. I really like her."

"That's alright then."

"Yeah. And we were up dancing all night."

"Yeah?"

"Yeah. I even danced five slow ones."

"I saw you dance with Gareth's friend."

"Oh, he's a moron. Anyway he left early." Stacey pulled the door open a fraction more and dropped the towel to the floor. "Did you really snog him?"

Tot flinched. "Who?"

"Gareth, of course. Who else?"

"Sorry. Yeah, we snogged. But you can't tell anyone."

"What's the point of snogging someone if you can't tell anyone?"

"I have told someone. I've told you." Tot had never spent this much time on Stacey's doorstep. "Can I come in?" The pause was long. Too long, and she felt just inches away from losing her grip on the smooth curve of Stacey's world.

Stacey let the door swing open and headed up the staircase. "Yeah," she said without turning. "But you can't stay long. I'm going out." She left Tot to close the front door.

When Tot reached the bedroom, Stacey was sitting in front of her dressing table. It was kidney-shaped and had movie star light bulbs and a yellow-and-blue-checked cotton skirt. Tot sat on the edge of the bed, ready to impale herself on any hurt feelings Stacey might care to hurl her way. She listened to the list of boys who had been danced with: the blond boy with the buck-teeth, a boy called Jim, a boy called Roger who was Jim's cousin from Tunbridge Wells and who was staying with Jim while his mother had a hysterectomy. Stacey had even danced with Keesal.

Before she could stop herself, she said, "That's only four."

Stacey glared at her in the glass.

"But four good ones," Tot said, backpedalling. "Four really good ones." She couldn't help but think about the Blond Boy and the way his hands had covered her like a man's might. She felt cold and pathetic, like an iceberg about to lose a chunk of itself.

Stacey tightened the belt of her robe and explained why she was going out and why Tot wasn't invited, her voice plastic and bright, still brittle edged. "It's a school disco," she said. "Kingsleys only."

"But we always go to things together."

"You're not a Kingsley. You can't come."

"I could be."

"No, you couldn't."

"I could be your sister."

"No sisters."

"I could gate crash."

Stacey frowned in the glass. "Don't."

"I could. I could get dressed up and…mingle, like I belonged there. I could do that."

"Don't! Anyway, you need a ticket, and you have to go to our school to get one. The head said that keeps out…undesirables."

"At Kingsley? Jesus, if they kept out the undesirables, there'd be no one there."

The old Stacey would have bit at this, and they would have jumped into their favourite fight: Kingsley Comp versus Waterford Tech. And Stacey would have won because it was her turn to win. But this Stacey said nothing. She merely pulled a pair of knickers and a pack of tights from the drawer. There was so much unsaid in the room. So much that wouldn't be said, and both girls knew it. Stacey wriggled into the panties and, tearing the plastic cover from the package, shook out the tights; they were white with seams. She rolled down each nylon leg and carefully eased them on. Tot grabbed the hanger holding Stacey's dress from the back of the bedroom door and handed it to her. The dress — grown-up: a solid dark blue with glittery capped sleeves and a tight wrap skirt — was obviously borrowed from Janine, Stacey's big sister.

Stacey took the hanger and wordlessly put the dress on. She fluffed her now dry hair in the mirror. "You won't, will you?" she asked.

"What?"

"Gate crash. You'll get caught, and then I'll get into trouble."

Tot picked up a lipstick from the dressing table and leaned in towards the mirror. She smeared the stubby stick across her lips.

Stacey tried to grab it. "Don't waste it."

Tot dropped the lipstick in Stacey's open handbag. "You'll need that. If you get lucky and some boy kisses it all off."

Stacey blushed.

"I could walk you down there," Tot said, pulling her jacket back on. "Promise I'll not come in. I'll just walk down there with you, and then I'll walk home…on my own."

Stacey shook her head. "No need. Jim and his dad are picking me up."

"Jim?"

She nodded. "From last week."

"Is he your boyfriend now?"

Stacey shrugged.

"You must know if he's a boyfriend or not."

"Then I suppose he's a boyfriend."

Tot sat on the edge of the dressing table. She spat on her finger and tested the heat of a movie-star bulb. "What makes you know?" she said, the spittle hissing on the glass.

"What do you mean?"

"How do you know he's a boyfriend and not just a boy-space-friend?"

"He smiles at me a lot." Stacey buckled her shoes and inspected herself in the mirror. "He smiles and he sits with me at lunchtime and his dad's giving us a lift to the dance." She picked up her handbag. "I think that makes him my boyfriend."

Tot didn't reply. She was thinking about Gareth and his bedroom and the way he locked his little brother in the wardrobe.

"Tot?" Stacey zipped up her handbag.

"What?"

"You haven't told me much. About Gareth. Did he shut-lip kiss you or did you let him French?"

Tot inspected her throat in the mirror. "Do you know how to do a love bite?"

Stacey shook her head.

"Wanna practice? So you get it right...if you have to do one?" She tugged off her jacket and rolled up the sleeve of her cardigan.

Stacey shook her head. "My dad says love bites mean you've done it with a boy. All the way."

"That's shit. Love bites are just like bigger kisses. And it's proof."

"What of?"

"That you love him. Like enough to want to eat him. Like he was dinner or something." She sucked at a chunk of flesh on the top of her forearm, peering at Stacey over her elbow.

"I don't think Jim's ready for love bites. I mean, we're just talking at the moment...and going with his dad to the disco." She edged past to the door. "I can't believe you let Gareth Strand French-kiss you."

Tot stopped biting her arm and inspected it. An angry blue-red crescent rose from her pale freckly skin, a tiny row of tooth indents at the top and the bottom that disappeared as Stacey turned out the light.

15

Dan had grown used to eating alone. He couldn't remember the exact point at which his solo dining began, but he did remember that his decision had been born of disappointment, and that it signalled the beginning of a formal distance between himself and his wife. It was the space into which an unknowing had flown and nested. The disappointment, the realization that perhaps he loved his wife more than she loved him, resulted from a conversation — or rather from the lack of a conversation. Millicent had been a soap opera aficionado. She watched them all from their very beginnings, from *Crossroads*, the ins-and-outs of a Midlands motel, to *Coronation Street*, the ins-and-outs of a northern housing estate. They were the Universal, she said, the Ideal; they spread human beings and their faults wide open in her living room. In their presence, she was viewer rather than voyeur and could judge without being judged. Every sinner was punished; every occasional saint praised. The soaps might not show life as it was, she told him, but they showed her life as it should be.

His self-banishment to the kitchen had begun with a plane crash ... or was it a missing cowman? Either way, it had begun at six-thirty in the front room on a weekday evening (he was sure of that) with *Emmerdale Farm*, the rustic ins-and-outs of a Derbyshire farming community. This source of pleasure ("a rare pleasure") was apparently marred by inconvenience. It was inconvenient, she said, what with Dan not coming in from work until six-fifteen and her having to sit there at the kitchen table watching him eat with his mouth open and then having to rush each forkful of her own dinner in order to catch this, her favourite show. So inconvenient that at the theme tune's opening bars, she had taken to disappearing — mid-sentence and mid-meal — to finish her dinner in the front room in front of *Emmerdale Farm*.

Dan had become used to finishing his evening meal alone, to serving himself a little pudding, then clearing away the table mats and salt and pepper pots and stacking the plates in the sink, before heading out to the pub for a pint or three, or to his shed for an evening of fixing things or reading or just for an hour of quiet sorting through.

Weeks before he retired from the ink factory, the soap opera's plane crash/missing cowman story surfaced, and he had offered that perhaps they could eat their dinner in the front room, at least until the black box (or cowman) had been found. So they changed their habits and settled down in matching armchairs to weather the soap storm together. The crisis had abated, the missing item found, and *Emmerdale* settled back into its old comfortable routines. But he and Millicent had not settled back so easily. They had not returned to the kitchen table. She told him, a little pout on her lips, that she liked eating in the living room in front of the television, that she didn't see why she had to rush around bolting her food in order to keep up with her favourite show. It wasn't, after all, her fault that he didn't get home until six-fifteen.

He hadn't kicked, in part because he had been offered no real opportunity to do so. But mainly, he had agreed to eating in the living room because he was an appeaser, a sucker for the easy life. She had softened in the face of his capitulation, telling him it would do them good to spend a little time together in front of the television of an evening. She pushed their armchairs closer together. She brought the bottle of Amontillado and two sherry schooners out from the drinks cabinet and rehoused them on the coffee table on a silver-plated filigree tray. She bought a box of *After Eight* mints.

But he didn't like the change. It wasn't that he disliked soap operas. It was more that he missed the tiny window that dinner in the kitchen had cracked open for conversation: after their move to the living room, when he tried to talk to her over his tray, she waved away his comments and questions with an irritated hand, her eyes never leaving the screen. Not that meals in the kitchen had been a setting for repartee. More, the easy exchange of what he remembered as pleasantries: *pass the salt, this pork is tasty, how was your day?* The loss of some small thing when all one has are small things is monumental. This loss, coupled with the realization that Millicent wasn't prepared to miss one minute of a fantasy life in order to be present for him and their real one, caused him to throw, rather quietly and half-heartedly, a plate of sausages, gravy and mashed potatoes at the television. He had missed, his plate hitting the wall, its contents slowly sliding down the wallpaper to gather in a greasy pool in the shag pile, and Millicent, getting up to change channel for *Eastenders*, told him that if he thought she was going to clear that up, he had another thing coming.

He had removed to the kitchen to eat his pudding and had stayed there ever since.

*

But this kitchen, Elaine's kitchen, the kitchen at 17 Stanley Close, bore no resemblance to that large, quiet space he had chosen over Millicent and *Emmerdale Farm*, the space in which he had not sat for almost three weeks. Mealtimes in the Thompson household resembled a scene from a Hogarth etching. That evening, Elaine, hot and messy, multi-tasked with a plastic ladle, using it to dish up food, to point menacingly at the children, and to demand, with a succession of sharp, gravy-splattering raps, absolute attention. Elaine, her ladle delivering meatballs and sauce, reprimands and warnings, was intent on making sure her family had enough of whatever she thought they needed. Dorothy, her son squirming and writhing in his chair like a hog-tied Houdini, had given up trying to feed the boy and had resorted to eating his dinner herself. She absentmindedly shovelled pasta from a bowl rimmed with a frieze of cartoon tanks into her mouth with his spoon, her hand dwarfing its tiny blue aeroplane handle. Tot wasn't eating anything. She merely pushed her meatballs up the sides of her bowl like Sisyphus. Dorothy released Trampus from his chair, and he crawled beneath the table, striking everyone's shoes with his mother's fork like a crazed xylophonist. No-one was listening to Elaine, who finally recognized this fact and left the table to begin the washing up, muttering something about fools and Penryth. It was Bedlam, and he wasn't sure if he loved it or loathed it.

Before he could decide, Tot leaned in close to whisper in his ear. She said she needed to talk to him about something. A problem, she whispered, and he couldn't help but feel a little proud that she had chosen to confide in him rather than in her mother or her sister. He knew she was snaking through a boyfriend minefield in tweeny wars. Her needing his help made him feel…useful. Younger, somehow. It made him feel relevant, as if he knew something that someone wanted to know, had something worth saying, some nugget of intelligence to hand over that would be acted upon. He whispered that he would come up and talk to her after supper, after he had helped her mother with the pots and pans.

She had been waiting for him cross-legged on her bed. The room had changed little since that night he had slept there, the night he had left his home in Sleaford. He was still surprised by its neatness: a Rolling Stones poster he had given her hung exactly in the centre of the wall opposite the window; a stack of laundry lay folded on the stool; and Millicent's tea caddy now sat in the middle of the shelf of snow globes. He reached up and took it down. Sitting on the foot of her bed, he studied it, giving his granddaughter time to summon up the necessary courage to broach what could be, for a twelve-year-old girl in the sweet throes of boyfriend turmoil, an embarrassing subject. He thought hard about the advice he would give. An eternity had passed since he had wrangled first love, and now that he sat and thought about it, he wasn't sure if he had every really been successful. It was true, he and Millicent had been happy for the first few years. Getting to know each other's little ways had been fun. But then Donald arrived and Millie grew tired. There was never enough time — to look after the baby, to earn money, to look after each other. But that was the way of things back then, wasn't it? Those years between the wars had been confusing. Everything had changed for everyone. Nothing could be relied upon. A man lived in his moment and tried not to think about the future, about how long that future might last, or where it might take him and the things he loved. Romantic love had seemed absurd…a luxury item. At least, it had felt that way for him. And yet, things seemed no different nowadays. Look at Donald and Elaine. What had gone wrong there? They couldn't lay the blame at the feet of war or rationing. What was their excuse for not getting it right? Maybe their burden was the fallout of the sixties with all that free love and sex. Maybe the flower-power children never grew up, never knew what it was to make a thing last, even if the thing seemed already worn out or ill-fitting for its task. So what hope for Tot, eh? What advice could an old man give a twelve-year-old girl? There were some constants though, weren't there? Some things that never changed? He wanted to tell her that she had a lot more time than she thought she had. And that this time could be both blessing and curse, and how good things, things with no grab handles, tended to rush past, while the bad seemed to be coated with Velcro — or sometimes honey — and either way, they stuck to you like burs.

So when Tot pulled his half gallon of Bells from under her pillow and placed it on the bedside rug, it wasn't surprising that all his words left him. She crouched down next to the bottle and spun it. His fiddling with the tea caddy had loosened its screw lid, and this became his focus, his excuse not to look at his granddaughter or at the whiskey bottle turning at his feet. But the round caddy didn't entirely fill his field of vision; he could still see Tot and the Bells. He thought about his wife inside the caddy and imagined how much she would have revelled in his predicament.

He screwed her lid on tight.

Tot halted the spinning bottle with the heel of her hand. "You can't hide things like this," she said. "Not down low. Not when there's a toddler in the house." Leaving the bottle's neck pointing towards the closed door, she stood up. "I mean, we had to go through this place putting all the cleaning stuff and medicine and anything sharp up off the ground so Tramps wouldn't be able to get to it." She took the caddy from him and returned it to the shelf. "Mum had me crawling around on my hands and knees so I'd be able to see what he'd get into."

Dan's immediate instinct was to deny and defend. After all, this wasn't the first time he'd been found out like this, his stash discovered. There was the day Millie decorated his shed as a surprise for his sixtieth and found a bottle of Balvenie — a decent single malt — in the sawdust bucket. She'd wanted to know why he was hiding things from her again, why he couldn't keep his whiskey in the drinks cabinet like a normal man. He'd discovered attack was the best policy and snapped at her, indignant and puffed up. He had never challenged her before, and part of him felt courageous in taking a stand. He remembered her shock at his reaction and the way she quietly replaced the bottle in the bucket and backed out of the shed. He also remembered the coldness that rose from the base of his stomach in the seconds before he had shouted at her and that lingered even with her departure. He had poured himself a slug of the Balvenie and given the sensation a name; he called the feeling in his stomach *Justifiable Anger*.

And then there had been the sofa incident. Their son, just before he disappeared, had driven down in a truck to buy an old leather sofa from them for fifty pounds; Dan had been aware and a little ashamed that this purchase had been his son's way of trying to ease another bout of financial unpleasantness which arrived as ever in the wake of Millicent's recklessness with the housekeeping money. He had arrived home earlier than expected and encountered his wife and son manhandling the sofa down the back alley. The pair had misread the look of panic on Dan's face as yet further embarrassment at the increasingly public nature of his and his wife's shaky finances, and his son had tried to lighten the mood. He had set his end of the sofa down and begun mining the cushions, making the joke that any valuables unearthed would reduce the purchase price accordingly. Millicent joined in and found an assortment of coins and a fluffy stick of liquorice. She presented her finds with huge smiles, their rarity lighting up the shady alley. Until Donald, down his end, came up a miniature bottle of vodka. And then another. And then another.

Nine in all, the kind they hand out on airplanes. Not hidden between the seats but stuffed inside a cushion. Not enough bottles to categorically brand a man an alcoholic, but certainly enough to warrant an explanation. The same coldness had formed in Dan's stomach as had gathered when the Balvenie was discovered. This time he named it *Indignation*. He had sat down on the sofa, unscrewed the top from one of the bottles, and downed it in an easy swallow. Donald, embarrassed at the situation, did what he knew how to do; he followed suit and joined his father on the sofa, uncapping another of the bottles and clinking it against Dan's in a conspiratorial toast.

Millicent had taken the other seven away. She returned with a can of Pledge and began to clean the sofa, rubbing at the worn leather as if to wear the hide from its wooden frame. She threw a duster at the two men on the

131

sofa. Donald had caught it and half-heartedly buffed the armrest. Dan, feeling his point made and his pride restored, had left the two of them cleaning and disappeared into the kitchen. He remembered feeling lucky, clever even at having shown them who was boss and the error of their over-reaction.

But now, this time, his granddaughter having found his stash in the music drawer at the base of the piano, he just felt tired, and when the familiar coldness welled up, he called it by a new name. He called it *Fear*. Fear of what, he wasn't sure. But there was no mistaking it. It stroked the inside of his stomach with frozen, glassy fingers. He stood up and turned to the window, closing his eyes, feeling a little sick, a little light-headed.

He heard her nudge the bottle with her foot. It hit the metal leg of the bed with a chime.

"Just keep it in the drinks cabinet in the front room. Or on top of the wardrobe." She climbed up on the bed and took the unicorn globe down from the shelf, polishing its smooth dome on her shirt. "Or you could just throw it away," she said.

He picked up the bottle. It was almost empty. Enough to last him…how long? Until the supermarket opened tomorrow morning? And when had he begun to buy whiskey by the half-gallon? He closed his eyes again. Two weeks ago. He'd bought the first the day after he found out about the house. The day he bought home the flowers.

*

It had been difficult to carry home two bunches of tulips and a record player, plus a carrier bag of whiskey and ice-cream soda from the village. But he had managed it without mishap, and as he proudly set his purchases down on the hallway carpet by the stairs, he knew it would work.

His offerings would re-balance the scales, settle the bill he felt was outstanding. Both Elaine and Dorothy would know what it was to receive flowers from a man who had no agenda, no ulterior motive. And they both needed a little of that in their lives. Men had not been kind to either of them, and he liked to think that he might be the one to step up and restore their faith. Tot would have her first real record player. He'd seen her with that tiny transistor radio stuck to her ear too often. That was no way to listen to music. You'd think her father would have taught them that. With your own record player, the world opens its arms. He could give her Wagner, Ella Fitzgerald, even a little Sinatra wouldn't harm a girl's development, balance out all this glam rock nonsense she seemed to be in love with. He had even remembered Trampus; in the off licence, he had lingered at the shelf of ice-cream soda and recollected from his youth its sweet tongue rush. He had bought a bottle and was looking forward to being the man who introduced Trampus to the wonders of carbonation. He could do all this, and then he could retire to his bedroom with a tall glass of ice, the Bells, and call Mrs. Phemister from the hallway telephone.

Without doubt, the kitchen was always the busiest room in the Thompson household, and he had spent most of the walk home happily anticipating the scene: Elaine would be working at the counter, listening to Radio 4 and cooking dinner, while Tot and Dorothy crowded the table with homework. Maybe Tramps would be playing under the table…or perhaps by now he would be tucked up in bed — he hadn't quite fixed the youngest on the family stage yet. But there were years ahead for him to fashion a strong great-grandfatherly relationship — a long-distance relationship — with this newest Thompson. He headed down the hallway to the kitchen whistling, anticipating their pleasure, and an evening of telephone calls to Sleaford to lay the groundwork for his homecoming. But when he opened the kitchen door, he found the room quiet and Elaine alone at the table. Even the radio was silent on the windowsill. He was surprised and not a little disappointed; he had been hoping for a roomful. His daughter-in-law sat with a pad and a calculator in front of her. A large manila envelope stuffed full of papers lay to the side. It was the envelope and its hidden contents that bore the full force of her frown.

When she saw him in the doorway, she covered the calculator with the pad and put down the pen. She looked both embarrassed and terribly angry at the same time.

"What are you up to?" he said, setting the tulips on the table, hoping her answer might give hint to the problem she was grappling with.

She pulled one of the bouquets towards her by its newspaper wrapper. She studied it for a moment before burying her nose in the crimson and black-streaked parrot tulips, hiding her face in their waxy petals.

"Like 'em?" he asked. "Those are for you. A little thank you."

She didn't respond. It was as if she were frozen in the red and black blooms.

He tried again. "Shame about tulips," he said. He took the other bunch and inhaled deeply, theatrically almost. "Doesn't seem right, does it? To be so pretty but to have no smell?" He sat down opposite and reaching out, took her hand in his. "What's the problem, Hen?" he asked. "Why so serious?"

She lifted her head from the flowers and pulled her hand from his. "I'll put these in water." She scooted her chair backwards, and the room filled with the screech of metal on linoleum.

He played with the stems of the remaining bunch. They stuck out from the newspaper wrapping and were wet, the water puddling in fat drops on the green marbled Formica. "These are for Dorothy," he said. "I figured she's too old for sweets, right?"

Elaine pulled a vase from under the sink and filled it from the cold tap. She eased the wet paper from the flowers and fed their stems into the wide vase. They splayed against the rim like invalids, each bloom now pathetic and garish. She tried to gather the bunch's leggy stems together, but however she arranged or propped them, the bunch collapsed, each tulip falling away against the vase's glass edge.

"You need marbles in there to hold those stems. Or some chicken wire. You poke the stems through the wire in the water. That's what Millie did." He began to unwrap the remaining bunch, careful to support the heavy crimson blooms. "She was a clever woman, my Millicent," he said. "And classy, you know?"

Elaine placed the vase on the table and sat back down. "Perhaps she used nine-carat gold mesh in her vases, Dan. Or solid silver marbles maybe." She shook her head as if to dislodge something that was caught there, something livid like a wasp.

"Silver marbles? What do you mean? I don't understand…"

"Maybe she just tipped a whole bloody bag of diamonds in there to keep her stems straight!"

Dan was confused. It wasn't like Elaine to bad-mouth someone, even Millie. He felt he should say something in his wife's defence. "Come on, Elaine. I know you two didn't get on, but she is dead, after all! How about a little respect?"

"Respect? Is this respectful enough?" She plucked a letter from inside the manila envelope and slid it across the table to him. "It's all in there. In black and white, Dan. Did she ever respect anyone? Even you?"

He took the letter. It was from the solicitors' office that was dealing with Millicent's estate. But he didn't read it or even unfold it. Instead, he just looked at it, frowning. "I don't understand, Love…"

"Me neither, Dan. I don't know what she was doing with the money — with your money — but it's all gone. The bank account, the savings…even the house. It's worse than gone. It's *more* than gone."

The letter that contained words like debt and bankruptcy was typed on heavy cream paper. He thought about the bottle of whiskey out there in the hallway by the front door. It was the kind of paper that showed its pedigree by its very weave. He thought about Millicent and Aintree and Epsom on the television, the horses with their sheepskin nosebands, their wonderful names — *Red Rum, Darling Boy, The Equalizer* — the way she would lean forward in her chair, an invisible whip in her hand, her voice urgent and tight. He thought of one-armed bandits, of betting slips, of the brown envelopes that arrived after she got sick and couldn't hide from him anymore.

Elaine went on. "You knew, right? You had to know, Dan. I mean, didn't you wonder why she made me and Donald her executors? Most husband and wives just leave it all to each other, don't they? So you had to know there was something…off. Right?"

What did *he* know? What was happening? It had been such a long time since he had been able to answer questions like that, even when he was the one doing the asking. So it wasn't avoidance, was it? Not really. He just didn't know anything anymore. He had given up with questions and their answers. He just kept on. He just did what he needed to do. He made the tea, he cleaned the kitchen, he tidied his shed, he had a drink. He had another. And then another. Other people's questions — Millicent's, Donald's, the odd remaining friend's — they dried up in the dearth of his answers. People didn't ask questions of him anymore, and he didn't ask any of them. His world had become tight, sealed up. It ran in blocks of time, regulated by drinks, his moods governed by how much or how little he had had and by how easily the next might be found. As to Millicent and money, he had known something was going down, that she was battling demons. Different to his own, but demons none the less. The pair had become almost kindred in their non-communication. Complicit in each other's nightmare. Closer in a shared silence than they had been for years.

As he and Elaine sat looking at the letter in his hand, silence hanging over the table, Dorothy launched into the kitchen and headed straight for the larder. He could hear her rummaging around behind him, opening the bread bin, moving tins across shelves, ripping open a mesh bag of fruit. She surfaced with an apple and a jar of peanut butter and sat on the corner of the table. He dropped the letter out of sight onto the seat of an empty chair.

"Whose is the record player?" she said, leaning back to grab a teaspoon from the kitchen drawer behind her, then taking a spoonful of peanut butter straight from the jar. "The one in the hall."

"It's for Tot," Dan said. "But these are for you." He pushed the tulips towards her. They lay on the damp newspaper like strange, bright fish. He thought she might complain about the disparity of the gifts, but she didn't. She fingered the frilly red petals as if they were alive. Oddly enough, she looked as if she might cry. And all he had wanted to do was to make her happy.

"They're pretty," she said.

"Not as pretty as you are," he replied. "Get ready, Lass. Men — good men — will buy you van-loads of flowers."

"Oh, for God's sake, Dan!" Elaine shouted, banging the calculator on the table. "I'm telling you you're ruined and all you can do is drone on and on about good men and bloody flowers."

Dorothy put down the spoon. "Ruined? What do you mean, 'ruined'?" She looked from him to her mother. "Ruined how?"

Elaine stretched her head from side to side and massaged the back of her neck. "I think you should take your apple upstairs, Love. I need to speak to your grandfather."

He shook his head. "Enough secrets," he said. "There's been enough in this family. If she's old enough to be a mother, she's old enough to know that being old doesn't make you clever."

"Then you tell her. I've got to get dinner ready." Elaine pushed the calculator and pad towards him and began pulling packages from the fridge.

He looked at the calculator and then at the numbers scribbled on the pad. "I had a feeling…that things weren't right with money." He lined up the calculator and the pad on the table and fiddled with the pen. "I mean your grandma was always selling things. Remember the sofa?" He laughed. "She even sold the car once." Contrary to his intention, his laughter sounded heartless, callous. "I knew money was coming in and out…more out than in. But I didn't know why. Not for certain."

"And you never asked?" Elaine's voice was small and shrill. "How could you not ask her? How could you be so blind, not seeing what was going on right under your bloody nose?"

"Like you asked, you mean? Like when your thirteen-year-old daughter was getting knocked up? Like that?"

Dorothy stabbed her spoon at both of them. "Whoa! Hang on! Don't turn on me! I just come in here for something to eat, and then Granddad gives me flowers — which I didn't ask for — and you're shouting at him and now it's all about me! How did that happen?" She grabbed her bag from the table, knocked the jar of peanut butter to the floor, and banged out of the kitchen. They listened to her thump up the stairs and waited for the slammed door.

The door slammed. The kitchen settled quiet again around their ears.

"I'm sorry," Dan said. "I didn't mean it. About Dorothy. Who could have known—"

"It's alright," she interrupted, her back to him. "You're right. I should have known."

"Oh, we should all know a lot of things. It'll all come out in the wash, Lovey. You'll see."

Elaine turned, an onion in her hand. "There's no money left, Dan. There's a second mortgage on your house, a line of creditors up the street and back, the bank...it's all in the letter. You're bankrupt. She bankrupted you. That's not going to come out in the wash."

He thought about the whiskey again and the plans he had had for the evening. They had begun with a few glasses by the window; he liked to watch the day fade and the lights over Treeverton glow up the rubbish dump. Then a few phone calls ... to Tommy at *The Hook and Parrot* to say he was coming home and to thank him, to Mrs. Phemister next door to ask her to air the house, and then he was going to get out the road atlas and plan his route home to Sleaford, think about finding a buyer for all those chickens.

She leant on the table, her hands wet and red. "You don't seem bothered!"

He looked up. "We all have our secrets, Elaine. The things we're not proud of. We've all got them. It seems spending money we didn't have was Millie's."

Elaine sat down and rubbed her eyes.

"It isn't that I'm not bothered," he continued. "But, I mean, what can I do? If she spent all the money..."

"She spent it AND some!"

"But whatever she did, it's done and she's gone."

The two of them sat for a moment, the only sound the clock and the faint noise of Dorothy singing a nonsense song to Trampus in the room above. He picked up the manila envelope from the table and papers slid out. More heavy cream letters from the solicitors. He rubbed a sheet between his thumb and forefinger. "Expensive," he said, looking up at Elaine.

She smiled quietly. "Only the best for Millie. Even in death."

"You've read all this, Love?" He looked at the letterhead. "Messrs. Davis and Trent are sure? It's all gone?"

She nodded. "You'll have to sell the house to pay off the creditors, Dan."

"Will that cover it?"

"You might have a little left over. And your state pension, of course."

"Well, that's better than nothing."

"I've got a pie to make," she said, standing up and turning back to the chopping board. She picked up another onion and rubbed at its paper skin.

"Tot home?" he asked.

"In her room."

"Then I think I'll go up, give her the record player." He leaned down to retrieve the jar of peanut butter and returned it to the table.

"Dan?"

"Yes?" he said, pausing at the kitchen door.

"You'll stay? With us?"

"It's a really nice player, Elaine. Takes '45s and albums. Smart tartan case—"

"You're more than welcome to stay, Dan."

He studied the door handle, then turned back to Elaine with a bright smile. "Got her that Goat's Head Soup LP. Mick Jagger. The one with the lips. Like the cushion in the bath." He pursed his own in a bad imitation. She smiled. He opened the door.

The sound of Dorothy's singing grew louder. She was singing the boy a song about houses made out of cardboard held together with sticky tape. He felt held together with sticky tape. Cheap sticky tape.

"Thanks, Elaine."

"Dinner's in an hour."

He nodded, the sound of her knife striking the chopping board filling his ears and slicing through the singing.

*

Two weeks ago, in the hangover of bad news, he had stood in her doorway clutching a portable record player, a man bearing gifts. Today, he stood by her window holding a whiskey bottle by the neck as if it were a wild animal: unpredictable, irresistible, dangerous.

"You could tip it away, *Dangrad*," Tot said again.

She was gathering up the snow globes from the shelf one-by-one and dropping them carefully onto the bed, allowing one each time and space to settle before dropping the next. Finally, she took down the tea caddy and sat with it, cross-legged on the pillow. He watched her lay out the globes in two rows on the pink chenille bedspread. They were like snapshots, strange events caught inside glass, each dome home to a frozen object: a stately home, a castle, a cartoon character. Some contained animals. Others contained pop stars. One was home to the moon and the Gemini spacecraft. One contained a blue unicorn pawing at a rock. Each scene waited for snow, however unlikely, however impractical. She put the round caddy at the head of the two columns, its opacity in the presence of all that transparency adding to the fascination of what the wooden case concealed. She picked up the globes in quick succession and shook them hard until the entire bed was a flurry of obscuring snow.

"Dad drank," she said. "Not much, but he drank." She picked up the unicorn globe again and spun it in her

141

hands until the snow was an eternal blizzard around the blue, horned myth inside. "Mum used to tell him he had a P.R.O.B.L.E.M., but he said the only problem was her."

"It's not a problem, Love. Just a drink now and then. Helps me sleep."

"It's blue," she said, "because it's a unicorn and that's okay. If it was just a horse, I wouldn't like it being blue. But unicorns are magic. They can be any colour they want to be. This one has green hooves. Look." She held it up for him to see.

"I'll keep the bottle on top of the wardrobe. The piano was stupid. I didn't think."

She offered him the unicorn globe. He carefully set the bottle down on the rug before taking the globe from her hands.

"You can wish on it," she said. "You just close your eyes, wish, and shake it hard. If the snow falls on the bits you thought it would, your wish comes true. It's my magic."

He looked at the globe. The blue unicorn had one green hoof up on a rock, the other lifted in air. The rock was wide and low. That's where the snow would fall. On the rock. He put the globe down carefully on the bedspread.

She stood, catching her balance on the bed for a moment, before returning the unicorn carefully to the shelf. He helped, handing her the others one-by-one. As she reached up towards the shelf, her sleeve fell back, revealing a line of tiny, round purple bruises, each one fading into brown around the edge like an old flower. He took her by the wrist, pulling her arm out straight and pushing up the sleeve of her cardigan.

"How did you do this?" he said. He gently pressed one of the bruise-flowers with his finger. "Does it hurt?"

She looked at him for a long moment, saying nothing.

"How did you do this?" he repeated.

"I didn't. You did."

"Me? What do you mean? When?" his voice rising, incredulous.

"When I asked you about the boy in the woods. When you were in bed."

"Why would I do that? What boy?" Dan couldn't understand what she was telling him. "That Keesal from number seven? Did he do this?"

She shook her head. "You did it," she said again.

"I don't understand," he said, tentatively matching his fingertips to the bruises on her arm. "Why would I do this?"

She retrieved the unicorn globe from the shelf and held it out to him. "Shake it."

He took the glass ball, closed his eyes, and shook it. When he opened his eyes, the rock was bare, the unicorn's back legs lost inexplicably in a drift of silver snow.

16

The fabric was slippery and treacherous; the pins did not want to stay put, and Elaine thought a hot iron might tame the material just enough to make its hemming easier. That was all that was required. Some patience, a little hand stitching, a final good press, and another order for *Colette's Creations* would be complete. She opened the door to the hallway cupboard and pulled out the old ironing board, its bad-tempered legs unfolding as she dragged it squealing to the front room.

When they asked, she told neighbours and friends that business was thriving. And it was. While the money went out as quickly as it arrived — towards a new sewing machine, an interlocker, electric shears — the money *was* coming in. She had blitzed the village with business cards, handing two to anyone who asked how things were going, slipping them into the folds of magazines in the library, pinning them to all the notice boards from the newsagents across the road to the high-end hairdressers past the church. She had press-ganged both kids into making a poster for the church noticeboard. Elaine had even asked Dan to help. And he came through, visiting every Bishop's Croft pub to tuck a card behind its payphone and had promised to check back regularly to replace cards that had been taken.

So an evening that didn't involve either sewing machine and fabric, or typewriter and invoices was a rare thing. If friends had told her four years ago she would be moving into her forties as a business woman, the proprietor of an almost successful home sewing company, she would have dismissed their forecasts as fairy tale. She would have told them her sewing was purely relaxation, a little hobby. But then, four years ago, she had no inkling that she would be facing her forties as a single mother. If she had known, she might have stabbed her finger with a knob pin and chosen to sleep away the next decade at least.

Perhaps she had been asleep her whole life, exhausted by its realities. Or maybe she had been living the life of a somnambulant, outwardly awake but inside caught up in a numbing fantasy. Either way, her husband had been her prince, but it had been his leaving that opened her eyes, not his kiss. She awoke to find herself alone in a realm of fear and spent weeks if not months asking the bathroom mirror — her only confidante — what she had done wrong and whether the other woman (because as far as Elaine was concerned, there *had* to be another woman) was fairer than she. Her interrogations always concluded with the same question: how on earth she was to survive with two girls and no man in the house? The answer had come in the form of elf hats.

When Donald left, her Stanley Close neighbours drew close — which was odd since she had always pushed them away, telling herself that, thankfully, she and they had nothing in common. They were either, as she termed it, "earth mothers" putting her to shame with their homemade baby food and plaited Indian sandals, or they were older women who reminded her of her mother-in-law and who always wanted to know more than she was prepared to tell them. It was one of these older women, a Mrs. Kenton, who insisted on breaking Elaine's reserve with a request: Mrs. Kenton had seen the card for *Collette's Creations* in the library and could Elaine make fifteen elf hats by the weekend? Mrs. Kenton, a volunteer at the Willowswitch Infant School, had been let down by a Treeverton company who had delivered the costumes for the children's annual pantomime but who had failed to supply the hats. The performance was the following weekend. Mrs. Kenton stood square on the red doorstep, a bolt of green felt propped against the windowsill, and waited for her answer.

Elaine had taken the fabric and transformed it into the required number of pointy hats by the following afternoon. Word spread, and while there wasn't a call for elf hats on the Bishop's Croft estate, there was a need for a cheap and convenient sewing service. Within a week or two, she had orders: Stanley Close's women turned up at her front door with their men's trousers that needed taking in, up or out, and with folded lengths of cheap spring cotton to be made into dresses and skirts for distant summer holidays. Nowadays, she turned down more private alterations than she accepted; her reliability and price had made a name for her with the local theatre groups, and she loved the challenge that work provided. She never knew what she would be making. It might be a nymph costume and a donkey's head, or a ball gown that came to pieces for Cinderella's midnight descent down the castle steps.

Whenever she heard herself say that business was thriving, the image that came to mind was not that of a healthy plant or child, but that of a woman seizing hold of her life. Four years ago, when Donald left and she was faced with raising two girls — one pregnant — she felt punch drunk. But she had rallied around the bare fact that there was only one person in her corner, and that she would have to learn to be both fighter and sponge-man, manager and promoter. She would have to be the wise old referee and the swimsuited girl who paraded with the round cards.

She grappled with the ironing board, setting its legs and positioning it in the daylight afforded by the bay window. She plugged in the iron and filled its reservoir with water from the tiny chrome milk jug she kept for the task. The iron hissed in the background as she removed the silver chaps from the dummy and spread them carefully across the board, smoothing her hand over the slightly prickly fabric. Its glittering shine did not mirror her mood. She would be forty this month and it seemed harder for her to be as sure as usual about life and its prospects. Things felt as if they were teetering, out of balance. She was fearful not only because of what was happening — she felt her days becoming stale, a constant round of sewing and

146

motherhood — but also because of what was not happening: there was her birthday to plan, and for the first time, she couldn't summon the enthusiasm.

From as far back as she could remember, even into her childhood, she had spent her birthday away from home. She had brought the tradition, one inherited from her mother, to her marriage. At first, as a new lover, Donald had found her need to be away from the mundane on this one day of the year endearing. He had played along, organizing secret destinations. One year, he took her to Calais on the ferry, and they came home with baguettes, good French wine and too much cheese. Another year, they had flown to Ireland for lunch in a tiny cafe at Dingle, overlooking the Blankit Islands. They had sat in the café all afternoon drinking strong tea and planning their retirement, how they would raise sheep, how he would shear and she would knit in front of a peat fire, how every night they would get tipsy and sweet on Guinness and champagne. For her twenty-fifth, he took her to Brighton…in a hot air balloon. They had found the dressmaker's dummy ("a near-antique" according to the shopkeeper) in a tiny shop in The Lanes. They had forgotten they didn't have the car, and the dummy had had to stand between them all the way home on the train.

Later, when both of them had been overtaken by the grind of marriage and babies, Donald stopped finding the birthday tradition endearing and wondered instead why they went to all the fuss. She had continued the tradition alone, taking the children with her on daytrips to zoos, to museums, staying out anywhere all day, returning late on the last bus, a child either side of her, everyone sleepy and fretful. When does tradition become compulsion?

High-pitched wails from the kitchen drowned out the iron's steady wet hisses and were punctuated by the steady clatter of a metal spoon on a china bowl and by her eldest's quiet singing to her son. Elaine regularly forgot how much noise a toddler can make. Sometimes she forgot she even had a grandson in the house. She nosed the iron gently across the fabric, the cloth turning momentarily dark, before its shine — its tiny threaded dazzles — returned. Dorothy had amazed them all. Elaine had imagined the arrival of Trampus would push them all back into the drudgery of nappies and night feeds. But Dorothy had surprised her: she had refused to return to school, saying she wanted to be a "real mother." Elaine had stepped in, trying to help, but Dorothy, after listening to her advice, pushed her away and got on with raising her son in her own way.

The interval between Donald leaving and Trampus arriving had been little more than a year. The three of them — Elaine, Tot and Dorothy — had spent that year digging out separate spaces in which to deal with loss. Elaine had tunnelled into sewing; she blamed her resulting isolation from the girls on her need to maintain an income, to keep their boat afloat. Tot had left the house to find her peace, spending evenings somewhere else…anywhere else. Dorothy removed to her bedroom, like some Victorian woman-in-waiting. When Trampus arrived, he pulled his mother into his world of need, and on the way, Dorothy leaned hard on her mother and little sister for balance.

The boy had become the centre of their lives. Elaine and Tot assumed the roles of supporting actress to Dorothy's leading lady, with the kitchen as their stage: baby food warmed on the stove; toys and picture books piled haphazardly on the table; the playpen in the warm corner by the boiler above which was strung ever filling lines of nappies and flannel bibs. When Trampus was teething, they pulled the little sofa from the cold lounge into the kitchen, and many nights, the three of them lay napping, curled up together, none of them willing to move for fear of waking the baby.

The baby's neediness had persuaded the three of them that they were not a sinking ship that had been abandoned; they were a sound ship from which one passenger had chosen to disembark. But as Trampus had grown, as he had grabbed hold of his own small measures of independence, the ship began to flounder once again, as if it could not remain on course without his need at the helm.

Elaine took a handful of pins from the saucer and stabbed them into the ironing board's padded cover. Then she ran the iron's sharp nose along the chaps' folded hem line, securing the crease with pins. It disappointed her that they were not so close now. As Trampus shifted from passive baby to intrepid toddler, Dorothy had put her spare energy into rekindling, Frankenstein-style, her relationship with the boy's father. Tot retreated again and Elaine couldn't seem to reach her; the child spent all her time at friends' homes as if her own was too much to handle. Elaine's reaction to all this had not been to redouble her efforts at mothering. Instead, she had thrown herself into her business, and business was doing well. She enjoyed working with the local theatres and had discovered a side to herself that she liked, becoming what her father-in-law described as "artsy." She had cut her hair short and dyed it red. She threw out the printed cotton dresses and flat sandals and bought black. She splurged on bright scarves and shawls. She felt as if she had been recast as a real woman, sloughing off the worn roles of both mother and wife.

She did not miss her husband.

Sometimes, however, she missed the idea of a man. She worried she would never again be held. She worried she might forget how to be held, how to soften into someone else's body. She worried she might, through fear, enter into a relationship with a man she didn't like, purely to be held. Recently, the most innocent encounters had become charged: her hand and that of a stranger's meeting over the same fruit in the supermarket; sharing a seat with a man on

149

a crowded bus; her hairdresser's hands on her neck; the stripper's strangely erotic feet planted square on the seat of her kitchen chair.

Elaine stretched, the knots in her back reminding her of the impending birthday. Why not a 40th in Penryth in the well-muscled arms of a twenty-two-year-old stripper? Why the bloody hell not? She settled into the armchair by the fire to hand-stitch the hems. Around her, the house was now void of human sound and yet it was full of noise. The washing machine agitated, the dryer hummed, buttons and zippers tapping a percussion inside the machine's metal drum. The radio played the shipping forecast from Dan's room on the other side of the wall, the meteorologist listing the locations: Finnestare, Dogger — places Elaine had never been to. Like Penryth. Like the arms of a twenty-two-year-old stripper. Her needle picked up tiny loops — hem to trouser, trouser to hem — her needle moving rhythmically, the fabric turning smoothly between her fingers. Completing the final stitch, she bent her head to bite the thread through, then shook out the chaps before laying them across the arm of the chair and checking her watch. 3:00 p.m. Two hours before he would arrive to collect the outfit. Enough time surely for Dan to finish spray-painting the final quick-drying coat on the spaceman tubes. Enough time, perhaps, for her to come to a decision about her birthday.

"Dan!"

No answer. He must still be in the shed painting the damned things. She checked her watch again before heading out to the back garden, hoping that all would be ready by the time Simon Dolan arrived.

*

"Dan?" Elaine pushed the shed door open, its old wood sticking and complaining. The inside was gloomy, cave-like, in contrast to the bright sunshine of a winter afternoon that lay across the garden like a cool benediction. Her father-in-law sat hunched over the worktable in the corner as if he were concentrating or working on something very small and intricate. The silver tubes were slung across the rack that held the garden rake and shovels. She touched their concertinaed surface. The paint was dry.

"Dan?" She touched his shoulder and he woke with a start.

"What the hell...!" He sat up, toppling his garden chair.

She stepped back, her hands held up, and was about to apologize when he interrupted her. "No, No," he said. "Welcome, welcome to my *farlour, little ply*!" He pulled down another chair from the hooks set into the eaves above and opened it out for her. He patted it. "Come join me and the spiders."

The shed was indeed a haven for spiders. Webs hung thick and dusty across the murky window above the table and stretched up into the corners. And yet the shed's contents — loungers, power tools, jars and jars of nails and screws, the girls' old bikes — were clean and orderly. Dan had done a good job of rationalizing the shed after pulling out the spare bed and mattress almost a month earlier.

She sat down alongside him. "What are you working on," she said.

"Nothing."

"When I came in, you were busy doing something." She peered at the table which was clear. Nothing in progress. No small thing under repair.

"Napping. I was napping. It's what we old men do," he said. His face was flushed and his hair stormy from sleep. "Whereas you, my dear, have no need of naps. You, my dear Miss Jean Brodie," he said in an affected Scottish accent, "are in the prime of life. The *Lime of your Prife*."

Elaine leaned forward, towards the old man's smile, and sniffed. Something. Something sweet, yet old. Not just the smell of a man who had spent too many hours in a dusty shed, but more the smell of...a pub.

"Have you been drinking, Dan?" she asked.

He looked bashful...almost coquettish. It was a terrible look for an old man to have on his face. He simpered. "Just a little one. Just a little nippy. Medicinal, you know." He held up his finger, its nail black and bloody. "Caught it in the drawer." He studied his finger minutely as if he had never seen it before, then leaned in close to Elaine, his simper switching to something more...calculating.

"Kiss it better?" he slurred. "Kissy Kissy, Millie-Millie?" He puckered his lips obscenely. He was obscene.

She frowned. Millie? He thought she was Millie. Dear God, on top of everything else she had to handle, her father-in-law was losing his bloody mind. She shook her head. "Kissy-Kissy won't cure that," she said. "Your loving daughter-in-law" — she stressed her title — "will have to get you some ice." She spoke loudly, as if she were talking to an idiot. She bent down to open the drawer, wanting to check its bite, mindful that Tramps was at the intrepid stage and that the shed was a magical place for small children. Dan tried to bat her hand away from the drawer's knob, but too late; the drawer opened smoothly and stayed open to reveal two bottles of cheap vodka and an almost empty half-gallon of whiskey.

She took a moment as the incongruity of the bottles inside the workbench drawer sank in. "Jesus, that's a lot of medicine," she said. "You must be a very sick man, Dan."

He leaned back in his chair, the idiotic smile returned to his face. "And you are a very beautiful woman, Elaine. And my son..." His voice trailed off, as did the smile.

"Donald."

The smile was back. "My son *Donald* was a...was a...*fluddy ball...a fluddy fluddy ball.*"

"Let's get you inside so I can look at that finger."

She pulled the old man from his chair, and he put his arms around her waist. "A bloody fool, Elaine," he said and she heard his words hot and wet on her neck, before she felt his tongue slide into her ear, before she pulled back in the gloom of the shed and before she slapped her drunk father-in-law hard across his cheek.

*

3:20 p.m. She could hear Dan sleeping it off in the room next-door, his snores annoyingly random and loud. Drunken fool, she thought, checking her watch. Bloody drunken fool: the son, the father, and the holy fucking ghost...who was presumably a man as well. All of them fools, a waste of bloody space.

She stood at the ironing board giving the costume its final press. She had done a great job. The outfit was perhaps her best work to date. Beautifully made and functional. Now, if she could corner the market on adult apparel, she would be made. No more strawberry tutus. It was a lovely fantasy to turn over in her head.

She pulled back the net curtains and looked out onto Stanley Close. He was late. There was no sign of his car. In fact there were no cars, no movement of any kind. Of course, vehicles were rare during the day. All the husbands drove off to work by eight-thirty, leaving the Close to its women and its road wide and strangely empty. But today, the Close seemed quieter than usual. The Green at its centre was empty save a few pecking crows. No women, with children or with shopping bags, walked in or out of the Close. The air looked still and heavy with the threat of storm.

She checked her reflection in the glass of the bay window, stretching the skin taut over her cheekbones with her fingertips and lifting her chin. The glass gave her back a smooth, attractive woman.

But Elaine knew the deceit of un-silvered glass, that it didn't hand back an entire picture; there was a lack of detail, of depth, a glossing over of shortcomings. And that was its lure, the deception ever present in the glass of car doors, of train windows, in dead television screens. But no glass, not even the starkly lit and silvered bathroom cabinet faced every morning could hand her back an accurate reflection of how she felt inside, of that out-of-kilter feeling she had, her grappling for balance between the rush of fantasy and the fierceness of the everyday. She was perched midway on a see-saw: on one end was an illicit birthday weekend in Penryth with a stripper called Simon who was almost twenty years her junior, and on the other the reality of family and sewing and the prospect of turning forty alone. The temptation to scramble along the see-saw's length, to topple headfirst into Penryth even as it smashed into the ground (which it surely would) was overwhelming.

It was then that she saw an old yellow van turn into the Close. It had to be him…and she wasn't ready. She pressed the iron across the ridges of the hemming, each individual stitch disappearing, invisible, in a hiss of steam, her free hand removing the pins and dropping them back into the saucer as she went. The van was outside the house now, its roof a thin yellow stripe above the overgrown privet hedge. The pins rained down on the Monopoly dog which had been joined in the saucer for some reason by the silver top hat. She heard the engine idling, and she nudged the counters with the point of the iron.

Was the dog tiny? Insignificant? Or was the top hat huge? Why the hell didn't he ring the doorbell?

Final ends. She took a pair of sharp scissors and cut each trailing thread; those at the hem, at the inside leg where the Velcro attached, at each popper along the crotch. His van must have been there now for at least three minutes. She carried the outfit to the window and inspected its seams in the light. Perfect. The van was still there.

She would go to Penryth. The fabric sparkled in the light through the curtains. She would hand the costume to Simon and tell him yes, she would go to Penryth and sit in the green room with him before he took to the stage. Dan could sober up and take care of the girls. She would help Simon clasp the tiny hooks on his tubing through the eyelets on his braces. She could do this. She'd take extra thread for repairs. She heard the engine die and the van door slam.

Folding the costume neatly, she dropped it into its cardboard box on top of the silver-sprayed hoses and sealed the top with packing tape. She walked through the narrow hallway to the front door and stood by the meter cupboard. But she felt stupid waiting there alone in the hallway, facing the front door with the box in her arms. She could hear the coffee machine hissing in the kitchen and the iron hissing in the front room. Outside a bird sang, a robin perhaps, and she could make out the thin drone of children's voices from the playground of the infants' school around the corner. There was Dan's snoring from the dining room. And then the sound of shoes on the concrete pathway. Soft shoes. Not Dan's steady leather-soled tread. Not Dorothy's clacking high-heeled approach, or Tot's lazy scuffle. Elaine found herself edging backwards up along the hallway and into the living room. She stood behind the curtains in the bay window, the box clutched tight to her chest. The door bell rang. One long extended chime.

She held her breath and leaned sideways an inch so she could see between the drapes, through the glass. She could see his feet on the red door step. He was wearing sandals again. Leather thong sandals. In March. His big turtlehead toes curving upwards. She jerked back, then walked slowly to the sofa and sat down, placing the box on the coffee table. If he looked through the window, through the nets and the heavy chintz drapes, he would be able to see her sitting on this sofa in front of the coffee table overflowing with magazines and kids' picture books and board games. He would see her and knock on the glass. If he knocked on the glass, she would let him in. He would ask again about Penryth and she would say yes and set in motion a train of events that might not easily be halted. If he knocked on the glass, she would know she was meant to go to Penryth.

She listened to the bell chime again, drawing her knees up to her chest and hugging them close. And then to the sound of soft shoes on concrete, the creak of the gate, the fall of the latch, the sound of an engine firing, a car pulling away. And then nothing, apart from the bird now singing in the laburnum by the hedge.

She went to the window in time to see the yellow van pulling slowly out of the Close. She unplugged the iron, and picking up the saucer of pins, went back to the sofa and sat down on the edge of its cushions. She rocked a little, wondering what would have happened if she had stayed in the hallway and opened the door, or if he had knocked on the glass and seen her on the sofa. What would she have done? What would she have said? She put the saucer on the coffee table and studied it as if the answer might lie there, might be readable in the pattern of pins, in the relationship between the Monopoly counters and the silver-threaded needle. Readable like tea leaves upended for a fortune teller.

She pulled the Monopoly box out from under the coffee table and removed its lid and folded board. Inside, in each neat plastic compartment, sat the banknotes, the Community and Chance cards, the plastic houses and hotels, and two silver counters: the racing car she and her daughters always argued over, and her absent husband's favourite, the boat. She picked up the dog and the top hat from the saucer and weighed them, one in each palm, for a moment, before placing the silver dog gently back with the car and the boat. Then she unsealed the costume's cardboard box and dropped the top hat inside. She'd post the box. Tomorrow.

Now, there would be just three monopoly counters to choose from. One for each of them. She replaced the folded board and lid, and slid the box back under the coffee table. It was easier this way. No arguments. No men in the game. No complications.

17

Keesal lumbered along beside Tot, kind and shabby, as they made their way down the crowded walkway that ran between the school quad and gymnasium. The matter of his Valentine card and the confetti had not been revisited, and it was this mutually tacit solution that enabled the pair of them to hang on to their friendship, one that had begun in the aftermath of her father's disappearance and in the wake of Keesal's appointment as whipping boy for the sometimes cruel adolescents of Stanley Close. The friendship had served them well, the awkwardness each felt when flying solo morphing into a comforting and buffeting camaraderie when they flew one behind the other: Tot's sense of abandonment abated; and the bullies in the street seemed less able to intimidate Keesal and turned their attention to other less protected targets.

They parted ways at the entrance to the gym, splitting off to head up the stairs to their respective changing rooms, the building's huge angled glass walls shooting bright sun squares onto the concrete walkway and into the storm of students that streamed into the building behind them.

Tot wasn't built for gymnasiums. She was the wrong shape for the ropes suspended from the girders that honeycombed the ceilings and hung down to the shiny sprung floor. She was the wrong shape for hooking her feet under climbing bars and hanging upside down. She was definitely the wrong shape for the trampoline, news of which was the buzz in the girls' changing room. Story was that it had arrived during the Easter holidays and had been installed in the corner where the mats and medicine balls used to live. Tot, harboring no illusions that the trampoline might be her saving grace, ignored the hubbub and headed for her usual spot in the corner of the long, form-lined room. Head down and facing into the corner, she quickly put on her gym kit. It was a practiced dance of veils; she could get changed without exposing a thin inch of potential embarrassment.

Intent on her task, she had not noticed the changing room emptying around her, the girls moving en masse to the parapet that ran the length of the gymnasium. She laced her gym shoes and ran to join them, edging through their gaggle until she could claim a place and look down into the gym. From above, the new trampoline looked benign, blue and bouncy, like a surprise one might discover in the garden at a rich kid's birthday party. The loud girls, the instigators, moved away from the parapet, loping down the gymnasium steps in twos and threes, the other girls following, flowing like bees, like workers after queens. Tot stayed up at the parapet looking down.

The first-year boys, including Keesal, lined the glass walls, hugging their arms across their narrow chests like shy boys often do. They shared the gym with the older lads who were doing loud circuits, each station littered with debris: cracked leather medicine balls, skipping ropes, a wooden box of basketballs, green padded mats. The younger boys, their gym kits still bright and new, flattened themselves against the walls, watching in open-mouthed awe as Mrs. Bickerly, the gym mistress, began a sophisticated routine on the trampoline. They had not yet found the bravado that would begin to build, like pearl, around the grit of their apprehension.

On her final descent, Mrs. Bicklerly, imposing in her blue tracksuit, stretched out her arms, bent her knees to absorb the energy, and brought the bouncing to an immediate and smooth halt. She deftly dismounted and cajoled the boys from the wall into an orderly queue alongside the trampoline. At the head of the queue stood Keesal, as awkward in his gym kit as he was in his school uniform. He slouched rather than stood, rubbing the uppers of his canvas shoes on the backs of his bare calves, keeping his eyes firmly on the ground. When Mrs. Bickerly called his name, he climbed up onto the trampoline, moving gingerly into its shifting center.

The gym paused and became still, sensing new blood. Boys shooting hoops suspended their game to watch, one slowly bouncing his ball, its methodical slap of rubber on wood a metronome. Boys shimmying up the ropes hung silent. Press-ups, sit-ups and skipping all stopped as Keesal stood motionless in the center of the trampoline listening to Mrs. Bickerly who spoke too softly for Tot to hear. All around was the smell of the floor's new varnish and the sound of the ball and the stuttered tock of the clock that hung high from the parapet.

Keesal's first bounce was low and pulled sniggers from two boys hanging from the wall bars. The girls fell silent. His second was higher, more controlled, and the boy with the basketball caught it and held it quiet in his hands.

Tot left the wall and walked down the steps into the gym. She leaned on the vaulting horse that stood at the foot of the staircase and watched. With each bounce, there was more and more air beneath his feet. It hurt her neck to watch him. He spread his arms as Mrs. Bickerly had, and Tot noticed the way Keesal's shoulders bunched down through to tiny, hard biceps. When had that happened? When had he grown those?

He rose still higher with each bounce, his face set as if he didn't see the staring boys or the gawking girls, or even Mrs. Bickerly shouting instructions from the edge of the trampoline — as if he were in a trance. His eyes were fixed on something no-one else could see. The sniggering boys became quiet, frozen as Keesal ascended again and again. The girls stopped pushing and elbowing each other, each one focussed on the boy on the trampoline. He had turned into something new, someone new. His body was tight and controlled. He landed exactly where he wanted to land, bounced as high as he wanted to bounce. Tot was mesmerized and wanted the moment to stretch on and on like elastic.

But there were other kids waiting at the trampoline's edge, and Mrs. Bickerly, her voice containing a touch of regret, told Keesal to wind it up and dismount. His bounces became smaller and smaller, his arms extended to balance all that slowing, his face still fixed with a strange beatific concentration. Mrs. Bickerly again told him to dismount as if she wasn't sure he had heard her, and at that moment, he landed, bent kneed, all motion absorbed. He turned to face the boys at the edge, the turn somehow disconnecting him from whom he had been in the air, reconnecting him back to the old Keesal — scruffy, awkward, constant Keesal — and it was this boy who, facing the wrong way, climbed down the short trampoline ladder, who tripped on the last rung, and who fell flat on his face on the shiny wooden floor. The boys on the wall bars began to laugh — too loudly — and resumed their climb. The boy with the basketball shot for the ring. And the girls forgot Keesal and began to chatter, the volume mounting to a steady buzz. The next boy climbed the short ladder and took his place in the centre of the trampoline. Equilibrium had been restored.

Keesal limped towards the vaulting horse and slid down onto the floor, inspecting his scraped knee, scrunching the skin to see if it was going to bleed. It did. Tot sat down next to him and pulled a handkerchief from her shorts' pocket. He took it and dabbed it against the graze. When he tried to return it, she pushed it back at him.

"Keep it," she said. "It's an old one."

He folded the handkerchief into a padded square and held it against his knee. "Thanks."

"Don't mention it." Tot stood up and rubbed her sweating hands dry on the soft suede of the horse. "Keesal?"

"What?"

"Where does your mum buy her saris?"

*

Saris! What a stupid thing to ask! But in that important moment it was all she could think of. Dangrad had told her boys were simple creatures — like amoeba, he said — and that you should start out with questions they could answer without their having to think too much. In fact, the questions and their answers should require no thought at all. He had made some suggestions, given her some examples. If she wanted a boy to talk to her, she should ask him what team he supported, or what he had watched on the television last night. She might ask him where he went on his holidays. Easy stuff. And the questions must be light. Boys didn't like dealing with heavy questions. Dangrad said that heavy questions felt to boys like quizzes or exams and to men like interrogation. Both boys and men were reminded of all the things they had got wrong. Keep it light, he had said. Keep it easy. Keep the answers unimportant.

But when Tot thought of Keesal, she didn't think of football or of television. She thought of his kitchen in the spring her father left and of a rainbow of freesias in a jelly jar on the table. She thought of Keesal's mother stirring something aromatic and sharp at the stove, a tea-towel wrapped around her waist as an apron, its dull white weave a foil to the fabric of her sari, always bright, always lush in its folds. So Tot had thought of saris, and maybe that had been a dim question, but it had been easy and light, and the questions she had rehearsed with Dangrad had not been intended for Keesal.

*

"The thing is, Tot," her grandfather said, "you can't let them know what you want up front."

"What do I want?"

"What did you call them? The start-up things?"

"The Beginning Things."

"That's it. You can't let a boy know you want him to be your boyfriend. And never mention the 'L' word up front. Never say 'love' to a boy. And when he is your boyfriend, don't hold his hand when his mates are around."

"Never?"

"Not unless he grabs your hand first. And if he does that, don't ever mention that he grabbed your hand first."

It had been the kind of day that seemed to have been raining forever. The sky's grey had settled in low over the trees and rooftops. Birds squeaked from branches, the rain running off leaves and roofs into rivulets that converged and coursed down the garden's concrete path, turning the borders shiny with slick mud. The plants all bowed down, their heads wet, their foliage folded, sodden and heavy. Tot had run out of things to do, and boredom had driven her to her grandfather's room. He was leafing through a photo album, mainly pictures from when he and Grandma were young, before they were married. She sat next to him on his bed, and when the last page of the album had been turned and the final picture explored and explained, he closed the book.

"How did you make Grandma fall in love with you?" she asked.

"Oh, I don't know that I did, Tot," he said. "You women just set your hats at us and that's it." He laughed, leafing back to a page in the middle of the album and handing the open book to Tot. "Talking of hats, that's your gran at Margate," he said, pointing to a photograph of Millicent in a boned swimsuit and a broad straw hat with a fuzzy feathered brim. "My favourite."

She took the album from him but studied her grandfather rather than the photograph. "No, really." she said, pressing him. "How do you do it? What do you do…up front…if you want it to be proper. A real…relationship."

"That's a hard one, Tot. I suppose we start by asking questions. We ask 'em questions they like answering. We all like talking about ourselves, right? But with boys? Let me see." He leaned back on the pillow, his arms crossed behind his head. "Well, you could ask them about football and television. Ask if they've got a dog. Where they went on their holidays."

"And then what?"

"They'll tell you things, and you remember them, and then when you bring those things up later, they'll think 'Bloody hell, she remembered.' That's really a boy's 'Heart Want.' That someone remembers what he said."

"Heart Want?"

"Yeah. Boys 'want' on two levels, Tot — with their hearts and then with their willies. Their willies tell 'em they want to put their hand up your skirt."

"What do their hearts tell them to want?"

"To be important. That someone other than their mum loves 'em."

"All boys?"

"All boys."

"Even Gareth?"

Her grandfather stood up and crossed the room to pull the curtains, shutting out the rain and the heavy skies. He peered at the photograph of Millicent on the wall. "All boys, Tot," he said, standing back and straightening the picture.

"And then what?"

"Well, then they realize that there's more to girls than tits and…" Her grandfather had paused a moment in front of the picture, thinking, as if pulling memories from far back in his mind. "…they realise there's more to girls than getting their end away."

"No, I mean what do you actually DO after you've asked them questions about their little brothers and their dogs?"

"Well, then you lean in a bit, giggle when they say something you think they think was funny. Make 'em feel good. Strong. Brave. You know the stuff, Tot. I don't have to tell you all this!"

"But you don't let them touch you?"

"Not yet, no. Make 'em wait, Tot. A boy will rush straight for…for the end things. It's how he's wired. It's your job to show him the start-up things…"

"Beginning Things."

"Right, Beginning Things like dancing and talking on the phone and going to the pictures. Talking." He smiled. "Things like *Corks in the Wuntryside*."

"Like *Porks in the Wark*?"

"Yeah, like walks in the park. Then, when he's not feeling so needy, he might find he likes the Beginning Things as well and doesn't do them just because he thinks you like them, when all he really wants to do is to put his … how did you put it? Ah, yes…*ningers down your fickers*."

Tot dropped the album on the carpet, and both she and Dan crashed heads as they bent to retrieve it. "You remembered." she said.

"Remembered what?" he asked, rubbing his head.

"What I told you that night. After the disco. About that boy. The one who wasn't who I thought he was."

"'Course I remembered! My *Diddle Larling* tells me about some boy trying it on with her in the woods!" He caught her in a hug. "'Course I remembered! You think your old granddad would forget a thing like that? After you came in to tell me 'specially?"

She laughed. But it was a laugh that didn't crease her eyes. Like the bruises on her arm, the things her grandfather had said lingered in her memory of that night: the things he had called her, the things he had not remembered saying or doing.

"So," he said, "why don't you let your old granddad take you out tonight on a date? Show you how it's done?"

"Really?"

"Yeah. Where do you want me to take you? Up the Chippie? *Pork in the Wark?*"

"Let's go to the Pig Bingo. At St. Lawrence's church. If we're quick, we'll make it. It starts at seven."

"Ah, romantic!"

"It's all that's on. There's never anything to do in this village…"

"Bishop's Croft, the bustling metropolis…"

"Mrs. Flannery said there's two pounds of sausages for a line and a joint of pork for a full house."

"The language of love." Dan took down his cap from the hook behind the bedroom door and skewed it at an angle over his eyes. He adjusted it in the mirror. "Let's see what you remember about lesson number one," he said. "Sit there, on the edge of the bed."

She did as she was told and looked up at her grandfather.

He continued: "Lesson one. Ask me something. Anything you don't really need to know … or even want to know. Remember, keep it light. Keep it easy."

She thought for a moment, then said, "Good evening, Mr. Thompson, how's your mum?"

He bowed stiffly from the waist. "Not too good, I'm afraid. We buried her in '35."

"Nice funeral?"

"Lovely flowers, thank you." He looked straight ahead with an expectant smile playing on his lips. He nodded at her encouragingly.

"And her dog?" Tot stood and picked up her jacket from the bed.

"Dead, too. Bad case of the mange. We couldn't stand the smell and had to shoot him." He held out his hand. "Would you like to go to Pig Bingo with me?"

She took his hand. "I'm glad the funeral went well. I love Pig Bingo."

He smiled. "See how it works, Tot? You ask questions, I answer them, I feel good, I ask you out on a date. Shall we go?" He helped her into her jacket and put his arm around her shoulders, steering her through the kitchen and towards the back door. She liked the feel of his arm across the back of her neck. It was heavy and his hand rested in air, not touching, not closing anything down. In the alley, he opened the gate for her.

"They might not do that, Tot," he said.

"What?" she asked, squeezing past him.

"Open doors and things. That might actually be one of the End Things now-a-days."

"I can open my own doors."

"Maybe not an End Thing. Maybe a Middle Thing."

He latched the gate and they headed across the Green towards Willowswitch Lane and the village beyond. Tot kept in step with her grandfather. He was whistling, murdering a tune, stopping every now and then to share a story about love and Millicent, about his memories of growing up and of girls in his street. She listened, her hands jammed warm in the pockets of her jacket, lost in pleasure that he had remembered her telling him about the boy in the park...but that he hadn't remembered squeezing her arm until it bruised. He hadn't remembered calling her a whore. His forgetting was as comforting as his remembering.

*

The pebble-dashed community centre was set behind St. Lawrence's, which itself was set back from the street, wedged between the doctor's office and the old library. The church was a large stone-and-flint studded building. Not tall and cloud-piercing, but sort of low and friendly. In an effort to both attract wildlife and reduce costs borne by an ever shrinking congregation, the grounds had been allowed to run wild, and that night, lit by the security lamps, grasses bent down in the rain to straggle across the gravel pathway that led from the street to the church's heavy porched door. The door was carved from dark oak and set deep inside the porch. Under the low beamed roof, all was dry and orderly: to one side of the door was a glass-fronted notice board that listed the times and names of each of the day's services; to the other was an A-board advertising the evening's bingo. A series of wet and puckered paper arrows taped to the church's stone walls led Tot and Dan around the side of the dark, unruly churchyard and to the modern community centre at its rear.

The double doors to the vestibule were open, and warm yellow light spilled out onto the pathway; however, inside, the entrance to the main hall was guarded by a fierce, toothy woman whose hand rested firmly on a stack of bingo cards, her table surrounded by a cluster of noisy villagers, mainly women in wet coats and plastic rain hats, umbrellas furled and dripping onto the black and white chequered floor.

They took their place in the line, a warm fuzz of steam forming above them, the queue's smell a combination of old clothes and casserole. When they reached the front of the line, Dan slipped his arm from Tot's shoulder, handed her his jacket, and bowed low to the woman with the bingo cards. Tot moved away to hang their coats on the already full hooks and stayed there to study the event board that hung alongside the main doors. She scanned the flyers' headlines for something interesting: *Summer Fete in June...Knit a Blanket for a Saigon Baby...The Big Book Comes Alive.* She noticed that the flyer advertising last month's

Youth Club Disco was still pinned to the board, obscured by a hand-written note offering cut-price piano lessons.

"Good evening, lovely lady," she heard her grandfather say. "Two for Pig Bingo and may the best man walk off with the swine's trotters." Tot turned to watch her grandfather in action, the woman's face defrosting in the warmth of his flirting, and the threat of a smile struggling with her mouth.

"How many cards, Sir?"

"I am a novice at the game...of life, of love, of pig bingo. So one will suffice. One for me and one for my young companion, who has the freshness of a Beaujolais but not the sweeter bouquet of a mature Merlot."

Tot thought she was going to throw up, but she couldn't look away as he bent down to take the cards and, before the woman realized what he was doing, dropped a kiss on her outstretched fingers. He headed for the notice board, and Tot watched the blushing woman recover her composure and scan the waiting line of people, defying them to snigger at her being wooed.

"*Dangrad*, you're a nightmare," Tot hissed, trying hard to hold onto her laughter until they got inside the main hall.

"Look and learn. Lesson in Love Number Two: Everyone loves a compliment." He handed her one of the bingo cards. "And Number Three: He who invites pays the bill." He stood in the doorway, scanning the room. "How about over there? By the stage. You go grab some seats and I'll get us both a cup of tea."

She looked across the room towards the stage and shivered. What had been February's dance floor, the setting for Gareth and the Blond Boy's manoeuvres, was now a parade ground of tables, chairs and old-age pensioners. They all faced the front, pens in hand, bingo cards spread out on the tables before them. Their blue china cups of tea and plates of biscuits and scones were pushed to one side.

They all watched the stage where the automated bingo ball bouncer — a glass and steel contraption — stood. Alongside the machine, on a barstool, sat the compere and caller, an old man in a sparkly tuxedo. At his feet, in front of a plywood painted cut-out of a pig, was a stack of wrapped packages that Tot assumed contained the prizes: sausages, bacon, chops, the coveted hand of pork roast. The pig was set upon a plinth of tinned sausages and beans, and around its neck hung a string of blinking fairy lights.

She took a seat at an empty table to the side of the stage and waited for her grandfather to return. He was deep in conversation with a woman at the serving hatch — the same hatch from which Mrs. Patel had handed out fizzy drinks and crisps. She watched him balance biscuits in the saucers of the two cups of tea and weave his way across the room to sit down next to her. He winked and slid a cup and a felt-tip pen across the table before bending over his bingo card, his reading glasses rammed firmly on his nose, as intent on the card's numbers as he would be on a betting slip at the Bookies. She watched him uncap his pen and lay it perpendicular to the card. He looked around the room, smiling as if at some secret joke, then lowered his cup of tea under the table, resting it on the edge of his chair. He took a hip flask from his inside jacket pocket and tipped a slug of something amber into the cup. He turned to see Tot looking at him, a frown on her face.

His smile turned nervous. "Just a nip, *Dittle*. Keeps out the cold." He held up the flask. "Want some?"

She shook her head and uncapped her own pen. The man on the stage picked up the microphone and pressed a button on the side of the bingo ball bouncer. It spat a white ball up a tube and into his hand.

"Welcome, Ladies and Gentlemen, boys and girls, and those as yet undecided, to the Bishop's Croft Pig Bingo Extravaganza." His voice was as flashy as the lights around the pig's neck, and the room quietened, straightened its cards and uncapped its pens. "Eyes down for any line and half a pound of finest streaky. Two fat ladies, Eighty-Eight."

With one hand, Tot picked up her pen and crossed through the boxed eighty-eight with a firm line. With the other, she fingered the folded sheet of paper in her pocket, stolen from the notice board.

18

Keesal had been surprisingly knowledgeable about his mother's saris. On the evening of the trampoline episode, Tot sat at the Patel's kitchen table where Keesal was spreading glue on the tiny plastic parts of a World War II Spitfire. The way he hunched over the plane, his fingers sticky with adhesive, his tongue clamped between his lips in concentration, put him at odds with the boy on the trampoline. It was as if they were two different people. She looked away and tried to concentrate on the scarf she was knitting. It was for her mother's birthday, and now she discovered she had been purling when she should have been plaining. Annoyed with herself, she slid the knitting from the needles and began to unravel in careless disgust.

Keesal looked up from his plane. "Alright?"

"This is all buggered up," she said.

Keesal pushed the plane away. "Mum, can I show Tot your saris?"

His mother turned from frying fish at the cooker, spatula in hand. "Whatever for?" she asked.

Tot gave up with the knitting and jammed the mess into her school bag. "Because I like them. And I don't understand how you keep them on."

"Ah, it's an art I learn, Tot. A world of my mother's windings and tuckings in." Mrs. Patel went back to her fish. "Just wash your hands first, Okey-Dicky?"

"DOKEY," said Keesal. "It's Okey-Dokey, Mum."

"Well, if it's Okey-Dockey with you, my boy, then it's Okey-Dockey with me. But clean hands, yes?"

Keesal, shaking his head, grabbed a giggling Tot by the hand and led her up the stairs to his parents' bedroom, detouring momentarily at the bathroom's washbasin.

At the foot of his parents' bed stood a large trunk, intricately carved with birds and twining branches. He flipped up its bronze-coloured catch and opened the lid.

Inside the red-velvet-padded chest were the saris. On top, Keesal explained, were the ones his mother wore on standard days — the plain cottons, their colours bright, but not garish: clear blues and greens, a dark red, another in mauve. He eased these to one side, unearthing an explosion of cranberry and gold. The scent of mothballs filled the air.

"She calls this her 'disco' sari," he said.

"Do your mum and dad still go to discos?"

"No. Dad can't dance what with his having just the one leg and all. But she wears it at Christmas. And on Dad's birthday…and she wore it when India won the cricket."

He wiped his hand on his trousers and gently pushed the disco sari aside. His hand had reached the bottom of the trunk now, and only one sari remained. It was silk — the palest caterpillar green shot through with nubbly silver and ivory threads. Its weave was highlighted with gunmetal leaves and spirals. He stroked it with his finger.

"Flippin' hell! That's beautiful," Tot said, her eyes wide. "Can I touch?"

He pulled his finger away and shook his head. "No, better not. It's her wedding sari." He began to tidy the chest's stack of saris, easing each one back into its place, smoothing out the creases as best he could with his palm. "I should have been a girl, but she's keeping it anyway."

"I'd make curtains out of it if I was your mum. Or a bedspread. It's a shame to keep it shut up in there." She was impressed. Not just by the saris, although they were beautiful. But by the way that Keesal handled them: there was a recognition of something important in the gentle way that he pushed the everyday saris aside to reveal the beauty of those beneath, the way he wiped clean his already clean hands, the way he stroked the warp and weft softly with the tips of his fingers.

She watched as he continued to tidy the saris, the glorious beauty at the bottom protected by the bright primaries of the everyday. When he had finished smoothing the top sari, a cool clean blue the colour of the sky outside the window, he sat back on his heels and took her wrist. Wordlessly, he eased her hand down the velvet inside of the trunk, through all the layers, until she touched the cool silk of the wedding sari. She could see the trailing foliage with her fingers. He released her wrist and she closed her eyes, weaving her hand up through the saris until she reached the blue of the very top. When she opened her eyes, Keesal was watching her with a slow smile on his face.

"Kee-SAAAAL!" His mother's voice broke the moment from the hallway below. "You two alright up there?"

"Just looking at the saris, Mother," he called, gently closing the chest's lid and covering it with an orange candlewick dressing gown.

"Then say all your bye-byes to Miss Tot. It's time for dinner."

A faint hint of mothballs remained in the room, which was silent, save the clock ticking from the bedside cabinet.

"What are you doing on Wednesday night?" Tot asked, concentrating hard on rolling the belt of Mrs. Patel's dressing gown into a tight wheel.

"Nothing."

"Wanna come out with me."

"What, on a date?"

Tot shrugged and snapped the coiled belt against her thigh. It unrolled along the length of her leg.

"Okay," he said. "Where are we going? Do I have to dress up?"

She turned around and shook her head. "Big Book Meeting. At St. Lawrence's."

"Big Book? A book club?"

She shook her head again. "They've got coffee and biscuits." She pulled the flyer from her pocket and handed it to him. He studied it for a moment, then looked at her frowning.

"'*The Big Book Comes Alive.*' You're asking me on a date to an Alcoholics Anonymous meeting?"

"You don't have to come if you don't want to."

"Are you an alcoholic?" he asked, now fiddling with the dressing gown belt himself.

"Course not! I just wanna find out some stuff. Anyway, it sounds…interesting and if you don't want to come—"

He re-read the flyer. "I'll come."

She plucked the crumpled sheet of paper from his fingers and stuffed it back in her pocket. "Keesal, it's a secret."

"What? The date or the fact we're going to an AA meeting?"

"Both."

"So it *is* a date?"

She nodded, not meeting his eyes.

"Well, I get the meeting. After all, it is Alcoholics *Anonymous*. But what about the date? Why's that a secret?"

"Because I need to see someone first. To tell them something. Then the date won't need to be a secret."

Keesal stood up and rethreaded the belt through the dressing gown's loops. "Okay. Wednesday then."

"Wednesday."

19

The women of Stanley Close settled difficult things over tea. It was as if the ceremony of teapot and kettle, of sugar bowl and milk bottle, provided the boundaries within which even the trickiest of conversations might be safely navigated. And it was to such a ceremony that Elaine found herself invited after bumping into Stacey's mother at the entrance to Stanley Close. Each woman carried a vinyl shopping bag full of groceries. Each was drab in a belted mac and head scarf, wrapped up against the cold March wind that blew in from the east, that plucked the last of the winter's leaves from the trees hunched between the houses and the dump, and blew them and the faint aroma of garbage into the women's faces.

Now they sat either side of Pat Wright's kitchen table, a brown ceramic teapot, a bottle of silver-top milk, and a blue and white sugar bowl between them. Elaine had anticipated the conversation. Given that Pat's Stacey had encountered a half-naked man standing on a chair in the Thompson kitchen, it was inevitable.

Pat milked both cups and poured tea. "So," she said, a smile stuck to her face like a parking ticket on a windscreen, "how are things, dear?"

The two had not always been friends. When Elaine first arrived on the Close, she had found it hard to fit in. She had felt above all these women with their hoardes of children, their aprons and their hair in plastic pre-weekend curlers. She found it painful to remember how ridiculous she had been back then, before Donald had left, before she realized what it was to live without money, without ease — financial or emotional — to have her own hoard to support. She took a sip from her cup and reached for the sugar bowl. "Things are interesting, Pat." She shook her head at the offered tin of biscuits. "But let's cut the crap. You want to know why there was a semi-naked astronaut in my kitchen."

"Well, I have to say I am sort of interested in this man who, as my Stacey so eloquently put it, 'had his arse hanging out.'" Pat took four chocolate biscuits and arranged them in her saucer. "You know me, Elaine, I keep myself to myself, but Stacey said he was one of them exotic dancers. It's none of my business, but I have to ask myself: why has Elaine got an exotic dancer in her kitchen?"

"He's a client. He was there for a fitting and the girls just walked in...at the wrong moment. And I had a mouthful of pins and couldn't say a word in my defence."

"Defence?"

"Okay, not defence. Explanation."

The explanation hovered above the two women at the table as they sipped their tea to the accompaniment of the washing machine and the irregular snores coming from the room above, where Mr. Wright was asleep after a late shift at the ink factory. Elaine shook her head and reached for the biscuit tin.

"Oh, bloody hell. He's asked me to go away with him, Pat." She stacked three biscuits next to her saucer. "To Wales of all places. Penryth." She snatched the top biscuit from the stack and ate it with something akin to rage. "Who goes to Wales on a dirty weekend? I mean, why isn't he stripping in Torquay...or Brighton even. I mean, Brighton's made for dirty weekends. But Penryth? Penryth? It's just my bloody luck to get invited to a dirty weekend in Penryth..."

Pat Wright was stirring her tea as if to dissolve the spoon as well as the sugar.

"...and he's only twenty-two. Built like a brick shithouse and twenty-two, for God's sake..."

Pat continued to stir.

"...so of course, when he comes round to pick up his costume, I pretended I was out. There I was, frozen in the front room, crouched down below the sofa like some fugitive from good sense. And there he is, banging on the door knocker like he's sending bloody Morse code. And does he give up? No, does he hell. Just stands there knocking away, rat-a-tatting and peering through the letterbox. Relentless. I can only imagine what he'd be like in bed..." She paused, then shook her head.

Pat dropped the spoon in her saucer and bit down hard on her second chocolate biscuit.

"...and there's me, thirty-nine years old, and not having had sex for three years, and feeling about as dried up as an old leather gardening glove left out on the path all summer. Could I go? Of course, I can't bloody go. Two kids plus a grandchild and a father-in-law camped out in my dining room." Elaine picked up another biscuit, bit off half and used the other half to point at the woman across the table, "But Pat, when you think about it, why the bloody hell shouldn't I? I mean I've spent the last twenty years looking after a useless, stupid husband, a daughter who gets herself knocked up despite all my efforts over the kitchen table, and a youngest who spends more time out of the house than she does in it. Well, bugger them all. Bollocks to the lot of them. This mouse is about to turn..."

"Worm."

"What?"

"Worm. It's the worm that turns. A mouse...well a mouse just...squeaks. Or eats cheese."

"I'm done with squeaking. I'm going to have a wild, wild night with an oiled-up stripper. In Penryth. I am, Pat. I bloody well am."

Wordlessly, Pat Wright pushed her substantial bulk away from the table and stood to fill the kettle again. When she had emptied the pot into the sink and dropped in two fresh teabags, she turned to look at Elaine. "Squeak or no squeak, I think we need another cup of tea. Don't you, dear?"

Ten minutes later, another pot of tea had been drunk and yet another kettle filled, and Elaine's dark anger was exhausted, spread across the kitchen table along with the biscuit crumbs and splashes of tea. She sat back in her chair and sighed, the breath emptying her. For four years, she alone had shouldered all the family's hardships — Donald's disappearance, Dorothy's pregnancy, her own sick and dying bank balance — in a silence that her few friends defined as "good natured" but in reality was full of fear and resentment.

Over two pots of tea, she had emptied her bag of disappointments and shown her neighbour its soiled lining. Not only did she resent her absent husband, but she resented her ever present children. She was tired of them strewn across her house like dirty laundry. She resented their demands for her time and attention, but at the same time, she resented their ability to leave her alone without a word in a house whose echoes spoke to her of plans gone awry. Those echoes, on bad nights, told her that this loneliness was all her fault and that it was here to stay. The echoes told her over and over that this was the lot of a middle-aged woman whose husband had run, that this was all there was and all there ever would be. She told her neighbour how she sometimes just wanted to run, and how, right now, she hankered after ill-advised and shallow sex with an exotic dancer. She told Pat all about Simon, about his toes, the way they turned upwards like turtle heads, about how he smelled of *Ambré Solaire* in the middle of March.

And in the telling, the sky had not fallen in. Officials had not arrived to take away the children. While she hadn't expected damnation to arrive in the form of black iron thunderbolts, she had expected Pat to snap the lid back on the biscuit tin hard and wave her a terminal goodbye from the back door step.

But Pat had done neither. She had kept the tea coming and now she was smoothing out the current copy of *The Observer* on the table and running the tip of the sugar spoon down the front page's index. She licked her finger and turned to a page near the back and read aloud: "'Flash Moron and friends. Adult comedy and cabaret at *The Firkin and Philanthropist*. 8:00 Wednesday. A quid on the door.' Is that your man?"

"He's not my man. But yes, that's him. He doesn't strip on Wednesdays."

"His night off?"

"Yeah. He just introduces the first act and then closes."

"With his clothes on?"

"Almost. I mean, he wears the Lurex chaps..."

"The ones that have his arse hanging out?"

"Yeah."

"The ones that are too big for him. Because he lost all that weight at Weight Watchers and the ones that do *fit* him are still sitting in a box in your bay window?"

"Yeah."

"Oh, then that does it."

"Does what?"

Pat swung the paper around so Elaine could read the advertisement in the "What's On" section. "Seems to me that Mr. Dolan needs his new chaps and you need a check. And I need a night out. So what do you think about hitting all three?"

"You mean me and you? At the comedy night?"

"He gets his trousers, you get some cash, I get to see a strange man's arse. Seems like a deal to me."

Elaine read the advertisement. Maybe this was what she needed. Maybe if she had a night out, some fun, if she saw him in person, she'd know what to do. About everything. "We could get the bus," she said. "I'll pay."

"We'll go Dutch. And I'll drive. Borrow Ted's car."

"We'd need to leave around seven."

"Seven, it is."

Elaine laughed, a tiny soundless laugh. She felt frightened, like a girl again. But that was better than feeling numb, and she'd felt numb for too long. She finished her tea and stood up. "Thanks, Pat. And I'm sorry."

"About what?"

"About Stacey seeing…well, about what she saw in my kitchen."

Pat put the cups in the sink and returned the sugar bowl to the cabinet. "Don't you worry, my Love. She's almost grown, so I don't think it'll scar her for life. Anyway, from what she said, Mr. Dolan's rear-end is a thing of beauty, and true beauty never hurt no one."

20

While Tot had postponed a confrontation with Stacey for an entire week following the youth club disco, she had managed to avoid Gareth Strand for even longer. It wasn't that she was loathe to accept the role he had played in the Blond-Boy-In-The-Park production. It was more that she felt the need to retreat, to regroup, to consider her own role in the whole sorry performance. This reflection had taken time, and if it had not been for the trampoline, she may still have been in retreat, rehearsing her lines, examining again and again her character's motivation. But now, the moment was upon her: she needed to confront Gareth in the cracked window of time before her first date with Keesal. She wanted, for once, to finish something cleanly before she began something new.

But what was it, this thing that needed finishing? She had done her best to pitch it to herself as *romance*, but even she knew — had perhaps always known — that real romance required more intimacy than pillow talk and a larger stage than that afforded by a boy's bedroom. Whatever it was, this thing between them, she had to be the one to formally end it. If she didn't, she would be left with the hard truth that Gareth had directed everything — not only its beginning and its middle, but also its tragic and tacky ending.

*

She could have tackled him at the school bus stop on the afternoon following the trampoline and the saris. But the sight of him, cocky and arrogant, and the fact that Blond Boy was hanging around grinning on the edges of the group, kept her silent. She stood separate from the others. When the bus arrived, she sat next to Keesal as usual but pleaded a headache and spent the journey resting her cheek against the window's cold glass.

She could have waylaid him in the park, where he and his friends half-heartedly played football before heading home for their tea. It would have been possible to march across the grass, tap him on his shoulder, and lead him off to the side. There she could have heard his rationalization, about how it was all a misunderstanding, about how he and the blond boy were no longer friends. She could have listened — patiently — and explained that despite all that, despite his apologies about the Blond Boy/Bait-and-Switch/Lost Shoe — she needed the Beginning Things from someone else rather than just all the Ending Things from him.

Or she could have sat on the wooden bench at the entrance to Willowswitch Lane and waited for him to come home from the park. As she waited, she could have rehearsed exactly what she wanted to say, and then, when he appeared around the corner, bouncing the ball, she could have walked up to him and delivered her lines.

But she didn't.

The thing was too enormous to instigate, its stakes too high. She got off the bus at the end of Willowswitch Lane and sprinted home. She could feel Keesal staring after her all the way down to Stanley Close.

*

After tea, Tot sat in the bay window in the front room and hooked the net curtain back behind the fruit bowl so she could better watch the Close beyond. Just 5:30 p.m. and all was already dark. Lampposts evenly spaced between the houses spilled yellow light out onto the road that circled the Green. Beyond the Close, Willowswitch Lane stretched its own chain of lights out towards the village.

She thought back to the summer when, far into the evening, front doorsteps had been full of friends rapping door knockers, gathering the gang to chalk hopscotch, skip rope, to play mob-handed on the grass. But this chilly evening, the lamp lit pavements were empty, the front doors closed and quiet. She missed that time when Stacey and she were inseparable. And try as she might, she couldn't stop thinking about how her best friend now went to parties without her. Or rather she went with a boy. With Smiling Jim and his chauffeur father.

"Watch him, Ventura! Watch him!" her grandfather shouted at the television, uncapping the lid from another bottle of Guinness.

The Thompsons were all squashed on the sofa watching the wrestling on the telly and eating Mars bars. Tot picked up her jacket from the back of the armchair where she had left it and made for the door.

"You going out?" her mother asked, not looking away from the television.

"Foul!" her grandfather shrieked. "Nagasaki's got him by the waistband! Did you see that, Elaine? Did you?!"

Tot stood behind the sofa and watched the men grapple in the wrestling ring. One of them, Lee Ventura, the one with his shoulders on the canvas, wore silver trunks and gold boots. The other, Kendo Nagasaki, the one sitting on Ventura's head, sported a black and red laced mask and matching leotard. He had never been unmasked: the Western world, as her grandfather was fond of telling them all, had never seen his face.

"Just going for a walk," she said. "Up the village."

"It's a school night, Tot. Be back before eight." Her mother fished the discarded top from the Guinness bottle out of Tramp's mouth and dropped it in her apron pocket. Tramps returned to filling his mother's kicked-off shoe with Lego bricks.

*

The walk from Stanley Close to the village was one she had taken thousands of times and one that she knew well. The journey required no thought since there was nothing new to look at, nothing new happening. Its monotony was welcome and freed her up to think about what needed to be done and to rehearse what needed to be said. The list was long. She still intended to slap Blond Boy's face again and get four quid off him to pay for a new pair of shoes. And then she needed to buy the shoes before Dorothy noticed the old ones were missing. She needed to get Dangrad to stop drinking. And she needed to talk to Gareth. She should have done that by now. She should have found the courage today to just walk up to him and pack him in.

It was her intense consideration of the Things That Must Be Done that resulted in her not noticing Gareth Strand sitting on the bench outside St. Margaret's House, the modern and low-slung old people's home that stood at the entrance to the village and across from the church. He was engrossed in a book. Blue/white fluorescent light spilled from a ground-floor window behind him. He and the open pages were in brightness whereas she still stood in the dark. She had had no time to rehearse her "This is the End" speech and had to decide whether to walk past him without saying anything or whether to wing it.

She stopped a few feet from where he sat and chose the latter. "You visiting someone?" she said.

He started as if slapped and seemed embarrassed or lost for words. She wasn't sure if this was because she had spoken first and in public, or whether it was because he had been caught with a book in his hand. "My mum," he said. "She's in a...a meeting." He jerked his head back towards St. Margaret's behind him.

Tot was unsure whether to sit down on the bench or to walk on. She knew she should sit down.

"I'm watching him." He looked across St. Margaret's neat lawns to where his little brother padded up in a parka, ran in and out of the clipped privets. "We're getting chips on the way home." The security lights cast an odd green glow over the boy and the home's gravel drive.

Tot knew she had to stay there and talk to him, even though she wanted to carry on walking. If truth were told, she wanted to start running. She anchored herself with another question. "What are you reading?"

He inspected the cover of the paperback as if he had never seen it before and then held it up for her to read.

"*Call of the Wild?* Never heard of it," she said.

"Jack London," he told her. "It's about…a dog."

"I didn't have you down as a reader…or an animal lover." Feeling braver and oddly in charge of herself and of the moment, she sat down. Next to him. In public. He didn't answer, and they sat there shivering in his silence. She pulled her jacket hood up and huffed into her hands. She didn't know how to begin. If she started with the park and the Blond Boy, they would have to fight. If she started with her and Keesal, they might not fight, but then everything would be her fault; she would be a "two-timer" and all that he had done would be forgotten in that fact's wake.

She scuffed the sole of her shoe against the pavement. He still held the book in his hand, closed and cover uppermost. "You shouldn't have done what you did," she said. He didn't reply. He was making it hard for her, forcing her to make all the decisions. "In the park. That night. I thought you loved me."

The village was closing down around them. It was getting late, the affairs of the day coming to a close, the shops already shutting, and shopping bag-heavy women waiting for the last bus back down to the estate. Men were driving through the village on their way home from jobs, to dogs that needed walking and to daughters who were giggling with their friends in bedrooms compiling lists of things to do when they were grown.

He studied the book's cover. "It's about this dog that runs away from people and other dogs — two little yappy poodle things — and he ends up with these wolves." He looked up at her. "It's like he becomes a kind of a wolf." He shrugged. "That's what I think it's about anyway."

She wondered if he was trying in his own cack-handed way to say something about what had happened. She could force him somewhere else. She could make him talk about what needed to be talked about in real words, clean and simple. Instead, she asked, "Does he prefer being a wolf?"

"You're not listening. I said he's not *really* a wolf. He's a *kind* of wolf. But at least he's not a poodle. He ends up on his own, ends up something else...something better than a wolf."

"You owe me four quid. I was going to get Blond Boy to give it to me. But you should give it to me."

"What for?"

"He threw my shoe in the woods and they weren't mine."

Gareth stuck his hand in his jeans and drew out a handful of scruffy notes. He peeled off four and gave them to her.

She sorted through them, turning the notes so the Queen smiled out in the same direction from them all. "I'm going out with Keesal Patel tomorrow night."

He didn't reply. He just picked up the book and smoothed it open with the flat of his hand. She heard its spine crack.

"So that's it," she said. "You're not my boyfriend anymore." She folded the notes and put them in her jacket pocket.

"I never was," he said, not looking up from his book. "It was just a laugh."

21

The following evening found Tot sitting on another bench but this time with Keesal at her side. He had changed out of his school uniform into jeans and a blue sweatshirt that bore a white number eleven stitched to its front. His trainers were scuffed and grubby, and his hair was still damp as if he had taken a bath not long before leaving home. He smelt like a memory of her father.

She took the number eleven as being a sign, and when the eleventh person walked along the church pathway towards the community centre and disappeared from sight down its basement steps, she herself headed for its double doors.

"Come on then, if you're coming," she called back to Keesal, who immediately jumped up and trotted along beside her as if he were determined not to walk into an AA meeting all on his own.

The basement was full. In the middle of the room was a rectangle of pushed together and scratched folding tables around which ranged an assortment of men and women. At one end of the rectangle sat a blonde woman in her forties. She wore a cream, cabled Aran jumper and matching mini skirt and resembled a tying-up post on a harbour quay. Not everyone had taken a seat. A knot of people stood in the tiny kitchenette at the foot of the stairs, filling china cups from a tea urn. Water pipes looped around the ceiling above their heads, and the room felt chilly and smelled a little damp.

Those seated at the table chatted to neighbours or sat reading what looked like blue bibles. Some sat silently as if lost in meditation. Back in the kitchen, people shook each other by the hand, passed cups of tea over heads, and proffered serviettes, spoons and sugar bowls. A tin moved from person to person, its cargo of biscuits diminishing.

Tot and Keesal paused at the foot of the stairs as if an invitation might be required, but no one seemed to notice them.

"Where do you wanna sit?" whispered Keesal.

"Over there," said Tot. "On them chairs by the radiator."

The Aran woman pulled books from a cardboard box and slid them, one after the other, down the length of the table, like some barmaid dispensing beers in a Wild West saloon.

She clapped her hands: "Come on, you lot," she called to the kitchen stragglers. "It's eight o'clock. Let's have a meeting."

When the stragglers had taken their places at the table and the room's hubbub had died down, the woman continued. "Let's go round the room and introduce ourselves so you can learn who I am and I can learn who you are. My name's Tammy, and I'm an alcoholic." She nodded encouragingly at the man sitting cross-corner to her.

He coughed and wiped biscuit crumbs from his moustache. "I'm Jimmy the Ears, alcoholic."

And so it went on until the fifteen or so people had introduced themselves. They were an eclectic assortment and Tammy wasn't the lone female; there were two more. The first was a pink-haired girl who wore track-suit pants and a bleach-stained black t-shirt. She said her name so softly that Tammy had to ask her to say it again.

"Alcoholic called Chance," she said, a little belligerently this time, as if there were only two volumes: regret or aggression. "As in 'Last'."

Next to her was a smartly dressed woman who didn't look up from her crochet as she said that her name was Karin with an 'i' and added that she had 'an issue with red wine.'

There were several older men who looked like builders or plumbers, one who might have been a bank manager, three young men who announced themselves as medical students and merely there to observe, a couple who held onto each other as if, untethered, they might float away, a man who smelled of paint, and another who sat tightly folding a yellow flyer into an origami hat...or a boat perhaps.

When everyone at the table had said their names, Tammy, stretching tall in her seat like a woolly meerkat, peered across the room at Tot and Keesal on the bench.

"Still Tammy, still alcoholic," she said. "And you at the back? Would you like to introduce yourself, young man?"

Keesal fidgeted and looked at Tot, who merely shrugged and studied her fingernails. "My name's Keesal," he said, "and I'm...I'm a first year at Treeverton Tech."

A few people at the table laughed, but Tammy clapped her hands to silence them. "Welcome, Keesal. Welcome. And your friend?"

Tot stood up. "My name's Tot and...well, I'm here because I think if someone goes to bed with their clothes on and doesn't remember stuff, but then the next day they're back to being normal...I don't know." She tried again. "My name's Tot," she said finally, "and I need to find some things out."

Aran Tammy smiled and then turned to the group. "Is everyone okay with opening this up tonight as a Beginners Meeting? We've got some students and a few newcomers and we're on the schedule as Closed, but we can go Open if no one minds." She waited. Most people at the table nodded, some did nothing, but no one objected. She slid her own book across to Chance. "Hand that back to Tot and Keesal. They can share tonight," she said and turned her bright smile up a notch. "You're in the right place," she added. "Welcome. Never too young to come through the doors."

The room felt suddenly quiet and heavy. In fact, everyone at the table seemed heavy with their own thoughts. It stayed that way until Tammy opened the ring binder on the table in front of her with a snap. "I've handed out three readings: How it Works, The Traditions and The Promises. Can I have them read in that order, please?"

The meeting was a revelation. Or rather, what was said was a revelation. Nothing was held back. When Aran Tammy asked if anyone had something going on in their lives that might make them take a drink, Freddie, the man who was folding the flyer into a boat, began by saying that he was fine. That life was fine. Really. It was just that his wife had left him, that he had slapped his youngest daughter, and that he was looking down the noisy end of a court appearance. Jimmy the Ears flung out from the end of the table that a drink wouldn't make any of that better, and that Freddie should get his arse to a meeting as often as he could. Chance said she hadn't had a drink since yesterday and felt as if her nerve endings were running down the outside of her skin. She said her mother didn't understand why she was making such a fuss about a few drinks. She said she hadn't had sex with a punter since February. After each revelation, each bold story, someone chimed in with his own tale, and told the Folder, the Last Chancer — whoever it was who had shared something — to keep coming back, to call another drunk, to read the book, and to do something called the steps.

At the end of the hour, Tammy pulled a plastic fishing tackle box up onto the table. "Who wants a chip?" she said, opening up the box and paddling her fingers through the compartments. Freddie the Folder picked up a red plastic disc which turned out to be a reward for not having had a drink for thirty days. There was a green one for sixty days, blue for ninety, purple for six months. Diamond Karin with an "i" picked up a silver five-year chip, and everyone cheered and clapped. When she collected it from Tammy, the hug she received made her disappear inside Tammy's wooliness.

"How d'you do it?" Tammy asked her, beaming.

"One day at a time," Karin replied. "One day at a time."

The chairwoman picked up a white chip from the box. "And now back to the most important one. The Twenty-Four Hour. Is there anyone in the room who would like to join our way of life, just for today? Anyone want to stop throwing up and start growing up?"

The room was silent and yet encouraging. Everyone waited, smiling. Tammy held the white chip above her head, her eyebrows raised, her smile still warm and real.

Tot stood up. "I'll have one," she said.

Everyone applauded, and Tammy beckoned her up to the front. As she walked the length of the room, people clapped her on the back. Even Karin with an "i" stopped crocheting and patted her shoulder.

Tammy handed over the white chip. "It's never too early to join our way of life." She said it more to the room than to Tot. "Unfortunately, you're never too young to be an alcoholic."

Tot held the disc in her palm. "No," she said. "It's not for me. It's…for a friend." The people around the table smiled back at her. "Really," Tot said. "It's not for me."

"Keep coming back, Love," said Jimmy the Ears.

"Yeah, keeping coming back," said Last Chance.

She slipped the disc in her pocket and walked back to Keesal. "Let's go," she whispered, as the rest of the room was standing and piling books back in the cardboard box and pouring more tea from the urn into their cups. "We can get some real chips on the way home." Suddenly aware of rule three and wanting to do everything right this time, she added, "Chips are my treat."

*

By the time they left the community centre basement and reached the High Street, the fish and chip shop was shut, and around it, on either side, the village was still and silent. It was already dark, and a slow mizzling rain fell. It soaked into Tot's hair, sparkling it with beads of not-quite-rain. Keesal reached out and took a hold of her hand. She didn't pull away, and his grip became slowly firmer, surer as they walked down through the village. They walked back past the curry house and *The Rose and Crown*. They walked past the youth club and in the direction of home, the thin band of trees at the park's furthest edge standing blue-mauve against the sky. Tot wasn't sure where all this went next. Dangrad had only taught her the first three rules of dating, and she didn't know what number four might allow.

But now Keesal was holding her hand, and she was winging it again. She thought about what she might do if he kept hold of her hand and walked her across the road towards the park, towards the trees and the sedge grass. She felt full of questions: *What would she do when Keesal tugged her across the road? Would she go? If she were to go, how far would she go?*

They paused, the glare of the security lights by the park reaching across to their side of the road. Keesal rubbed her knuckles with his free hand. "Cold," he said. "Your hands are freezing." Then he reached up and ran his palm across the spirals of her hair. She could see the bright beads of not-quite rain spangling against the brown edge of his hand. *She would cross the road to the park and the trees beyond. It would be the Thing she wanted. She would cross the road.*

Suddenly, laughing, he rubbed her head hard with both hands, tousling and tangling her hair, and ran off down the pavement. At the corner, he grabbed hold of the lamppost and swung round it twice. "Race you to Willowswitch," he said. "That'll warm you up!"

Then he took off down the lane. She stood for a moment, watching him disappearing, knowing he was still laughing, just a boy running like crazy along a pavement. She looked across the park to the trees.

And then she was off, chasing after him, running like a girl at first, her arms and legs clumsy, unused to the motion. By the time she rounded the corner, she was running like an antelope, like a Masai warrior, like Sebastian Fucking Coe. She was running like a boy.

"Keesal!" she shouted. "Keesal!"

He didn't stop running. He just looked over his shoulder, still laughing. "What?!"

"Where did you go for your holidays?"

"Wales!" he said. "Brecon Beacons!"

The gap between them was getting smaller.

"Why haven't you got a dog?"

"A what?"

"A DOG!"

"Dad's allergic. Why?"

"I'm catching you, Keesal! I'm catching you!"

22

Dan couldn't remember the last time he had woken up. He couldn't remember sleep pierced by either alarm clock or dawn chorus, couldn't fathom a morning that began with a kiss and the morning paper. He didn't doubt that perhaps his days had begun like this in an earlier life, but in this life, this life now, they opened with a 'coming to,' the circus of his day beginning with a drum roll on his heart. Not a light rapping, a gentle rolling call to attention, but a bass drum kind of roll, one that required a fat man to stomp up and down on a pedal.

His heart's irregular beating filled his ears, his breathing an impossibility until he could squeeze its ins and outs inside the space between each beat. If those spaces weren't filled with breath, he might deflate.

He looked at the clock. It was 3:00 a.m. as it often was when the drum began. He had given up trying to work out how many hours of sleep preceded these episodes of 'coming to'; while the timing of a previous evening's first drink was usually fixed in his head, the downing of its last was lost. To still the drum, he practised block breathing. He used Fives. Breathe in for five seconds. Hold for five. Breathe out for five. Hold for five. He pushed his thumb into the mattress — one — and then each finger — two, three, four, five. First one hand and then the other.

When his heart had slowed, he reached down, hoping to encounter the smooth surface of a neatly folded pile of clothes beside the bed. He had discovered that he could learn a lot about a lost evening by the topography of his room: a smooth plateau of shirt and trousers on top of socks and shoes meant he had probably taken to his bed early and drank himself to sleep; but a loose landslide of garments strewn across the carpet told of a bout of rage or melancholy. Worst still was a room's absence of clothes: the mornings he discovered a trail of clothing leading from the lounge to the kitchen, from the kitchen to the bathroom, told the tale of night's insanity. For some reason he had yet to fathom, his worst behavior and maudlin rages were always conducted semi-naked. He had woken in Sleaford several times to find his shirt and trousers in the alley by the back door. He didn't want to think about finding abandoned clothes on the staircase of 17 Stanley Close. The thought made him feel sick.

But there they were, in a neat stack: shirt, trousers, underwear, his socks married, and his belt in a tight roll. Evidence of a docile drunk. He concentrated on his heart rate, sliding his hand back under the covers to take his pulse with sweaty fingers. He was coming back to normal. Whatever normal was.

He pulled the covers over his head and tried to move back into the warm dislocation of sleep, closing his eyes, tightening then relaxing his muscles, first his feet, then his calves. When he relaxed his thighs, he was aware of the weight of the blankets on his legs and of the darkness behind his eyes and was struck by the idea that coming to from a blackout was perhaps a little like being shot from a cannon. He imagined that a man — a man wedged inside a cold dark tube, immobile, alone — might be pushed towards prayer in the hush of a braying crowd gone quiet, knowing the silence contained a clown, a lit taper, a fuse.

Night after 'night, ready or not, Dan cursed the clown and prayed for the net.

*

He spent the day helping Elaine with the spring cleaning. He had the odd notion that if he touched every surface of the house, or even better, had a hand in fixing or improving those surfaces, he might feel as if the house were his home. After all, the creditors' meeting in March had turned 17 Stanley Close into the only place left that he could call a home.

He had moved at least a ton of pea shingle from the pile at the back of the shed to the ornamental border that Elaine had begun but then abandoned as a project the year Donald left. He had fixed the fence, sanding and attaching a top rail. Now, he was back in the shed, screwing coffee jar lids to the bottom of a wooden shelf in readiness to rehouse the miscellany that Elaine currently kept in a bucket labelled "Metal Things."

The shed had been castrated in the wake of his son's leaving. Elaine had hung flower-print curtains at its windows, and the peg board tool rack was almost empty. The tools that did hang there were cheap and seemed light in his hands. He had wrecked the wheelbarrow — a flimsy affair more suited to weeds than gravel — and had made a pig's ear of the fence with a plastic sanding block. He longed for the tools back in the garage in Sleaford. Tools with weight and wooden handles. Tools that would soon be sold.

He was sitting on a folding canvas chair, centring a metal jelly jar lid on the underside of the shelf, when Tot walked through the shed's open door and sat in the corner on a bag of hardened cement.

"I wanna know four and five," she said.

"Four and five what?"

"Love lessons. One is 'Asking Questions,' Two is 'Flirting' and Three is 'Paying.' What's four and five?"

"Why do you want to know," he said, not looking up from his work.

She didn't answer immediately, shredding the corner of the paper cement bag. "I've done those three. I want to know what comes next."

"A man could spend a lifetime on those first three and still not be ready for number four." He marked the centre of the plastic lid with a soft pencil.

"I'm ready."

He slid the pencil back behind his ear and picked up the hand-drill. "Well, four and five are tricky."

"Why?"

He put the drill down. "The first three are really just friendly lessons. I mean, they apply even if you just want to be mates." He held up his hand, counting off each lesson on his fingers. "One shows you're interested in your friends. Two...well, two's really just paying compliments: it's a nice thing to do. And three's only fair: if you want to do something, you had better be prepared to pay for it."

"Aren't four and five friendly as well?" Tot rifled through the drill bit tin and found a skinny one. She handed it to her grandfather.

He fed the bit to the drill and turned the chuck. "You use one, two and three to make sure you like the chap before you get serious. You can't take getting serious lightly." He slowly drilled a hole through the lid, curls of white tin spiralling up around the drill bit.

"Tell me number four," she said.

"Push that bucket this way."

She slid the galvanized bucket towards him.

He pulled out a screw and he held it up to her. "We're looking for anything that looks like this," he said. "No nails, no hooks, no extraneous 'metal things.' The days of the Metal Things Bucket are over." He rifled through the top layer of the bucket's contents and emptied a handful of screws into a glass jar. Tot followed suit with a smaller handful. "So, Lesson Number Four," he said. "Two parts. 'A' is walk away."

"Walk away?"

"Yes. 'A: Walk Away'."

"But what if we really like each other? Why do we have to walk away? That's stupid."

"Now it's nails," he said. "Anything with a point on it." He picked up a panel pin and dropped in another jar.

"You've got to walk away and have a think before you go to number five."

"What's number five?"

"Doesn't matter what number five is. Do number four first. A then B."

"B?"

"B: Ask Yourself the Question."

"Which is?"

"If you could stay away right then without hurting their feelings and chalk up all the questions, the flirting and the first date down to fun and friends, would you? That's the question you have to ask yourself. And if you think you could walk away and stay away, you had better do it sharpish. Because once you do number five, you've got someone else's feelings in *your* bucket." He held the bucket's handle and rattled the remaining metal things. "And that's a heavy bucket to hang onto." He held out the jar with the panel pins, and she dropped in an assortment of nails in different sizes.

"Go on then. Lesson Five. What is it?"

"Pecking."

"Pecking? What's pecking?"

He sorted through a cardboard box for another lid and marked its position on the underside of the shelf. "It's an old fashioned term, my Sweet. Pecking is kissing with your mouth closed. No tongues. No grunts or groans. No roaming hands. Just a kiss."

"Hmmm," she said.

"Pecking moves you on from friends to more-than-friends. It's like the intermission at the movies. Shows it's time for everyone to get ready for the main feature."

"Time to get a choc-ice?"

"Yeah, time to get a choc-ice. If you're not staying to watch the film, no point in getting a choc-ice. Might as well just get the bus home."

"Can I practice?"

"Got to do one, two and three first. Remember: you can't miss out steps."

She nodded then stood up, brushed the seat of her trousers down, and left, closing the door behind her. A second or two later, there was a knock. Dan opened the shed door. Tot stood on the pathway outside.

"Evening, Dangrad. How's your mum doing?"

He sat back down in the deckchair and twisted the glass jar of screws up onto its lid until it was suspended from the underside of the shelf. He inspected his handiwork, testing the jar was secure. "Still dead and gone. *Ged and Don.*"

"I was sorry to hear about her dog."

"Me, too, Love. Me, too." He repeated the process with the nail jar.

"You're looking very dishy today, Dangrad. Would you like to come out with me on a date?"

"With a compliment like that, how could I refuse? Where are we going?"

"Surprise."

"How much will it cost? I'm an old-age-pensioner, after all."

"Twenty pence each, and that includes tea and biscuits, and I'm paying because I did the asking."

"Bargain! When are we going?"

"Tonight, Dangrad. Starts at eight."

*

He hadn't been surprised when Tot had told him to pull in to the car park alongside the community centre. Everything in Bishop's Croft appeared to happen in the building behind the church. He wondered if it might be Pig Bingo again. He couldn't remember what else was going on at the centre. He hoped it wasn't ballroom dancing...or God forbid, aerobics.

He locked the car and allowed Tot to take his arm. After all, she *had* done the asking and was about to follow through with the paying. All he had had to do was the driving. If he was a lucky man, he would get a peck on the cheek at the end of the evening, and he could retire to his room and his half-gallon of Bells.

As they walked through the double doors into the community centre, he heard pop music and a loud enthusiastic voice from the main hall beyond. "In and out, and in and halfway—hold it for four. ONE-TWO-THREE-FOUR! And re-LEASE!"

It was aerobics, and Dan wished he had put on his stretchy trousers. But Tot steered him past the main hall and down a short flight of steps that he hadn't noticed the last time he had been in the community centre.

The basement could have been a setting for another bout of Pig Bingo. A mismatched assortment of men and women sat at a pushed-together island of scratched metal tables. To the left of the steps, a knot gathered in front of a serving hatch where people — mainly men — helped themselves to biscuits from a battered tin and poured themselves tea from a huge urn. His granddaughter squeezed through the throng to duck below the hatch and surface on the other side. She pulled two cups from the kitchenette cupboard above and set them down on the counter. The man in charge of the urn, a skinny old man with hairy ears and wearing jogging bottoms and a snagged blue cardigan, gave her a fatherly hug and filled each cup with milk and tea. She dipped back below the hatch, collected the cups and some sachets of sugar, and carried everything carefully to the table. She sat down, beckoning over her shoulder for Dan to join her. As he crossed the room, people at the table turned and smiled at him. When he sat down, Tot slid him a cup of tea, and the man who sat on his left passed Dan a chocolate digestive biscuit and a blue hardback book.

"It's called the Big Book," the man whispered. "It's all in there. You'll be fine! Here we go!" He nodded his head towards the far end of the room.

Dan followed the man's gaze to a woman who sat at the top of the stretch of tables. In front of her were a ring binder and a gavel. The woman was in her fifties, attractive in a mumsie kind of way and dressed in a thick hand-knitted Aran jumper and matching skirt. She glanced about the room, smiling quietly, and appeared politely interested in all the conversations taking place around her. There was a self-contained calm to the woman that he found attractive. He picked up the sombre blue book. Bible study, perhaps? Maybe Tot had found religion. He hoped not. He wondered if it was too late to suggest that they head upstairs and join the aerobics class.

Before he could ask her what the hell they were doing down here, the Aran woman banged the gavel on the table, and the room began to hush.

"Good evening," she said. "My name is Tammy, and I'm an Alcoholic."

He didn't catch what she said next. He was too busy glaring at Tot, who was astutely ignoring him and sharing her biscuits with the girl sitting next to her, a girl with flamingo pink hair. The Aran woman finished her spiel, and the snagged cardi man with the hairy ears introduced himself as an alcoholic called Jimmy and began to read aloud from a sheet of laminated card.

Dan was angry. He could feel the old coldness rising up inside him. But what could he do? If he stood up and ran out, this bunch of drunks would probably think he really was an alcoholic. Even if they didn't, Tot obviously thought he was, and running out would make everything worse: she'd get upset and tell her mother; and then he'd get it in the neck from both of them. Thinking about it, Elaine was probably behind all this. She'd probably put the kid up to it.

So he sat and fiddled with the book. He rotated it in ninety-degree twists. Slowly at first, and then faster, spinning it silently on the shiny table-top. Who did this kid think she was? Twelve years old and telling him he was an alcoholic! He wouldn't have dared. He imagined doing the same thing to his grandfather and winced at the inevitable outcome. At the very least, it would have involved lots of shouting and a cuff round the ear. Yet his grandfather would have deserved the tag. He was an alcoholic. Dan thought back to the way his grandfather's dog used to turn up on their doorstep, whimpering and cowering low against the step. When Dan's father saw the dog, he put on his coat and headed up the road towards his parents' house and returned invariably with Dan's grandmother in tow. Dan would lie in bed with the dog listening to his grandmother crying in the spare room down the hallway and to his parents talking low and late into the night. His grandfather was an alcoholic. There was no getting away from that one.

"So, we have a newcomer in the room. Would you like to introduce yourself by your first name?" It was the Aran woman again, and no one was answering her.

Dan looked around the table. Most of the people were still smiling at him like loonies. The others looked nervous, fiddling with mismatched china teacups or making mini towers with their biscuits. The man next to him folded a meeting flyer into an origami hat. The woman sitting next to the folder, a well-dressed woman with highlighted hair and with what looked like real diamonds in her ears, nodded encouragingly across the table at Dan.

At him. HE was the newcomer.

He looked down the room to the woman with the gavel. What was her name? Tammy.

She smiled that calm, wide smile. "Would you like to introduce yourself by your first name?" she asked him again.

Tot kicked him under the table, and he coughed. "My name's Daniel," he said. "And I'm not sure why I'm here. I thought it was Pig Bingo."

Quiet laugher rippled around the room. Tammy rapped the gavel lightly on the table. "Well, Daniel," she said. "Pig Bingo is upstairs first Saturday of the month. Us drunks are down here every Wednesday trying to get to midnight without taking a drink."

The people at the table nodded a collective nod. A few grunted. Brainwashing, Dan thought. They're a group of sad no-hopers with nowhere better to go. But he liked the way she said his name. Daniel. No one called him that anymore. Not for years. She put a heavy stress on the first syllable, stretching it out. And she had looked squarely at him when she said it, those brown eyes taking over from her wide mouth and delivering the smile. She was pretty. He gave her that much.

"I'm Tammy, Alcoholic," she said again, as if it were a profession, like teaching or fighting fires. "Since we have a newcomer in the room, let's talk about what it was like for us and how we got here. Daniel, just listen tonight. See if anything strikes a chord."

There it was. His name again.

He did as he was told and sat back in his chair, nursing his tea. He could do with a drink. Not that he was desperate or anything. He could just do with a drink. No problem with that. There was probably a whole row of men just like him at the bar of *The Rose and Crown* across the road, sipping their beer and talking about their wives, their jobs, their gardens. And here he was in a damp cellar listening to a room full of desperados spill their guts. Even the women. The lady with the fancy earrings was telling the room about how she used to keep her red wine in the airing cupboard so her husband wouldn't find it and pour it away again. She didn't look the type. Millicent would have liked her.

They all took turns to tell the room who they were and share their stories. Some of them didn't sound like alcoholics to him. Just men with war stories. Some of them were pretty far gone though. That bloke with the ears, he WAS an alcoholic. Said he'd been inside for "Grievous Bodily Harm." G.B.H.. Jesus. Blamed it on the booze. He reckoned he'd been sober for twenty-nine years and put it all down to something he called a Higher Power. Dan thought he was talking about God and wondered why he didn't just say it straight. Why couldn't he just say he was a drunk who'd got religion?

Then a man at the far end of the table told his story. He told it with the polish of a man who had told the same tale time after time. The pubs were full of know-it-alls like him. Men who liked the sound of their own voices. Dan had met them all. The man said his wife had pushed religion down his throat for twenty years, and that he'd retaliated by getting drunk in his garage most nights. Then he'd had an affair. His wife found out and told him to stop drinking or else she was off. The man said he was a "grateful alcoholic." Everyone in the room looked at each other and began to smile. Dan couldn't work out why they were smiling. Grateful? It sounded bloody tragic to him. The man had lost the lot — house, car, life savings — and was sitting in a basement telling everyone how chuffed he was to be an alcoholic! Dan didn't understand it. They were all as mad as goats.

The woman with the diamonds interrupted his thoughts by pushing a small wicker basket in front of him. It was full of coins. There was even a note or two. He automatically dug into his pocket for some change, but Tot pulled the basket away from him and dropped in a twenty-pence piece. "Asker pays," she whispered and pushed the basket towards the girl with pink hair, who slipped in a few coins and then delivered it back to Tammy.

"Let's close with the Serenity Prayer," Tammy said, and the room stood in unison and formed a circle. On one side, he had Tot's hand in his, small and dry, and on the other, a man's, a sweaty hand that vibrated like a power sander. He couldn't remember the last time he had held hands with a man.

As the room droned on, bent-headed, through what sounded like a load of God-bothery nonsense, he glanced around. Everyone looked content. Some even looked happy. Even the man who had spent the evening transforming flyers origami-style into swans and hats was smiling. Dan thought about it. In a weird way, even *he* had quite enjoyed himself. It was nice to hear all the drinking stories — they made his own escapades seem quite...normal: he wasn't the only person who hid bottles down the sofa or in the sawdust bucket; he wasn't the only man who cried. He didn't think he belonged in the basement, but the hour he had spent down there had been rather nice.

Prayer over, the press of people moving up the narrow steps to the foyer and to the car park beyond caused a mini traffic jam on the stairs. He watched Tot slip under the arms of those up in front of her. She reached the vestibule above and stood chatting to the pink girl, their hair clashing horribly. He felt a tap on his shoulder and turned to see the Aran woman smiling that smile and holding out her hand. He struggled for her name.

"Tammy," she reminded him. "Glad to see you here tonight, Daniel. I hope you come back."

There was that long syllable again, and he wondered what she wanted. Was she chatting him up? It was a long time since anyone had smiled at him in quite that way or said his name like that. Before he could decide, the folding man, who was standing alongside them on the stair, wrapped his arms around her in a silent hug. She returned his embrace, and Dan was surprised, embarrassed even, at the tears on the folding man's face.

"Thanks, Tammy," the man said. "I mean it. I mean life's okay…I'm fine and all that, but thanks."

"Just keep coming back, Freddie. It gets different, then it gets better. I promise."

He nodded and wiped his eyes, then headed back to the table where he gathered up the blue books into little stacks.

Tammy turned to Dan. She shook his hand like a man and said, "You know, Daniel, you don't ever need to take a drink again…if you don't want to." With that, she disappeared up the steps, squeezing people on their shoulders and receiving hugs as she went.

*

Outside at the far corner of the parking lot, Tot was waiting by the car. She looked sheepish and he felt sorry for her. He thought back to his own grandfather and to what a cold bastard he had been to everyone — his wife, his kids, the dog. He trotted across the car park and folded her up in a huge hug, lifting her off the ground for a second or two before lowering her gently back down. They stood like that for a long time. It was his way of saying the date was okay, that he had, in a strange way, enjoyed himself. Aware of the pressure of her head buried against his chest, he looked across the car park at the row of cars parked against the church wall. The Aran woman — Tammy, he remembered — was arguing with a young man, a boy in his teens. But the boy was ignoring her, his sullen silence almost audible. Dan was glad the young man wasn't his grandson.

He tapped Tot on the top of her head. "Have you gone to sleep down there?"

She looked up at him, smiling. "Nope." Then she unwrapped her arms from his waist and made a big production out of taking giant steps backwards until she was some ten feet away.

"Where are you going?"

"Nowhere," she said. "Just walking away." Then she ran back, and reaching up, she wrapped her hands around his neck, pulled his head down to her level to kiss him on the chin. "Lessons four AND five," she said. "How did I do?"

"Not bad for a beginner," he said. "In fact, *Muddy Blarvelous.*"

He hugged her close and over her head, he watched the boy storm away from Tammy, then slink back. Before the boy got into the car, he turned and seemed to look square at Dan. He looked like a bad 'un. All moodiness and sharp edges. It seemed to be the fashion today, he thought. Like all those chains and buckles they were wearing on their trousers. He wondered how Tammy stayed so calm and serene with such a lout for a son and thanked God for Donald. Quiet, studious Donald. He'd been a good kid, good to his parents. He just wished the boy had spent a little less time playing the trumpet and more time with his wife and kids.

He opened the car door for Tot and then got in his own side, buckling his seat belt and adjusting the rear-view mirror to get one last look at Tammy before she drove away.

"What's lesson six?" Tot said, oblivious to the drama playing out in the car by the church.

He turned on the engine and eased the old gear box into first gear. "No lesson six."

"Then what do I do after the pecking?"

He let the hand brake off with a series of clicks. "That's up to the Pecker and Peckee," he said and eased the car out of the car park, past *The Rose and Crown*, its windows full of light and bonhomie, towards home and his bottle of Bells.

23

At first, Elaine thought that perhaps her stars were aligning. The house had emptied before Pat knocked at the front door, removing any need for her to explain to the kids and to Dan where she was going all dressed up to the nines: Dorothy had taken Tramps to spend the night at Christopher's parents, and Elaine was relieved that they were finally stepping up to the plate and that Dorothy had matured enough to hold the plate rather than dash it to the ground; Dan and Tot had disappeared on what the pair called "*a dot hate.*" She made him promise not to take her youngest up the pub and then felt bad for suggesting that he might do such a thing. After all, she was glad he was plugging into village life, glad that Tot was spending time with her grandfather. Given this auspicious start, she was hopeful that her evening would pan out as she had rehearsed it endlessly over the past week.

Her plan was simple and elegant: she and Pat would arrive at *The Firkin* and watch the comedy show from the obscurity of the bar; Simon Dolan would be bitingly funny in his role as master of ceremonies and adorable as a possible lover; at the end of the evening, she would give him his chaps and her invoice, and she and Pat would head for home, perhaps stopping at *The Blue Anchor* in the village for a bag of chips. Once home, she would sit down at the kitchen table with a cup of tea to mull over the prospect of beginning a "thing" with the grindingly attractive Mr. Dolan.

*

Of all the plan's stages, this last one — the tea in bed and the mulling over — was the shakiest. After all, hadn't she already decided that Simon Dolan probably wasn't the one for her? Recently, she had arrived in a place of decisions. The shifts over recent months had opened her up to the potential of change, to the necessity of loosening the buttons on life's coat a little. The ease with which her father-in-law had made the transition from south coast to Bishop's Croft, from homeowner to lodger, from financially secure to bankrupt had made her examine her own capacity for handling change. It was time perhaps for her conversion, for her to be back in the middle of things, to not let loneliness become a regular state of being. She knew the difference between "lonely" and "alone": "Alone" was a decision she had made, a way to navigate the loss of a husband and the necessity of raising a family. But "lonely," decision's silent sister, had moved in when Elaine in her need to look after her family, had failed to look after herself.

It would be hard to loosen up enough to risk all the security and safety that successfully navigating life alone had afforded her. What she really wanted to discover at this point, as she headed into her forties, was whether or not she was willing to allow risk back into the room, to offer it a seat at her table. She knew now that nothing was certain. She had thought, in an earlier life, that Donald was happy. She had thought they were cast in concrete. And yet he had left the table. He had picked up his things and walked away. Then she thought about Simon and the things he said, the way he looked at her. And when she thought hard on all of this, on all he had to offer her, she couldn't help but see him dancing naked on her table rather than sitting fully-clothed at her side.

But even though Mr. Dolan might not be worth the risk as a life partner, he might still make the cut as a birthday treat.

And so, she hadn't ruled out a weekend away with him: all she required of herself was that she be honest about the reality of such a weekend. Of course, it was all about sex. She wasn't so much a romantic as to think that Simon Dolan was intending to pack love and commitment into his overnight bag. Penryth would be a dry run. Or a slightly moist run, she hoped. A chance for her to practice, so that when a bonafide dinner guest turned up at her table, she would be ready to order.

*

All was as she remembered. The queue snaked up the stairs, a slow-moving serpent scaled with heavy overcoats and wet umbrellas. The girl with the bright dreadlocks was not on the door: a blonde girl, nondescript and bored, had taken her place. The bar was packed and a little steamy from the combination of wet coats and red-hot radiators, and the show had already begun. Pat joined the press of customers at the bar while Elaine commandeered two empty seats at the back of the hall. She could see Simon leaning against a pillar at the edge of the stage. Above him, throttling the microphone, stood a skinny blushing boy in a shiny suit, shaking and stuttering his way through what was perhaps his first three minutes of life as a stand-up comedian. Elaine felt bad for him, as she might feel for her own children doing badly at something they had dreamed of doing well. When the audience began to boo and jeer and spin beer mats and insults at the boy, she watched Simon run up the short flight of steps to the stage and hustle him off behind the heavy red curtains. From where she sat at the edge of the room, she could see a little into the stage's wings and caught sight of him with his arms around the blushing boy as if consoling him. Then Simon turned and ran back onto the stage to pelt the still heckling crowd with boiled sweets and chocolates and to denounce them all as "a bunch of wankers." Back in the experienced hands of the abrasive joker they loved and felt they understood, the audience howled its approval, and grinning, Simon introduced the next act.

And so the evening progressed in much the same way that Elaine had expected. The acts were funny and the audience cheered, or they were awful and the audience jeered and threw insults. Either way, Simon, in his role as Master of Ceremonies, glued the evening together, absorbing both insults and applause, and throwing out candies and gold-thonged charm. She caught herself wishing she had sent him the new chaps in the post — the ones he wore were dull and baggy, and the new ones would have sparkled as brightly as the man who wore them.

Each time he left the stage in the hands of the next act, he returned to the PA console where the girl with the magenta dreadlocks controlled the stage's lights and sound. Rather than sitting back to enjoy the acts, Elaine found herself watching Simon and the girl and wondering why Magenta was on the PA and not on the door. From the way the two of them huddled over the controls, Elaine thought that perhaps the girl was learning the ropes, ropes that Simon was teaching her. She found herself hoping that this was the case, that he wasn't draping his arms around her shoulders in affection but in instruction, that his fingers were on hers purely to guide them across the slide buttons, that his eyes were fixed strictly on the PA's dials and LED patterns and not on her dreadlocked delights.

When the final comedian left the microphone, and Simon had thanked the acts and the audience, and when the applause ended, the room began to empty. Pat excused herself and left to visit the Ladies, and Elaine headed for the bar so she could watch Magenta and Simon unobserved. The girl turned up the house lights then left the console in order to lug two huge speakers down the stage's short flight of steps. As Elaine watched the girl pack power cords and extension blocks into a metal trunk, she was oddly pleased that Simon didn't help her, that instead he stood on a chair at the back of the stage to unhook the backdrop, shake it out, and fold it into a huge duffel bag. He shouldered the bag, picked up his space helmet from the edge of the stage and jumped down.

Elaine leaned against the bar, empty save the barman who was stacking the washer with dirty glasses. He smiled at her in recognition and fished in his pocket for a moment before retrieving a roll of *Fisherman's Friend* mints and tossing it to her.

She caught it. "No broken glasses tonight, Eric?" she asked.

He shook his head and smiled. "One for the road, Sweetheart?"

"No, We're off in a minute. I just wanted to have a word with Mr. Dolan before we head out."

The barman nodded and returned to stacking the washer as Simon struggled through the arch into the bar carrying the duffel bag, the microphone stand, and his space helmet. When he saw Elaine, he dropped the lot and the space helmet rolled under a nearby table.

"Jesus, Elaine. Why didn't you say you were coming? You been here all night?" He bent down to retrieve the duffel bag and placed it on the bar.

"I didn't really plan on coming. My friend wanted to see the show…so I said I'd come. And anyway, I wanted to bring you the costume."

"Yeah, what happened? I came round, but there was no one in. Did I get the day wrong?"

"No. I was…under the weather."

"You feeling better?"

"Yes. Much better. The show was great. You … were great."

"Thanks. Why don't you and your friend come up to the green room. Have a drink with us. It'll be a laugh."

"Will it? Aren't comedians all — how did you put it — 'sad bastards' without a microphone in their hand?"

He smiled. "Good memory! But tonight was a success," he said. "Apart from the little kid in the suit, everyone had a good set, so they'll be full of it. Please. Come up and have a drink."

"Well, I'll have to ask Pat. And I'll need to go down to the car first to get your stuff…and my invoice."

"Sounds like a plan," he said, "and we can talk about Penryth." He looked around as if he had lost something. "Where the hell…?"

"What's up? What are you looking for?"

"My helmet." He circled the tables, peering under chairs and benches. "Ah, there it is!" he said, reaching a cluster of chairs grouped by the doorway. He crawled under a nearby long narrow table just as Pat, on her way back from the Ladies' Room, returned to the bar. She stood in the doorway watching Simon, all silver chaps and gold thong, struggle to reach his prize.

"Oh, yes," she said, turning to Elaine. "Well worth a pound. Every damn penny."

*

Pat was a dog that had slipped its leash. Elaine watched from the comfort of the old green sofa as her neighbour trotted from group to group, complimenting the acts, swapping stories with their guests, and grinning fit to bust. Pat knocked back her third free beer while skirting around a huddle of young things crouched over a messy stack of chalked menu boards. The top board was littered with paraphernalia: blades, pound notes and white powder. Pat eased past, apologizing, on her way to a pool table where Simon was playing a hard and silent game with Magenta. Onlookers offered the girl advice which she ignored. She was losing badly. Pat loaded her paper plate from the pistachio bowl before standing back to watch the girl miss an easy shot for the corner pocket. Low rock music played from ratty speakers set into the ceiling.

Elaine couldn't quite reconcile this version of Pat with the woman she rarely saw out of stretch yellow velour, a woman who seemed happiest when surrounded by children and within grabbing distance of chocolate biscuits and an electric kettle. Maybe it was all down to environment, she told herself. Perhaps it wasn't only children who were shaped by location, by the expectations of those who loved and bankrolled them. She wondered whether Magenta might lose some of her hard-edged mystique if she had two kids to look after and only machine-washable tracksuits in her wardrobe. She tried to imagine Pat with dreadlocks. She wondered when she might be able to hand over the spaceman suit and lure Pat away from the bright lights of *The Firkin* and its green room. Unlike Pat, she was growing tired of all the energy in the room. Even Simon Dolan was beginning to look a little too theatrical under the pool table's bright lights. She wanted to restack the chalk boards and point out the perils of cocaine. She wanted that bag of greasy chips smothered with salt and vinegar from *The Blue Anchor.*

Eric, the barman, was one of the game's onlookers, and he broke away from the group to stand with Simon at the edge of the pool table. He took a cube of blue chalk from his jeans pocket. There seemed to be something proprietorial about the way he offered it to Simon, holding up the cube firmly between his thumb and forefinger, as if inviting the comedian to twist his cue there while Eric held the chalk steady. He seemed to be making a point, somehow, but Elaine couldn't work out what that point might be. He didn't appear to take offence when Simon, laughing, took the blue cube from Eric's fingers and chalked his cue unaided. Eric merely shrugged and pushed through the cluster of comedians and hangers on who leaned and lolled against the wall watching the game, watching Simon beat the young woman as savagely as if he was a predator wearing down some beautiful but weak animal. Magenta winced as Simon's white ball smacked against its yellow and red cousins, ricocheting a selection off the cushions into the corner and middle pockets.

Eric sat down next to Elaine on the lumpy sofa, the very same one down whose cushions she had found the plastic Santa Clause just weeks earlier. He balanced his pint glass on the cardboard box containing the spaceman outfit that sat between their feet. She winced but said nothing, and they watched the game in silence for almost five minutes before Eric leaned in closely as if they were both allies in some kind of skirmish. She could feel his breath on her cheek. It smelled of beer and cigarettes.

"Simon's going to beat her," he said, "and he won't give a damn."

"No?" she asked.

"No. Watch. He has just three balls left — two yellows and then the black. Watch how happy beating her is going to make him." He leaned in close enough for his lips to graze her ear. "And she so much wants him to take her to bed." He sat back, his arm across the top of the sofa, a smile playing across his face.

Elaine moved away to perch on the arm of the sofa, not only to get a better look at the game but also to put some distance between her and Eric, who had begun to unsettle her. She studied the two at the pool table. Simon, who had swapped his stage chaps for a pair of jeans and a blue t-shirt, played barefoot. Magenta stood behind him with her arms folded, her pool cue tucked tight to her body. Her attention was on Simon, not on his cue or on the yellow the white was about to hit and pocket.

Eric scooted over so he sat next to Elaine, her higher perch placing his head at the same level as her breasts. He looked up at her, his eyes wide and innocent and yet terribly cynical. "See how she's looking at him? Like he's an éclair in a bakery window."

"Why would I be interested, Eric? I'm just here to deliver some sewing."

Eric didn't seem to hear her. "Simon can be such a tease, a little bitch when he wants to be." His voice slurred around the words. He picked up his glass and drained it.

Elaine turned back to study Simon, the cue held loosely in his long white fingers, his gaze on the ball. Suddenly he looked up and smiled towards the pair on the sofa. His eyes were full of something that seemed to be more than mischief. He turned his attention back to the game and dropped the final yellow into the far pocket. The cue ball spun before returning down the table and coming to rest four or five inches off the cushion. The crowd broke into a smattering of applause that stopped as Simon cued up on the black.

Eric stood and tucked his pint glass under his arm. He leaned down to whisper in Elaine's ear: "You're interested, Elaine" he said, "We all are." He straightened up. "Sink the bitch, Spaceman!" he called across the room and left by the side door.

"I always do," called Simon, not taking his eye for one moment off the black.

*

It was almost midnight and though she had only been in the green room for an hour, Elaine was exhausted. Pat had collapsed like a sugared-up kid at a party and was asleep, a little drunk, on the sofa next to her. Her makeup had run but she was smiling in her sleep like a clown. Many of the guests had left for a local nightclub, and Simon sat with the remaining four of five on bar stools ranged around the pool table. Eric had returned with a last box of bottled lager and had assumed his role as surly barman, uncapping bottles and sliding them dangerously across the table.

Magenta sat at the stack of menu boards, all paraphernalia gone, nursing a wine glass.

Elaine excused herself from a long and tedious conversation with a comedian from Canada who, earlier in the evening, had headlined and blown everyone away from the stage but on the sofa he had turned into one of the "sad bastards" that Simon had warned her about. When Elaine stood to head for the pool table, Pat slumped into the vacated space and the Canadian shifted both attention and conversation seamlessly to the sleeping woman.

"Simon, have you got a minute?" Elaine held the cardboard box under her arm.

"'Course I have, Sweetheart. I was waiting for Canada to dry up!" Simon slipped down from his stool and met her halfway across the room. He steered her away towards the farthest corner where a huge and grimy stained glass arch looked out onto the street below. A few tail lights streaked red on their way out of town, and through the glass, St. Albans looked smeary and ready for bed. "So, I'm sorry I've been schmoozing all night. I need to sweeten up some more acts for Penryth."

"Ah. So it's not a solo gig?"

"No. It's a warm up really...for Edinburgh in August. I've got most of them lined up. I just need to get Canada on board without having to bring Suit Boy, too."

"Why would you bring the boy? Didn't he die out there tonight?"

"Yeah, but Canada's taken a shine to him, and he's threatening to drop out if I don't give the boy a spot."

She set the box down on the wide windowsill. "Mentor?"

He laughed. "Almost. Canada's known for 'mentoring' but only if the mentee is male, young, and good looking."

"Got it. I didn't realize comedy was so...dramatic."

"Drama Queens and tragedy. That's the game." Simon tapped the box with his finger. "Is this what I think it is?"

She nodded. "It's all there. Chaps, braces, and silver tubes."

"Great. I should probably try them on. How about I wait until everyone's gone?"

Elaine looked across at Pat who was now snuggled up in Canada's lap. Canada looked uncomfortable and fidgety. "I should probably get Pat home," she said.

"Really?"

"Yes, really. We've both got kids to get ready for school tomorrow. We're not like…" she gestured towards Magenta and the cluster of comedians drinking around the pool table. "We need to get back."

"Fair enough. But let me try it all. Then if there's any problems, you can fix them before Penryth. You're okay about Penryth, right? It'll just be an overnight. Drive up Friday. Drive back Saturday. You'll be back home before anyone misses you."

Elaine handed Simon the box. "Ten minutes, and then I need to go."

Simon took the box and headed for the restroom.

*

It was a challenge getting Pat down the stairs and into the car, but Canada had been a trooper. Perhaps that was down to a remnant edge of chivalry on his part. Perhaps it was because Elaine told him she could put in a word for Suit Boy. Whatever the reason, Canada had picked up Pat, carried her down the stairs and loaded her into the back seat of the Capri. Elaine, after finding the car keys in the bottom of Pat's handbag, drove away, watching Canada in the rear view mirror smooth down his shirt, then bound back to the side door of *The Firkin*, no doubt to rejoin the party and Suit Boy. She hoped that Simon would discover the invoice where she had left it, tucked inside the visor of his spaceman helmet.

As they left St. Albans behind, its lights in the mirrors becoming indistinct and merging into a rain-dazzled blur of yellow and red, Elaine found herself thinking about the sewing tin and how it became home to things that didn't belong: the unopened fortune cookie motto, the mints, the Monopoly pieces. She realized she sometimes threw things, like the silver dog, into the tin because she was in a rush and trying to keep things tidy. But more often, she tucked things away inside the tin because she had not yet formed a plan for where or even if these things should be kept. Things like the motto and the mints. The traffic lights at the junction of the A41 and the turning into Bishop's Croft shone amber in the distance, and Elaine checked her speed, braking gently on the wet road surface. She should clean out that tin, find homes for the misplaced, and throw the crap away.

At the lights, she stopped. From the back seat, Pat snored lightly and murmured something about pistachios and cocaine. The lights changed to green and Elaine turned left into the village. The outline of St. Lawrence's was drawn heavy against the night sky, and the church's interior lights illuminated its stained glass saints on their candy-colored procession. Elaine had come to a decision. She would throw away the fortune cookie motto unread. She didn't know — or want to know — what her future held, but she did know one thing: it held no place for a stripper called Simon.

24

Dan wished that someone had taken him aside before that first meeting — the one that wasn't Pig Bingo — and clued him in that, whether he took the pledge or not, the next hour was destined to put a crease in his drinking forever.

If someone had, Dan might have been able to run for it, taking the basement steps two at a time and heading for *The Rose and Crown* and a pint of Abbot. If someone had, he definitely wouldn't have gone back to the basement the following week to collect a twenty-four-hour chip. If someone had just taken a moment to talk to him before that first meeting, he could be in the garden shed right now, retrieving his bottle from the empty Metal Things Bucket rather than picking pondweed from a pink nylon fishing net and feeling as guilty as sin.

He flicked the slimy weed into the grass at the edge of the canal towpath and dipped his net back into the inky water, fishing more for solutions than for sticklebacks or minnows. Maybe it *was* his destiny to stop drinking…or maybe it was his destiny to start again. Maybe his predicament wasn't down to people telling him or not telling him anything. Perhaps it was all tied up with this Higher Power/God thing they wittered on about at the meetings. But even as he tried to think it all through, trailing his net through the murky water, he could hear his sponsor telling him that Higher Powers were on the Third Step, and since Dan was still sitting on his arse on the First (the one where he had to put his hands up and say his drinking was the real problem,) he had no place even thinking about God. And that maybe it was his thinking that had got him into this mess in the first place. Sometimes he wanted to punch his sponsor. His net filled with another stringy clump of weed, and this time, he thought about letting go of the bamboo handle and watching the pink nylon mesh sink beneath the water.

*

If Dan's life had been a book, a good book — a book worth finishing — he would have driven home that night after the first AA meeting with Tot and tipped the rest of the whiskey down the bathroom sink. But his life wasn't a good book. So instead he had made himself a sandwich, said his goodnights, and taken the plate and a clean glass up to his room. He'd undressed, folding his clothes neatly, and got into bed. As he ate the sandwich and sipped his whiskey, he leafed half-heartedly through the blue book that he had stolen from the meeting. He found nothing in there that made any sense. It was a book about people he didn't know. Alcoholics and sad fuckers, a few Molly Mormon types thrown in for good measure. But it *was* a memento and Dan liked mementos. The book proved he had been there and he had picked up a pen and written the date on the inside of the cover: Wednesday 7th April 1976. Then he had screwed the lid on the Bells and stowed the bottle in the bottom of the wardrobe.

The following morning, he had woken up. Not come to, but actually woken up. He remembered listening to the sounds of breakfast from the kitchen on the other side of his door. Dorothy was singing along to some pop tune playing on the radio, and Elaine was interrogating Tot about the previous evening, asking where Dan had taken her and what they had done. Tot lied, telling her mother they had watched the aerobics class and that Dangrad was thinking of getting a track suit.

He reached across his bedside cabinet and picked up the glass from the previous evening. There was still a half-inch of whiskey in the bottom, and there was almost a full bottle in the wardrobe. There it was. Proof. Those poor bastards in the basement might well be alcoholics and thank God for AA. But he, Dan Thompson, was merely a problem drinker and he would get this problem under control in his own way. He drained the glass before getting out of bed and pulling on his work clothes. There were still hooks and hinges in the bottom of the bucket in the shed, and he needed to find them a permanent home.

But as he sifted through the bucket, something had rankled at him. Maybe it was that morning's half-inch of whiskey. Maybe it was the way the Bells wouldn't stop ringing at him from inside the wardrobe. Whatever it was, that afternoon, he found himself in the tiny library in the village, leafing through the rack of community information leaflets until he found one on Alcoholics Anonymous. It listed all the meetings. There were three each week in Bishop's Croft: the Wednesday meeting at the community centre, and two at the old people's home across from the church: one on Tuesday and one on Saturday.

He folded the leaflet in half and stuffed it in his back pocket. What else was there to do in this God-forsaken village, anyway? He picked up a Wilbur Smith. It had elephants on its shiny cover. What harm could it do to hang out with a few old men and listen to their insane stories? He handed the book to the woman behind the counter who stamped its inside cover and gave it back to him without comment. Outside, he sat on the bench. And, of course, he thought to himself, there was always Tammy, the woman with the wide smile and the long syllables. Across the street, he could see the sky white as a snapped sheet across the high-pitched roof of St. Lawrence's. What harm could it do?

*

The meetings had become his anchor. Not that he stopped drinking or anything. After all, as Tammy had told Freddie the Fold, the only requirement for membership was just a plain old *desire* to stop, and he felt he could lay claim to that desire on a daily basis: he had it every morning when he woke up. The problem was, as the day went on, the desire to stop drinking was defeated by a desperation to start. Sometimes, he battled the despair, and sometimes he didn't.

Tot came with him to the Wednesday night meetings, but she wasn't allowed to attend those at the old people's home. The group had made Wednesday's meetings Open which meant that anyone could go. But the Tuesday and Saturday meetings were Closed: you had to be an alcoholic to be in the room. Sometimes, on Wednesdays, she brought that Indian lad Keesal with her. They didn't sit at the main table, preferring instead the kitchen where they did their homework. Dan wondered what the deal was between the two of them. He thought back to the Valentine card and how disappointed she had been that Keesal had sent it. He wondered who the other boy was, the one she had really wanted the card to have been from. He wondered if she were still seeing him. Was a twelve-year-old's life meant to be so complicated?

His own was reasonably straightforward. The creditors had been fobbed off with the sale of the house and the poultry farm, most of his pension went to Elaine for housekeeping, and he kept a little for himself, for pocket money, and, admittedly, for when the Bells' ringing could not be ignored. He was diligent about the meetings though and was always there when they kicked off and was one of the last to leave. He liked helping to clear away...especially if Tammy was there.

She was very hot on what she called "her service work." She put her own sixteen years of sobriety down to reading the Big Book and doing the service thing. As far as he could make out, service work was unpaid AA work. It was making the tea, cleaning the cups, putting out the books and then picking them up at the end of the meeting. It was doing anything that needed doing.

Tammy said that if she were asked to do something for AA, she always said yes. Dan fantasized about telling her that a kiss would save his sorry arse from the demon drink, and that her lips on his would be a form of one-on-one service work. This wasn't the only thing he fantasized about. He sometimes wondered if the only reason he went to meetings was to hear her say his name: listening to her deliver that first long drawn out syllable made his head spin. And anyway, he reasoned, whatever his motives, they put his arse in a chair in a meeting three nights a week and he'd been coming for almost five.

As he waited in the inevitable traffic jam on the stairs at the end of a Wednesday meeting, he thought his dreams of a kiss were about to come true when she slipped her arm around his shoulder and whispered, her words husky in his ear, "Daniel, do you feel ready for a little…service work?"

He nodded, blushing, and she took his hand, pulling him back down the stairs and into the tiny kitchenette. She reached down into one of the cupboards below the center island and pulled out a cardboard box full of paper.

"Two hundred flyers, Daniel. They need folding into thirds, so the third with the date and the address is on the front."

He took one of the sheets and read it. An AA spring dance on June 12th. The flyer promised "sober fun and fellowship," two speakers and a disco.

Aran Tammy perched on one of the stools at the counter. The woolly sweaters had given way to cotton sundresses and cardigans, but the name had stuck. "So, could you fold these and bring them to the meeting next week? That'll give the office about a month to get them out to all the groups. It should be a good night. We're having it at St. Margaret's."

He nodded. It wasn't quite the service work he had fantasized about, but the thought of doing something for Tammy — even indirectly — made him grow warm inside.

"There is something else I wanted to ask you, Daniel," she said, patting the seat next to her.

He sat, still holding the flyer, pretending to work out where best to fold it and blushing like a boy. "Ask away," he said. "Daniel T. at your service, Madam."

"It's a bit tricky, Daniel," she said. "I don't want to embarrass you or anything."

She was going to ask him out. Even if it was just to the summer dance, it would be a start. He would buy a new tie, maybe even a nice, smart shirt, and pick her up in the car. They'd arrive, she'd walk around hugging everyone and smiling, then they'd eat some sandwiches and vol-au-vents, and then they'd dance and he'd kiss her...

"Daniel?"

She'd said something and like a fool, he'd missed it. "Sorry, Tammy, miles away."

"It sometimes happens like that," she said. "It takes a while for the fog to clear. We keep drifting off. It's like we can't stick to anything 100% and, well, that's what I wanted to talk to you about."

"Fire away. I'm all ears," he said and he meant it.

"I wanted you to do the folding. I mean, it's really important that we get these flyers out."

"I'll do them tomorrow," he said. "Maybe I could bring them round to your place?"

She shook her head. "Next week at the meeting will be fine. I actually wanted you to do something else for me as well."

"Name it."

"The dance is our anniversary. We've been having a meeting at St. Margaret's for thirty years. Can you believe it? Anyway, Jimmy is going to be our speaker before the dance."

"Speaker?"

"Yes, he'll stand up and tell everyone what it was like for him and what happened to bring him to AA. He'll finish up by telling us what his life is like now…in sobriety. He'll do about twenty minutes up there on the microphone."

"Scary," said Daniel.

"For us or for Jimmy?"

They laughed in the quiet of the kitchen. The huddle on the stairs had long since thinned, and the only sound was occasional bursts of conversation in the foyer and the rumble of cars leaving the car park.

"Thing is, Daniel, we need a thirty-day drunk to balance out Jimmy."

"What does that mean?"

"Someone who's got thirty days clean and sober in the program. We think it would be a nice contrast to Jimmy's story. There'll be people at the dance who might only have a day or so without a drink. It's hard for them to identify with a man who has thirty years. But thirty days? That might seem more…do-able for them. What do you think?"

"Yeah. Thirty days seems a lot more do-able."

She smiled again. "No, Daniel. What do you think about being the thirty-day speaker? Could you…qualify by then? By June 12th?"

She knew he was still drinking. All this time, despite his bluster and big talk at meetings, she knew he was still drinking.

"Thing is, Daniel," she said gently, "you'd need to —"

"Yes, I know. I'd need to stop drinking right now." He folded the flyer in thirds, running his fingernail down the two creases. Someone had hand-drawn the picture. There were streamers and trumpets…and cups of tea drawn where normally one might see champagne flutes. "Is it that obvious?" he asked her.

"That you're still drinking? No, not really. I just have radar for that kind of thing." She took his hand and pressed it between hers. "After all, drinking is what we do best, right?"

He nodded, unwilling to risk his voice on any other response.

"Time to try something else?" she asked.

He nodded again and picked another sheet from the box.

"So I can rely on you?"

"*Curtainly San*," he said, making two fresh creases. Tammy looked at him, confused.

"He means you certainly can," said a voice. They both looked up to find Tot watching them from the other side of the open serving hatch. "We'll fold the rest at the weekend, and bring 'em back on Wednesday. Come on, Dangrad. Keesal and me have got school in the morning."

He placed the two folded flyers back in the open box. Before he had a chance to stand, Tammy leaned forward, held his face between her hands, and placed a quick kiss on his forehead before disappearing out of the kitchen and up the stairs.

In the car, Dan struggled with the gear stick, grinding between first and third. Tot slipped her hand over his and shifted it smoothly into first.

"Lesson one. You could ask her who knits her jumpers," she said. "That would be the first thing."

*

The following day, he had begun full of resolve. He read the Big Book in bed from cover to cover, underlining with a green pen the things he thought were important. He read about the psychic change the book said was essential for recovery and hoped that he had already had one without realizing. To be on the safe side, he decided to pray every night before he got into bed, to do it properly on his knees. It couldn't do any harm. He decided that good nutrition and exercise were just as essential as a psychic change and considered the pros and cons of vegetarianism. He considered walks around the park and a conversation with Elaine about getting a dog. He made grand plans for his sobriety: when he had three months clean and sober, he would get himself a part-time job, maybe earn enough to rent a little flat somewhere. Tot and her friends could come and visit. He'd ask Tammy to stop over on weekends. They'd go to meetings together in town. He'd get involved in service work, maybe start taking a meeting into the jail in Treeverton. They could get married...or live in sin—

But then the shakes began. Tot made him an egg sandwich for breakfast without being asked and cut the crusts off. He ate it silently at the kitchen table, sipping his tea and crunching down two aspirins. He decided to go back to bed and sleep day one away.

*

Over the following twenty-nine days, life had gradually improved — at least as far as the shakes were concerned. He still thought about a drink all the time. He was grumpy and snapped at everyone. Even Tammy. But he went to three meetings a week and read his Big Book. He had even asked Jimmy the Ears to be his sponsor.

Looking back, the last thirty days had been different, and at times, Dan wasn't convinced that they had been better. But then again, if he were honest, he had no idea what better looked like. He supposed that what he had wanted and had not received was recognition — more credit — for the monumental step he felt he had taken. But as Jimmy took satisfaction in telling him every morning when Dan rang for his daily check-in, it wasn't about Dan and his ego anymore. Until he actually did something admirable, he shouldn't expect to be admired. Jimmy pointed out that a family might admire the drunk and his first week or so of not drinking, but after that, the family considered the new leaf turned and went on with their lives.

25

Dan had spent the morning of the dance doing the very thing his sponsor had told him not to: he rehearsed his speech in front of the bathroom mirror. He wasn't prepared to take Jimmy's advice and leave it all to God. It seemed to him that this was an easy thing for his sponsor to suggest. After all, Jimmy had thirty years of recovery to brag about that night at the microphone, and Dan only had twenty-nine–and-a-bit days. He was finding it hard to come up with anything positive to say about the experience, and on top of that, the mirror was telling him he looked a bit of a prat.

He thought that maybe the silent house was getting him down. Everyone was out. Elaine was at the launderette, Dorothy and Trampus were staying with friends, and Tot had gone out with Keesal into Treeverton to visit a new model aircraft shop. Dan told himself that maybe he needed to go out somewhere too, somewhere with some noise and some people. He was spending too much time in that bad neighbourhood called his imagination.

He spent half an hour pressing his suit and laying his clothes out on the bed. He needed to be ready to roll at six: he was taking Tot and Keesal to the dance in the car, and if they left at six, they'd be there in good time to get a seat for Jimmy's seven o'clock speech. And there'd still be time for him to calm down before he had to take the microphone himself. He put the iron away in the larder and picked up his jacket, unsure of where he was heading.

Outside, the summer stretched early and clean across Stanley Close, the sun picking out the candy colors of the cars. A cat cleaned itself on the pavement, its tongue licking long and slow through its black fur. A neighbour perched on the top of a ladder, a chamois in his hand and a bucket clanking against rungs as he rubbed at his windows. In the distance came the bells of an ice-cream van heading down from the village. Dan thought back to when he was a kid and to weekends on the river at Sandford, fishing for minnows and dropping down into the water from a rope swing. The memory of the soupy, warm river and of water rats and moorhens navigating the water made up his mind — he would walk down the hill and spend the day by the canal. That would calm him. How could it fail? And it was close enough for him to get down there, spend the afternoon by the water, and still get back in time to have a quick bath before they all left for the dance.

By the time he emerged from the mouth of the pedestrian subway that passed beneath the railway line, he was feeling serene and at peace with the world. How hard could it be? It was just a twenty-minute chat. He'd held court for hours in pubs, talking up getting drunk and the funny and tragic things that had happened to him as a result. All he had to do was add in a bit about AA, squash it down a bit, and he was good to go.

Serenity would probably have stayed with him all the way to the microphone if he hadn't stopped in at the newsagents next to *The Dog and Partridge*. He couldn't get the memory of those minnows in the Sandford out of his mind and he wanted to see if he could still net one. The newsagents had a cheap bamboo fishing net in its window, along with plastic buckets, and he had pushed through the door, smiling at his own foolishness and at the thought of an hour spent fishing like a boy.

Inside, the tiny shop was empty of customers and oddly packed to the gunnels with large cardboard boxes, their ranks forming a corridor that stretched from front door to counter.

"Morning," he called to the woman at the register. He shut the door, its tinny bell still jangling. "I'd like that fishing net from the window. And one of those little yellow buckets."

"For the grandkids?" the woman asked, squeezing between him and the boxes on her way to unlock the window.

"For me," he said, sheepishly. "Been years…I'd just like to catch one fish. Like when I was a boy. I suppose you think I'm an idiot?"

She had disappeared into the window display. "No, no!" she called, her voice disembodied and muffled. "Not at all. We all have our dreams, right?" She emerged with a yellow bucket in one hand and the net in the other. She handed him the bucket and propped the net against the counter before she squeezed back past all the stacked boxes on her way to the till. "That'll be sixty pence."

He handed over the exact money and she rung it up on the register. "Mine's to turn this into a knitting shop," she said. She gestured to all the boxes. "Wool, needles, patterns. It's a bloody nightmare really. Like I don't have enough to do! But Roger has faith."

"Roger?"

"My husband. He owns the pub next door. We're knocking through. I'm grabbing a bit of the public bar for the sheep."

"You're having real sheep?"

"No!" she laughed. "It's the name of the shop." She pointed to a long wooden sign that leaned against a newspaper and magazine rack. Two words, "The Sheep," were picked out in gold Gothic script against a black background. "Roger's going to hang it up outside next to the pub sign on the front wall. He thinks it's funny."

Dan looked confused.

The woman laughed then took him by the arm and led him outside. She pointed up at the sign that hung above the pub entrance next door. It read *Dog and Partridge* "Get it?" she asked. "The sheep bit and then the dog and partridge bit…"

Dan studied the wall, a smile slowing breaking across his face. "Ah, *The Sheep Dog and Partridge.*"

They both looked up at where the sign would hang.

"He thinks it's funny. It's all that matters, right?" she said as they both walked back into the shop. "Are you in a hurry?" she asked.

"*Rot nearly.*"

"It's a bit cheeky, but could you move a few of those boxes into the stockroom for me? There're in the way of the loo and I'm busting!"

"Well, we can't have that," he said gallantly. "Show me the stockroom."

When he emerged, sweaty and dusty, the woman was talking to a man at the counter, a man who turned out to be her husband. She introduced them and told Roger what a treasure Dan had been and how he had ended up moving the boxes that Roger had been promising to shift all week.

The landlord shook Dan's hand and said he owed him a pint, said he wouldn't take no for an answer, and that there was no time like the present. He threw his arm around Dan's shoulder and steered him out of the shop and into the pub next door where Dan forgot all about the net, the bucket, and the minnows.

26

It had been a month of walking backwards rather than walking away. She had modified her grandfather's fourth lesson to allow her to keep her eye on the thing she wanted. In the past, she had taken her eye from the prize, and the prize had either done the walking, never to return, or had dragged her mute to places she had not intended to visit.

So Tot kept Keesal in clear view as she mastered lesson number four.

She had faith in her grandfather's simple counsel and in its ability to bring the things she wanted — the Beginning Things — into her life. After all, even though lesson one's 'Asking Questions about Unimportant Things' had at first seemed silly to Tot, in practice the unimportant question had made important things rise like bubbles of oxygen to the surface. Like how Keesal could stroke saris with his finger like a girl might, but still remain a boy. Keesal had been good at answering questions and that had made lesson one easy. Lesson two — the Paying of Compliments — had been more of a challenge: Keesal was awkward around both flirting and compliments and they bent his chin to his chest and sealed his mouth shut. Lesson Three — Asker Pays — was somewhat academic due to the abysmally low levels of pocket money enjoyed by both Keesal and Tot. And often, there had been no clear Asker: they gravitated towards Keesal's kitchen in the evenings where he worked on model planes and she did her homework or read. More recently, they had spent afternoons in the park watching the cricket and sharing the cost of newspaper-wrapped chips and warm cans of Coke. On Wednesday nights, Tot paid, dropping coins into the AA basket before grabbing a handful of biscuits from the tin and sharing them with Keesal, the pair bending over their books and dusting crumbs from homework on the quiet side of the serving hatch.

But lesson four's 'Walking Away and Thinking About Everything' was the hardest. Walking away from something she wanted did not come easy to her. It never had. One night, eavesdropping from the kitchenette, she'd heard Tammy tell Freddie the Fold that maybe he should try something called "ninety-in-ninety" and that Freddie should go to ninety AA meetings in ninety days. Tammy said it helped make everything stick. So Tot, unable to imagine three months of retreating from Keesal, shortened it and committed herself to 'A Month of Walking Backwards.'

Apart from sitting together on the bus and in the kitchenette at the community centre, Tot had kept her distance. For an entire month. And in the space the walking backwards opened up, Tot discovered family. When her father had left, she had walked away from her family, too scared to rely on what had not managed to keep him close. Now, she stayed home, tethering herself to the house and to the people who lived there. She made her grandfather egg-mayonnaise sandwiches and more cups of tea than he could ever drink. She untangled reels of cotton from her mother's sewing box, tidied the contents of Dorothy's chest of drawers, and steeled herself to hours of Lego and Tramp's sticky fingers. At the dinner table, she asked her mother and Dorothy about their days and listened — really listened — to their answers, using their responses to fashion more questions. And in asking questions of those she loved, she found the courage to ask and answer questions of herself and to finally walk back to Keesal to ask him if he would go to the AA Summer Dance with her and her grandfather the following Saturday.

*

"So here it is, a sherry trifle without the sherry!" Her mother brought the bowl to the kitchen table as if it were a birthday cake and set it down between the two of them. Tot leaned across and peered through the glass. The trifle was a multi-layered paradise: at the bottom, sponge *Ladies Fingers* steeped in orange juice, a layer of custard, a layer of red jelly with yellow mandarin oranges, and then three inches of whipped cream topped off with a scattering of multi-coloured *Hundreds and Thousands*.

Tot looked from the trifle to her mother. "No sherry?"

"No sherry." Her mother pulled the apron from around her waist, hung it on the hook by the sink and sat down on the other side of the trifle. "So, tell me again. What's all this in aid of?"

"It's an AA dance at the Old People's Home."

"And they have speakers? What do they speak about?"

"Well, the first one is Jimmy the Ears…"

"The ears?"

"He's got big hairy ears. They're as big as my hand. Anyway, he hasn't had a drink for thirty years, so he's going to stand up and tell everyone how bad it was when he was drinking, and then he'll say why he stopped, and then he'll finish off by telling everyone how AA keeps him sober."

"Is that it?"

"Sometimes the speaker cracks jokes. But they don't really need to. People laugh even when it's not funny. They nod a lot, too."

"Nod?"

"Yes, like this." She stuck out her bottom lip in her own imitation of grave sobriety and slowly nodded.

"Oh."

"And then there'll be another speaker. Someone who hasn't had a drink for thirty days."

"And who's that going to be?"

Tot was silent for a moment. She knew who it was meant to be, but until he took the microphone, he was an unhatched chicken who could not be counted. "Dunno.

The flyer just said TBA. That means To Be Announced. I suppose they didn't know who it would be when they did the posters."

"Thirty days doesn't seem very long," her mother said, adding another spoonful of *Hundreds and Thousands* to the top of the trifle. "How many days does granddad have?"

Tot shrugged and lifted an empty cardboard box from under the table onto the chair next to her and carefully placed the bowl inside. "Thirty days is a long time if you're new," she said. "Sometimes newcomers are shaking and mumbling and going on and on about how everyone makes them drink and how if their wife or their boss or sometimes even their mum and dad would stop being a pain in the arse..."

"Language!"

"I'm just telling you what they say! Anyway, they say if everyone would stop being...a challenge, then they wouldn't have to drink. But they don't know what they're talking about because they're newcomers and haven't done the steps yet or got a sponsor.

"Steps?"

"It's complicated. You should come tonight and find out. It's for family, too."

Her mother shook her head and stood up, turning away from the table and towards the pile of dirty plates that waited on the counter. "I'm on a break from nights out," she said. "And it's not really my cup of tea, anyway." She turned on the tap, the water noisy in the plastic washing up bowl. "Where *is* your grandfather? I thought he was giving you and Keesal a lift?"

Tot looked at her watch, aware that only minutes had passed since the last time she had checked. "I don't know where he is," she said, "but he's late."

The chime of crockery against saucepans was joined by the sharp rap of the front door knocker, and Tot rushed out to answer it. "Dangrad must have forgotten his key," she called back to her mother.

She opened the door to find Keesal standing on the step. He had his shiny-just-got-out-of-the-bath look about him. She could still see the comb tracks running through his damp hair. He was wearing his school trousers, but he had put on a shirt that Tot hadn't seen before. It was wild. Iridescent blue and mauve shot silk with a granddad collar. He looked nervous and clutched a bag of biscuits — *Ginger Nuts.*

"Neat shirt, Keesal," she said.

"Thanks. My mum bought it for me." He thrust the biscuits at Tot.

"You can hang onto them until we get there," she said, pushing the bag back towards him. "My mum made a trifle. Without the sherry."

She ushered Keesal into the hallway and shut the door.

"Where's your granddad," he asked, looking at his watch.

"I dunno."

"We're going to miss The Ears if we don't get a move on. And I want to hear about him in prison and the Grievous Bodily Harm."

Tot's mother appeared with the box containing the trifle. "I don't think you should wait for granddad," she said. "Why don't you start walking up the village, and he can catch you up."

Keesal handed the small bag of biscuits back to Tot and took the big box himself. "My dad can take us, Mrs. Thompson," he said. "He's just washed the car."

"Sounds like a plan," Tot's mother replied. "Okay with you?"

They both looked at Tot who was lost in a memory of the time that Stacey went to a party without her and how she said that Jim's father would be driving them there. She looked at Keesal, all damp and shiny in the hallway, and remembered how jealous she had been of Stacey and of the fact that she was having all the Beginning Things without having to do any of the Ending Things first.

"Okay with me," she said, and Keesal left to find his father.

Tot stood in the hallway turning the bag of biscuits around in her hands. She felt strange, as if something was happening that shouldn't be happening. She was glad about Keesal and his dad giving them a lift, but Dangrad should be here. He should be driving them. If he wasn't here, where was he?

*

Tot and Keesal arrived at St. Margaret's with ten minutes to spare. The building was one that tried desperately to be homely and failed. Its pebble-dashed concrete and too-small/too-high windows clashed with an English box hedge running around its perimeter and up the edges of its long gravel drive. They had told Keesal's father they were going to a dance organized by the vicar of St. Lawrence's. They had lied for two reasons. First, there was the issue of AA: how on earth could a thirteen-year-old tell his father he was taking a girl to an AA Anniversary Dinner? and second, if Mr. Patel thought the dance was a church affair, he wouldn't insist on coming in with them.

Their logic was sound. Mr. Patel dropped them off and drove swiftly away, tyres spitting gravel in their wake.

St. Margaret's lounge was almost full, and Tot recognised a few faces from the Wednesday night meeting. Some partygoers stood chatting in small groups, the inevitable plastic cups of tea in hand. Others stood at the buffet table, unloading offerings — bowls and plates of home-made food: potato salad, sausage rolls, vol-au-vents. Diamond Karin with an "i" was in charge. It was hard to imagine her as a snot-smeared drunk with her hair and her life all messed up. And tonight, she was in her element, accepting the bowls and plates and arranging them beautifully on the long table-clothed trestle tables. Freddie the Fold, the evening's DJ, was busy unpacking boxes of records and equipment and challenging outlets with a tangle of plugs. "It'll be fine," he kept saying to no one in particular. "Just fine!"

The committee had done its best to make the room look party-like. Twisted crêpe paper garlands stretched from the light fittings to each corner of the room. Helium balloons trailed multi-coloured ribbons onto small round tables, and the speaker's podium — where Jimmy the Ears, suited and booted, stood tapping the microphone with his finger and checking for echoes — had been wrapped in silver and gold paper. But the committee had been able to do nothing festive with the green vinyl institutional armchairs which had been pushed back along the walls so as to free up the middle of the room for the evening's dancing. A few residents, half asleep, still occupied the chairs, unsure of what was going on either in the room or in the world at large.

Tot and Keesal delivered the trifle and biscuits to Diamond Karin before taking seats at the far end of the buffet tables. Tot waved at Jimmy, who quickly headed across the room towards them, a worried look on his face.

"Where's your granddad?" he asked Tot, checking the pocket watch he had pulled from his waistcoat. Jimmy was looking sharp; he had even trimmed his ears.

"I don't know," she replied. "Keesal's dad gave us a lift."

Jimmy shook his head. "I knew it," he said. "I bloody well knew it!"

"Knew what?" Keesal asked.

"Nice shirt, Kid," Jimmy slipped the watch back in his pocket.

"He'll be here," Tot said.

Jimmy ruffled her hair, something that people seemed to do a lot of recently and something she wished they wouldn't. "It'll all come out in the wash, Sweetheart." He tweaked her ear lobe between his long bony fingertips then wandered off to speak to Diamond Karin.

"What's his problem?" Keesal asked. "Oh, look. Bloody hell. Look at Tammy!"

Tot turned to see Tammy heading straight for them. She wore a long black silk dress, slashed to the thigh. An embroidered red dragon wound itself around the split, snarling and beautiful. But unlike Keesal, it wasn't the dress that shocked Tot into silence. It was the little boy who trailed after Tammy, his hand stuffed into a huge bag of *Cheesy Wotsits.*

Tammy bent down to hug Tot. "Where's Daniel?"

"I don't know! Why does everyone keep asking me?" Tot stared at the silent boy who had tucked himself tightly behind Tammy.

"It's just…" Tammy broke off. "Never mind. Time to introduce Jimmy." She stood up and almost tripped over the small boy behind her. She put her hand on his shoulder and propelled him forward until he stood in front of her. "Say hello, Melvyn," she said. "This is Tot and Keesal."

Melvyn put out his hand and Keesal shook it.

"This is Melvyn, my youngest," she said. "He's fed up to the back teeth with AA, but I couldn't find his brother, and I can't leave him at home on his own. This is Tot," she said to the boy. "She won't bite." Melvyn stuck out his hand and Tot swallowed hard, trying not to stare at Aran Tammy who had now become Tammy Strand, Mrs. Strand, Melvyn's mother and Gareth's mother, all rolled up into one tangled ball.

"Hello, Melvyn," Tot stuttered. "It's nice to meet you," and she shook Melvyn Strand by his greasy little yellow hand.

*

Jimmy the Ears had done the lot. He told the audience of how he survived an abusive childhood by stealing drinks: from the tables at family parties, from drinks cabinets, from the off licence, from the local supermarket. He had found early on that a drink, as he put it, "tightened all the loose screws." He told of how the thieving escalated, of how he graduated from cans of lager from the local supermarket to hot-wired motors and car stereos from the back streets of Waterford. His street education earned him fifteen years in prison for Grievous Bodily Harm where he shared a wing with the Kray twins…and got sober. He told the room — the alcoholics, their families and the three sleeping residents — that he had always looked forward to Thursday nights when a local AA group brought a meeting into the prison wing. At first, it was just a break from being banged up, a few new faces. But in the end, he looked forward to hearing about how life could be different, about how he didn't have to wait until he was paroled — life could start being different right away.

He wound up his speech talking about his Higher Power and how one of the Thursday jail men had said he could choose one of his own understanding: it didn't have to be the old-man-on-a-cloud variety, or one who rained down fire and brimstone. Jimmy told the room how he had tried to piss off his first sponsor by choosing Charlton Heston as his Higher Power. His sponsor, a man pulling twenty for attempted murder, told him that as long as Jimmy had a Higher Power who wasn't Jimmy, Moses would do just fine.

When Jimmy finished, everyone clapped like crazy until a resident, an old man tethered by an IV to a stand and wrapped in a white cellular blanket, woke up with a start and asked what time it was. Tammy took the microphone and, without missing a beat, she replied that it was time for a short break — long enough to get more tea and reload plates — at which point the second speaker, the 'Thirty-Day Drunk,' would take the podium.

They didn't have to wait long. By the time everyone had reached the tea urn and the buffet table, the second speaker arrived, fishing net in one hand and a carrier bag in the other. He strode through the doors and crossed the room to the podium, where he put his packages down and tapped the microphone. "One, Two," he said, smiling. "One, Two."

Tot watched her grandfather and tried to work out where he was. Was he in that place he went to when he'd been drinking, when he did things and said things he didn't remember? She looked across at Tammy and Jimmy who were sitting by the podium. They too were looking at Dan, unable to stop stark concern playing across their faces. And then there was Keesal sitting next to her, his plate full of sandwiches and trifle, smiling and totally unaware of what might happen next up there at the podium.

The room began to quieten down, expectant, waiting for the Thirty-Day Drunk to begin, to tell them what it had been like for him, what had happened and what his life in sobriety — all thirty days of it — was like.

Dan grinned at the room full of people and then picked up the fishing net. He dipped his hand inside the pink netting and pulled out a skein of pond weed and held it up. "Hello, everyone," he said. "My name's Daniel. I'm an alcoholic and I've been fishing." They all laughed — all except Jimmy, Tammy, Tot and the resident with the IV who had gone back to sleep. "That's one of the reasons I was late. I intended to go fishing this afternoon and ended up in the public bar of *The Dog and Partridge*." The people in the room stopped laughing and became very quiet. Dan continued. "Jimmy here tells me his first Higher Power looked like Charlton Heston." Jimmy smiled and looked at his shoes. "Thing is, I think mine might be a woman called

Dolores who wants to run a wool shop down by the canal."
The people in the room leaned forward, not sure if there
was a message coming or if their thirty-day speaker was,
after all, a zero-day speaker. Either way, there was drama in
the air, and to a room full of alcoholics, there was nothing
more intoxicating than drama — their own or someone
else's. "Anyway, I was standing there at the bar with a brand
new pint of Abbot in front of me, just about to say to hell
with it all, when Dolores comes in with my fishing net in
her hand. Said I left it behind in her shop and that she
hoped that it wasn't too late for me to catch my dream."
The audience looked confused but were used to speakers
who rambled and took some time to make their point. "So,"
said Dan, "I took the net and left the pint. As of right now,
I have thirty days sober..." The room broke out into
enthusiastic clapping. Dan held up his hands to halt the
applause "...and I caught my dream: a minnow, a little
stickleback."

Dan spoke for another ten minutes. He talked about
Sleaford and how he felt he had never fitted in, even as a
boy. He talked about Millicent and how he had been scared
all his life — of chickens, of claws and feet in general, of
commitment, of not measuring up. He finished by telling
everyone he was trying to do this thing one day at a time. If
he could end the evening by having a dance with his
granddaughter and going home to bed to think about his
day and to work out where he had done the right thing and
where he had done the wrong thing, he stood a chance of
waking up tomorrow sober and doing it all again. The room
applauded, Dan sat down with Jimmy, and Tot squeezed
Keesal's hand hard.

"THAT'S my granddad," she told him. "That's what
he's really like."

She was still smiling and squeezing as Freddie the
Fold put the first record on the turntable and people began
to abandon their seats and plates and head for the dance

floor. She watched her grandfather shake Jimmy's hand, give Tammy a long hug, and head out across the hall towards her. He had stopped to say something to one of the residents in the institutional chairs when he was over-taken by a tall boy in a black and white mohair jumper and jeans smothered in chains and buckles. Tot could only watch, aware her mouth was hanging open, as the distance between the boy and her diminished, until he stood in front of her.

"Would you dance with me?" Gareth Strand said.

And Tot, with a beautiful Beginning Thing suspended in the air before her, was unable to say a single word.

27

If Keesal Patel hadn't smacked Gareth Strand squarely in the mouth, things might have ended very differently.

She might have stood up and taken Gareth's hand, coming to the conclusion that Things in the Wrong Order were better than No Things At All. She might not have realized that even though Gareth was now doing the Asking, she had already done far too much Paying. Perhaps she might have danced with him, but seeing Keesal over Gareth's shoulder, she might have wondered how the smooth silk shirt would feel against her cheek.

Whatever might have happened, what did happen was that Dangrad had to pull Keesal off the boy on the floor. Keesal had thrown the first punch and looked set to deliver a barrage of others. As Dangrad hustled Keesal outside, Tammy and Jimmy helped Gareth up from the floor and took him to the nurses' station.

Freddie the Fold silenced the music and walked quickly to the podium, clapping his hands to get the room's attention. "Ladies and Gentlemen," he said, "that concludes the Bare Knuckle match. Please take your seats for Jousting with Lager Bottles, to be followed by Tag Team Throwing Up and Crying." A few began to chuckle, the tension dropping as their laughter became infectious. "Seriously though," Freddie continued, "it's one of the things we do best, right? Get a room full of alcoholics and there's bound to be a fight. Thing is, neither of tonight's two scrappers are alcoholics…or at least, we don't think they are!" More laughter. "Not yet, anyway! But what we do have is a young lady in need of a dance partner. Gentlemen?"

Freddie crossed the room back to the DJ stand and placed a record on the turntable. Rod Stewart's scratchy Scottish burr filled the room, Jimmy the Ears was the first at Tot's side, and they took to the floor.

"I'm proud of him," he said.

"Granddad?" she asked.

"Nah, that little Indian kid. Tammy's son is a right shit. Good to see him on his arse for once."

So Gareth really was was Tammy's son. How had she missed that? She closed her eyes and pressed her face against Jimmy the Ear's chest. He felt different tonight. She had hugged him so many times at the Wednesday meeting, but tonight, he was warm and soft against her face, not tickly and musty like when he wore his old snagged cardigan. She tightened her arms around his waist and concentrated on the music.

Everything was different: Jimmy was looking sharp; Keesal had been hauled off into the car park by her granddad; she was in here dancing to her favorite record; and Gareth Strand was somewhere on the first floor having what looked like a broken nose seen to.

"Jimmy," she said. "Do you mind if I sit this one out?"

"'Course not," he said and led her back to the ring of chairs at the edge of the dance floor. "I'm still on your card for later?" he asked, and she nodded.

"I need some fresh air," she said. "I think I'm going to take a walk round the car park."

*

It took a few minutes for her eyes to adjust to the darkness. As she waited, she wasn't too sure what it was that she would see. Maybe Keesal had really lost it, and Dangrad would have him pinned against a car bonnet somewhere. Or maybe he'd be crying, and Dangrad would have his arm around his shoulder. What she actually saw was Keesal and her grandfather sitting on the step by the side door. They were laughing, and her grandfather was dabbing at Keesal's hand with a handkerchief.

She walked over and sat next to Keesal. "Are you okay?"

Dangrad gave the handkerchief to Keesal and stood up. "I'm going to leave you to it," he said. "There's a lady in there who promised me a dance."

As her grandfather headed back towards the hall, Tot took Keesal's hand in hers. Two of his knuckles were split and bleeding.

Keesal winced. "Your granddad said they looked alright. Didn't think they needed stitches."

"Why did you do it?" She took the yellow linen handkerchief and tied it in a bandage across his hand. "Keep it straight out."

"I don't know. One minute I was just sitting there watching your granddad coming over, and then I saw Gareth and couldn't work out why he was there and then…then I was watching you." He pressed the yellow cloth against his knuckles.

"Don't press it! Just let it rest a minute!"

"One minute I was alright and the next, I just went mental. I don't know if it was some kind of delayed reaction about the Valentine card thing on the bus, or because boys like him have always been in my face." He shook his head and turned to look straight at her. "Do you get confused, Tot?" he asked. "I mean, do you get those times when you don't know what you want to do or who you are?"

She didn't answer. She thought she might know what he meant. Sometimes, when she was on Gareth's bed, she had wished that instead she was lying on the ground under the big leathery leaves in her mother's rhubarb patch. And then there were times when she was sitting with Stacey on the garden swing set under the polythene cover talking boys and television and shoes when she just wanted to be on her own. Sometimes, she was so happy she couldn't stop grinning, and other times, she held a pillow to her bedroom wall and slammed her head into it. Was that what he meant? Did he feel like that, too?

"I didn't want you to dance with him, but I didn't know why. Because, like, I don't dance and what's the harm, right? But I just didn't want him and you..."

She held her fingers to his lips. "This is our place," she said.

He took her wrist, then gently closed his hand over hers. "What do you mean?"

She pointed beyond the cars. "That's the park over there," she said. "And if you look about an inch past the corner of that house, that's the community centre. And over there, if you could knock down that roof, you'd be able to see Tenner's Wood."

"So?"

"Sometimes when I'm confused, when I don't know who I am or what I want, I go to all those places in my head and they're the same as they ever were. I mean, there are kids on the swings, and there's trees getting leaves and then losing them, and people getting married and dancing and getting toasters."

"I don't get it."

"It all just keeps going on — even when I'm confused. I just have to wait it out for a while, because all those places will still be there for me...when I'm a minute or a year or even ten years older...when I'm not confused anymore."

He didn't answer, but he kept hold of her hand. She could feel the difference between his warm skin and the cool yellow handkerchief wrapped around his knuckles. She leaned across and kissed his hand through the handkerchief — a quick peck — and swivelled round on the concrete step until she was facing him. She closed her eyes and leaned in, her face close to his. There was a faint aroma of ham sandwiches and trifle.

But he pulled his hand away and stood up. "I'm going to get your granddad," he said, his voice high and cracking like glass.

As it was, her granddad, swinging the fishing net and his carrier bag, was coming to get them. She watched as Keesal and the old man met halfway in the car park. They talked for a moment then headed towards the car.

"Tot!" her grandfather called. "Come on. Time to go."

She stood up and hurried towards them. "Why are we going?" she asked. "It's only eight-thirty."

"Seems Mohammed Ali here broke the idiot's nose."

"Are the police coming?"

"No, Tammy says it's about time someone rocked him on his arse. But she's taking him to the hospital and I said I'd meet her there later if she needs me. So if you want a lift home, you better come now."

When she got to the car, Keesal was sitting in the front with her grandfather. She slid silently into the back seat, unsure of how she felt about Keesal or Gareth…about any of it. She wedged her grandfather's fishing net on the back window ledge and stretched out across the bench seat. If she had to sit in the back, she might as well be comfortable. Her feet found a carrier bag on the seat and she picked it up, intending to place it in the foot well, but she couldn't resist looking inside. She pulled it open to find the tea caddy wrapped in a towel.

"What's grandma doing in the car?"

Keesal looked round, turning quickly, as if he expected to find a dead woman on the back seat next to Tot.

"I thought she should be there tonight," said her grandfather.

She took the caddy out of the bag and unwrapped the towel. "Why?"

"Because she would have liked to have heard what I had to say. She should have heard it. Years ago."

"Are you going to put her back in my room, or are you going to keep her in yours?"

Keesal shook his head as if his ears were full of water.

Her grandfather looked across at him. "It's an urn, Laddie. My wife's in an urn."

"It's not an urn. It's a tea caddy," Tot said.

"Why's Mrs. Thompson in a tea caddy?" Keesal asked.

"It was only meant to be temporary," replied Tot. "Until Dangrad worked out where he wanted her."

"Who's Dangrad?"

The car sped through the village, past the flint library, past the row of houses where Gareth, Melvyn and their mother, Tammy, lived, past the park with its swings and its dark row of trees that shielded the sedge grass from view, and onto Willowswitch Lane.

"Pull over!" said Keesal. "Pull over here!"

Dan pulled the car to a halt at the entrance of Tenner's Wood. "Just here, Lad?" he asked.

Keesal nodded and leant back across the headrest. "Tot, can I walk you home from here?"

Tot looked at her grandfather, as if for permission.

"It's up to the Pecker and the Peckee, right?" her grandfather said to the question she hadn't asked.

Tot nodded.

"Sounds good to me," she said, opening the car door. Keesal had already got out and stood waiting on the grass verge. She wrapped the tea caddy up in the towel and leaned across to place it on the passenger seat. "Granddad, what are you going to do with Grandma?"

"I don't know," he said. "I thought the canal might be nice. What do you think about a burial at sea…or 'at canal'?"

She sat back in the seat and watched Keesal out on the grass. "Maybe."

"Be good. Don't be late."

"I won't."

"I'll send out the bloodhounds if you're not home in forty-five minutes," he said, smoothly shifting the car into first gear.

"Okay."

"And then I'll send your mother."

"I won't be late!"

"And then Dorothy."

"Grandad!"

"Night, *Dittle Larling.*"

"Night, *Dangrad.*"

*

Keesal had walked into the woods and was waiting for her by the tree. It was the tree they had climbed every day the previous summer, packets of sandwiches and melted ice-pops in their pockets. Keesal always wanted to climb to the top. She had been content to sit on the thick lower boughs, above the heads of the occasional dog walker, but below the birds and their nests and the wide sky. It was the tree she had climbed the afternoon she found out her father had left them all. It was the tree under which Keesal had showered her with confetti on Valentine's Day, the tree from which she had run to the safety of Stacey's back garden and the swing set.

He stood with his back to its trunk. His shirt seemed to shine in the fragments of moonlight that fell through the branches.

She didn't know what was meant to happen next. They had done the Beginning Things and done them in the right order. There had been the sari questions, she'd done her best to flirt with him, and then she'd paid. She had done

The Month of Walking Backwards before she pecked his knuckles. But then Keesal had done his own Walking Away. And yet here he was by the tree. Maybe this was his Walking Back.

She stood in front of him, suddenly shy. He ran his hand down the back of her shoulder and across her shoulder blade. It was going to be alright, she thought. Things were happening in the right order. She began to undo the buttons of her shirt.

His hands stilled hers and she looked up. He was concentrating on a point over her shoulder, back across the trees, back towards the village. He didn't look at her as he spoke.

"It's not that I haven't wanted to do this," he began, "because I have. Sometimes when I'm sitting in the kitchen and you're reading and I'm sticking stupid bits of plastic together, I want to lean over and kiss you. Really, I want to touch bits of you. But then other times, I just want to stick bits of plastic together."

His hands were clenched, holding her hands and the edges of her shirt. His eyes were bright and he looked as if he might cry. She gently shook his hands off and began to do her buttons up.

"It's not that I don't fancy you, Tot, because I do," he said, an edge of panic in his voice, as if he was letting a wonderful opportunity run off barking down the road.

She stepped back and looked up at the tree. In the dark, only the bottom boughs were visible, the rest was a dark tangle. It was hard to discern one branch from another. "Get up on that first one," she said. "Up there!" She pointed up to the first low bough.

He hesitated for a moment before jumping up to grab the thick branch and pulling himself up the trunk of the tree until he was sitting astride the bough like a cowboy.

"Pull me up," she said.

He bent down, one arm tightly around the branch and the other stretched towards her. She grabbed it and he hoisted her up, not letting go until she sat facing him, both of them tight against each other, out on the bough.

"Now I'm going up to the next one," she said, standing to find footholds in the rough barked truck. When she was astride the branch above, she reached her hand down. "Let me pull you up," she said, and Keesal took her hand and clamboured up until he was at her side.

Tot looked up as far as she could see into the oak above her, its dark branches obscuring the moon. She knew it hung there, round like a magnifying glass upon them both, full and bright, and that if they didn't climb high enough to catch it tonight, there would be other nights to climb; that moon was going nowhere in a hurry. And even when she couldn't see it, it was there, hidden by clouds or by the world's smooth curve, but still waiting for her. It would always be there however long she took to slow down, to take a breath, to decide what things she wanted to do and the order in which she wanted to get them done.

ACKNOWLEDGEMENTS

I want to begin with thanking Kay Sexton, my best and oldest writing friend, who looked at an early draft of *The Beginning Things* and played me its songs and its caterwauling: I needed to hear both. Thanks also go to my Randolph College colleague Laura-Gray Street for spending a month in the summer of 2012 reviewing a later draft and for giving me back the confidence I needed to keep on keeping on. The following year, in a hot and stuffy classroom on Bowdoin campus, a tight group of Stonecoast MFA alums helped me breathe life into Elaine and her stuttering relationships. Bless you. And finally, as ever and always, a lion's share of my gratitude goes to Nan Carmack-Crytser and Mary Alexander who have been my writing's sounding board for almost a decade.

ABOUT THE AUTHOR

BUNNY GOODJOHN was born in London in 1960 and moved to the United States in 1999. She is published in both prose and poetry and her books include *Sticklebacks* and *Snow Globes* (Permanent Press 2007, Scribe 2008, Centrepolygraph 2008) and *Bone Song* (Briery Creek Press 2015). She teaches and directs the Writing Program at Randolph College in Lynchburg. www.bagoodjohn.com